D1232082

A Choice of Murder

BY THE SAME AUTHOR
(*published by Peter Owen*)

Fiction

The Story Teller
Pastimes of a Red Summer
Landlord
Quintet
Lancelot
The Death of Robin Hood
Three Six Seven
The Tournament
Aspects of Feeling
Parsifal
The Wall

Non-fiction

Worlds and Underworlds: Anglo-European
History through the Centuries

PETER VANSITTART

A Choice
of
Murder

FINKELSTEIN
MEMORIAL LIBRARY
SPRING VALLEY, N.Y.

PETER OWEN • LONDON

U.S. DISTRIBUTOR
DUFOUR EDITIONS
CHESTER SPRINGS,
PA 19425-0449
(215) 458-5005

00424 9024

The endpapers are based on a grave stele from Pelinna depicting
a Thessalian horseman wearing a chiton, chlamys and helmet.
Mid-4th-century BC, Paris, Louvre

PETER OWEN PUBLISHERS
73 Kenway Road London SW5 ORE
Peter Owen books are distributed in the USA by
Dufour Editions Inc. Chester Springs PA 19425–0449

First published in Great Britain 1992
© Peter Vansittart 1992

All Rights Reserved.
No part of this publication may be reproduced
in any form or by any means without the written permission
of the publishers.

A catalogue record for this book is available from the British Library

ISBN 0–7206–0832–5 (hardback)
0–7206–0851–1 (paper)

Printed in Great Britain by Billings of Worcester.

To Julie and Geoffrey Bush, and family

Never to be born was the best, call no man happy
    This side death.
Conscious – long before Engels – of necessity
    And therein free
They plotted out their life with truism and humour
    Between the jealous heaven and the callous sea.
And Pindar sang the garland of wild olive
    And Alcibiades lived from hand to mouth
Double-crossing Athens, Persia, Sparta,
    And many died in the city of plague, and many of
                                        drouth
In Sicilian quarries, and many by the spear and arrow
    And many more who told their lies too late
Caught in the eternal factions and reactions
    Of the city-state
And free speech shivered on the pikes of Macedonia. . . .

Louis MacNeice, from *Autumn Journal* IX
(by permission of Faber and Faber Limited)

Contents

Note

This story, not quite history, not wholly romance, is loosely based on Plutarch's account of Timoleon of Syracuse, *c.* 411–337 BC. In Syracuse, his mixed constitution survived some fourteen years before surrendering to the despotism of Agathocles. The days of the self-sufficient Greek city-state, of local loyalties and political autonomy, were over, capitulating to the Age of Empire. Macedon. Parthia. Persia. Rome. 'Timo' often pondered whether his efforts had perhaps been useless. This is not easy for me to answer.

P.V.

Corinth

1

Two spirits lived in the door, both invisible. One was friendly, leading you, soon after sunrise, into the brightness of street, water, sky. The other was gloomy, shutting the house when Apollo reddened the sea and light collapsed.

The rooms were small, some bright, others in shadow, a spirit flickering in each corner. Father and elder brother Timophanes remained outside talking in markets and the gymnasium, arguing with friends, with sailors, stall-holders, with wandering Sophists who took money to mock the gods. They played draughts in taverns, attended assemblies, and Father, Timodemos, sat on the Council.

His wife, Demariste, who at certain times became 'Mother', remained in the women's quarters, sternly managing the slaves, the stores of figs, goat's cheese, dried fish. Mead for the slaves, barley wine for others. Women slaves worked the looms, the bakery, the laundry. Demariste also kept the gods in good humour with prayers and offerings. The family, one of the oldest, respected the gods more than some others, Timophanes chuckled, speaking only to Father.

To be Timo, son of Timodemos, was to be grandson of Zeus. Father was acclaimed in assembly, foremost in Council, a Magistrate. He had shares in a merchant ship; had rescued an allied town from bandit mercenaries, returning to a welcome from all Corinth.

13

He had been elected Supervisor of Buildings, no less, and owned a farm, where the family went for olive harvests, tree planting, offerings to Hera, Queen of Heaven. There, a baby had been killed by villagers, who smeared the blood on a new wall, giving it life. A poet had sung a rude ditty about a goat, whose horn then crumpled. Long ago a millet-sower fell dead, hearing that a hill, or a hill woman, had cursed him, and Mylas Dirty Face boasted of embracing a centaur. The centaur was believable, not the embrace.

Across the farm courtyard, behind walls cracked by olive roots, was a hush, heavy but transparent, within which lay other slaves worn out, for whom attention came mostly from cats and the ugly and unwanted.

Some slaves had once been rich, but, losing all, sold themselves. Only Sikinnos had any importance.

Timo looked about him, exploring life. Timophanes had already done his military training and been heroically scarred, fighting rebels at Sicyon. He was strong and loud, pushing upwards, clearly god-chosen. He had veins of fire, bronze limbs, his dangling cone was long as a dagger, tough as boxer's gristle, very enviable. Only once had he allowed Timo to hold it, though almost at once shouting at him to stop. 'It'll knock you over.' He noticed Timo only when a little drunk.

Timo smiled. His own cone was starting to swell and lengthen, though not for six years would his head be shorn for Apollo and Hermes, for him to join Timophanes in manhood.

He would like a younger brother, to despise as Timophanes despised him, but Father seldom entered his wife's bed. Down in the City lived his 'Particular Lady', trained by Aphrodite herself, though only Timophanes ever mentioned her, usually ill-temperedly.

Mornings were promises, adrift on smells of barley, oatcakes, sometimes wheat bread: on the grind of wheels, on rising hubbub, on the wings of swallows that had seen Egypt, dim but dangerous, with animal gods, green stones, and what Father called ebony.

Walking to school, you must be accompanied by the pedagogue, Sikinnos the Grammarian, called Sikinnos in jest, after the tutor owned by Themistocles of Athens, scourge of Persians. There were always sights: a vessel being hauled over the slipway to the Gulf, a fight in the bird-market. Sikinnos said little, even when pausing at a charcoal brazier or latrine, but was watchful. Boys were often stolen, not only in alleys and broken lots but in the sunlit, jostling streets. Rape, pain, the little knife. Certain streets and gymnasiums were forbidden, certain youths evaded, because of feuds inherited from 'long ago', with causes hidden in family busts.

Sikinnos has taught him his letters. Though Father complained that these destroyed memory, he himself wrote much, on behalf of the Council. Not so Timophanes, for whom letters should describe only champions. He himself was his own ode.

Letters meant Homer, and the Laws, sung in chorus at great festivals. Father had praised Alcibiades, not for treachery with Persia, with Sparta, but for having a schoolmaster flogged for not honouring Homer.

Corinth, between two seas, was the eye of the world. All met here: Cretans, swarthy as tanners; Phrygians, stupid as a mule's daughter, Timophanes said; high-nosed Athenians; Persians, closed up and silent, fancying themselves lords of this world and all others. On her Isthmus, Corinth controlled the Gulf, despite father declaring that ships were less numerous, though from here the first triremes had sailed the Middle Sea, creating the future, making colonies in Ionia, in Sicily.

Corinth, Timophanes had an exciting way of speaking, is income.

Singing, dancing, playing hoops or blind man, stripping for a race, Timo felt Corinth pressing on him. Streets and docks, the Gulf, green and white mountains. Also statues, always about to speak, though, people said, seldom doing so. Tell our stories, the curved mouths, hard eyes, seemed to command. Listen.

Stories. Questions. Were the house spirits part of the family, or did each house have spirits which the family inherited? Why were some houses unlucky? Hush!

At school, you gazed at a boy on a bench: at once the boy was a sailor, the stool a raft, the floor an empty sea. You had a lexicon of gods and heroes. Hermes, half-smiling messenger, Athene sharp-sighted, of many counsels, guardian of Odysseus.

Sing the wrath, O goddess, the black anger of Achilles. Heracles, Jason, King Dionysius. Corinth also had her heroes: Oedipus the King; Periander; Cypselus, descendant of Heracles. Honoured were the Best of All, beloved even of cold Artemis, those who had lived for the City. On the Isthmus was the flat, dented rock on which Heracles slew giant Alcyoneus, stealer of Lord Apollo's cattle.

Listen to the tale of Medea, the young and beautiful witch. Betrayed by Jason she killed his wife. A poisoned robe set her on fire.

Deep in the night, yet dazzling, hovered the mighty dead whom Homer saw lying dearer to the vultures than to their wives.

There was language behind words. Vulture and eagle were signs of Zeus; the raven, of Apollo; crows of Hera. Also, the clammy silence of ghosts. Yesterday, older boys had sung

> Nine human spans is the life of the chattering rook;
> A stag's life is that of four rooks;
> A raven endures as long as three stags;
> A palm tree as long as nine ravens;
> And the lives of nymphs, daughters of Zeus,
> Are long as ten palms.

Numbers too contained words. The shrouded Great Goddess was also Three: part of the memory lessons taught by Cheiron the Centaur.

Much was not taught, best not asked. Furious Titans under the earth struggled for freedom so that the City sometimes quivered. In Hades was Sisyphus, who built a fort up there on the Acrocorinthus and had been buried where the Isthmus narrowed, for his ghost to protect the waters.

Gorgon masks on walls, on jars, glaring away demons, knew stories best left unheard. Perhaps of Crete, brilliant, gay, where *something happened*: earthquake, rage of gods, a gigantic bull. Timophanes could perhaps explain, but never did, though he enjoyed talking of bulls, noisily, as he did when cursing dog-eating Carthaginians. Often he was brooding, dark with frowns under that bright litter of hair; sometimes quarrelsome, even with Father; then grinning as he kicked a dog, slapped a slave or reminded his friends of scars won at Sicyon. He walked with gods, loved applause, was always with young men competing to share his cup, his couch.

Timo, in so vast a shadow, partly content in it, had no intimates, though he was well enough liked. Last week, escaping Sikinnos, he had climbed the glistening Acrocorinthus, citadel built by Diomedes, son of Tydeus, whose eyes flashed terror into Troy. Beneath Athene's harsh statue, gazing at the blacks, whites, greens slanting from high Geranea opposite, he prayed to be noticed by Kallias, an older boy, already a champion, whose grandfather had collared the bay wreath at the Pythian Games. O that Kallias would turn his lovely head! But, favoured by Heaven, looking straight before him, Kallias was as aloof as Timophanes, though quieter.

Timo sighed. One day he might dare offer Kallias a raisin cake, or murmur praise after a race, singing contest, dance. Kallias' voice, mounting over the lyre, could stop birds in the sky, or should do. Such thoughts made you a slave, but Kallias was tall, slender as Artemis, his cheeks were shield-bosses, hair scaled gold, eyes a summer sea. Perfection. When he recited, his gestures, glances, changes of tone forced even the masters into praise.

Lately, daubed on walls and columns, was a youth in purple tunic, bare-limbed, eyes wanton, tied under a mast at sea. Everyone knew the story. Soon mast, deck, swelling sails would be thick with grape and leaf, dolphins sporting, gods watching. Dionysos, lord of the vine. But what did it portend? Prophecy of rich liberties? A triumphant alliance? A political turnabout? Timo did not care: the bound youth was Kallias, who might need rescue and thus turn his head.

In class, in gymnasium and stadium, Kallias would be smiling, joking, oiling himself, scraping, unaware that he was loved. His mother possessed an alabaster chair, a talking bird, a Numidian cook black as Hecate's teeth, whose parents must have dreamed of ebony, but only Kallias' friends and lovers saw these wonders. His father was rich, travelled between the islands, headed one of the political groupings sometimes praised by Timodemos, though the two men seldom met. Timophanes strode into the future, proud of his scars, his Name, his followers. Kallias was ahead of all others. Timo, small, perhaps blemished, certainly ugly, trailed after them, unseen.

Girls? They seldom appeared in the real life, in markets, temples, at table, though occasionally parading at festivals and somehow protected by the nameless. Some, easily scorned, were still veiled. In barbarian lands they could fight in armies, but Hellas deemed this disgraceful. They had powers, of course. Look up, at

noon, when Apollo is Master, and up there, high on the Acrocorinthus, glimmers Aphrodite's temple where, they say, hundreds of
nymphs from Thessaly dance for the goddess naked, or in Coan
silks transparent as cobwebs. To love girls was like plague, like
madness, like poisoned arrows.

Timo contented himself with stories, when Father beat him,
Timophanes scowled, the schoolmaster sneered. When Kallias'
head was in the clouds, he felt the brightness darken. In dreams,
his brother's dagger lay in a red pool under a porch, a face grinning
horribly above a blood-drenched neck. Once a vulture, yellow as
fear, began to tear him.

'Don't do that, sir,' old Sikinnos rebuked Timophanes for tor-
menting Timo. 'You might hurt the young master.'

'Exactly!' Timophanes' smile was itself a vulture.

Always, behind the light, waited the unseen, domain of Hecate,
crone of night, whose statue was kept hidden. She controlled the
Furies, or used to. Night gave forebodings of failure, disgrace, you
could be sucked into moonlight and vanish for ever, like the
sorriest cockle-digger. Slaves muttered of Cretan omens: the bat,
the viper. Only in Sparta was fear forbidden.

Timo watched and listened. Dionysos might step from the wall
and proclaim himself King. Father was slower, sometimes spoke of
'Factions' and looked worried. Not long ago the Great War had
savaged all Hellas, Sparta and Parga, finally wrecking Athens.
Sparta became supreme, then Thebes, with her hero, Epaminondas, supported by Corinth. War might come again, as Theophanes
hoped, enjoying blood. In Persia, the Great King waited. He now
controlled Ionia. All life seems a matter of waiting your turn.

2

Classmates were leaving for communal dormitories, but Timo, for
whatever reason, remained at home, thus more isolated. Often he

was glad. Spiteful Tornos, dirty-fingered Charmides were scarcely the sweetness of mint after rain.

He waited his turn. Father grieved about Factions, Timophanes scented battles, demanding more scars. Corinth continued in state, prospector of towns and islands. Bustle and stir, processions for Aphrodite, for Heracles. Tall, slim-waisted aristos, many with hair fiery with rings and bunched behind, as in Old Times, lords of Corinth, pacing in sunlight or glinting at night under flaring cressets. Theophanes amongst them, with fiery eyes and broad fists.

Arching into the sky, loomed the Acrocorinthus. Towers, temples, ramparts, terraces, were crowded as ever, though people grumbled about spies. From there you saw, or thought you saw, all Hellas, in apparent unity. Mount Kythene, now near, now far, as Apollo willed. Lord Poseidon's great home on the Isthmus, the blue-haired Earth-shaker. Below, the harbour lay like a giant lyre, smacks dodging between swaggering merchantmen and triremes with dangerous beaks. Coloured sails brimmed, painted eyes on prows made the water aswarm with peacocks, with giant moths. Father spoke of trade failing, but the harbour was unmistakably loud and thronged. White ships, red ships, blue ships cutting the waves, a mast on the horizon beckoning. Once a black hull, black sails, had passed by, a plague-ship uncanny as Colchis where pale warriors rose from furrows after Jason sowed dragon's teeth. Where was it going? Forbidden all ports, sailing into starvation and madness, diseased mouths gnawing each other.

Timo was freer to range the streets, unsupervised. Timodemos asked fewer questions, sometimes appeared blind. On quays he watched embarkations to Athens, Lemnos, Ionia. Stacked, guarded were Sardian gold, Indian ivory, Spanish metals, Cretan dyes, the world's tribute. Charcoal from Archanae, acrid, unpleasant. Bronze was being packed for Thebes and for flower-loving Persia. Sunspots winked and glimmered on water.

Those scrawled figures of Dionysos remained, but were no longer discussed, though all agreed that something was going to happen: soon, some time, or perhaps had already happened.

Further into the City, streets led away from the frantic Agora where salesmen yelled prices, angry hucksters orated, painters with a flick, a jab, created a Theseus, an Ares. Magicians spun discs, against earthquake, prophets mumbled about the sky on fire above Thrace; gamblers argued about forthcoming Games and trainers' records. Talk was like sharp flints: the latest Sophist, the downfall of a teacher, a legal contest. On sale at corners were mules, grave-masks, bad quality slaves with dead eyes and decrepit hands, surly house-dogs, blinded crows and jackdaws, monkeys resembling skittish Creon-Next-Door. Persian peach trees, statuettes of fanged Cerberus. Stalls shone with fancy sandals, tasselled cloaks from Miletus, city of star-gazers, glazed Samosian cups, Lydian carpets, amber from the wild north, where Macedonian bandits knocked each other flat, to become High King. Amber was useful for the rites. Near the pepper-root sacks, ranged as if for sale, old men sunned themselves like lizards and eyed your bottom.

Miletus, Persia, Babylon, such names opened life, though Miletus, Timophanes sneered, had been crushed by the Great King.

Like Carthage, the Great King could poison the Middle Sea. No Corinthian, no Hellene save such as Alcibiades, Father had taught, could admire those Persian nobles, who cast themselves overboard to save Great King Xerxes from a storm. Xerxes called himself Beloved of God, so had a better chance of saving himself and should have grabbed it.

Corinthian streets were more enticing than Persia, than Carthage certainly. Smells of fried meat outsoared Babylon, while rival flax-sellers bawled foul jokes and crowds pushed and stumbled down the streets of cobblers, potters, furnaces, coppersmiths, past little taverns surging with quarrels, and laughter like the splitting of pine. Wounded men lurched by, bleeding, rough as Phrygians or Macedonians, which they probably were. 'Macedonians', Timophanes said, more than once, 'are boars. Good on the platter, better between your teeth.' Outside taverns collected former athletes, ruined champions, clumsy and graceless, faces rotted, bodies paunchy, hands and legs horribly misshapen, wet eyes begging between tricks of fat. They were far from the trim, naked lines on vase and bowl, on statues, from Kallias in the gymnasium. Father explained that such men now competed only for money. 'They even specialise, they develop their muscles out of all proportion! They reject harmonies!'

'Greedy louts.' Timophanes joined in, though none was certain that he absolutely hated money.

Timo promised himself to preserve harmonies, whatever they were. In the streets, in bed at night, feeling his cone growing, he felt stories still falling into him, mysteriously, from out of the air. He told them to classmates, they listened, they sometimes praised. Teachers also listened, but praised less, sometimes told him he was impertinent. Timophanes never listened, but threatened to cudgel him.

Rebelliously, he whispered: 'I saw a juggler. I know why Philo was given the bracelet', wondering at his own singularity that those at home pretended not to see.

He still enjoyed dice, balls, songs, the jokes and riddles old as Cronos – what is white, then red, then white? A blackberry – but was less part of them, complete only within himself. Perhaps he was talking too much. 'Great men keep silent.' Sikinnos repeated. Timo swore to remain mute as long as possible, though this was usually brief. 'Listen, a certain man met a giant. . . .'

Once he saw a man shuffling across the Agora, hands outstretched like the blind. Everyone shivered in the damp heat, stepping aside as if at a snake.

'What is it? What has happened?'

'He's marked,' whispers hissed. 'He's marked.'

None explained. A multitude of stories was implied, confirming Homer's words learned only last week:

> They exchanged shuddering glances
> Like those in a lordly household
> When, from far-off regions, a murderer
> Stalks in, seeking sanctuary,
> As though gripped by demons.

In Sparta, he would have been encouraged to quarrel, to steal, to develop guile and bravery, though flogged if caught. No one liked Sparta.

I am Timo, son of Timodemos, brother of Timophanes, devotee of Kallias, and my turn will come. Meanwhile, crouching from the wind on the rocky shores of the Gulf, he discovered a cave almost covered with bramble, and within a boat, its unfurled sail revealing a cyclop's angry head. At once he imagined Athene, lady of Horses, washing the sea; Thetis of the White Hands, mother of Achilles; then Artemis, who touched a cherry tree, and the tree died. His own head brimmed with deities; yesterday the class had learned the names of the Hesperides, the Graces – even the Fates.

Everyone was protected by a god or goddess, though Timophanes disclaimed any such need. His own, Timo's, must be
smiling, Hermes Kourotropas, guardian of boys. Demariste, on a
day when she was Mother, had said: 'We neither see nor know
gods. But we feel them.' Hermes was often close. Had he chosen
Hermes or been chosen? On such questions the world trembled.
But he must be cautious. Everyone knew that the nimble god's
smile, brilliant but sly, could deceive. He played with mortals like
dice. Hermes could be a statue, slim and bare, quivering into life,
an inviting youth blue-robed and rimmed with light. Or coldly
unamused, like Athene and Artemis. Usually he was a silent voice,
a pressure, slightly teasing, started by the shadow of a vine, a run
of soft silver over the waves, the stillness of this cave.

He glanced nervously at the walls, cracked like dark hide, the
small rocks, burrowings, bats' droppings, filled with the hum of
waves, then at the small boat, message from adventure. A cave
could tempt you down to green enchantment, twilit, free of pain
and death. Another story. A boy descends a cave, is welcomed
below, enjoys unending games and feasts in the green light, until
at last missing the bright air of Hellas, above. He begs to return, for
seven days. His companions sigh, but allow it on oath to reveal
nothing of their land. But of course, back in the Agora, in tavern
gardens, he blabs, and never again finds the cave, his wits are
gone, he wanders away, his fate known only to a wise dolphin
from whom we learn the tale.

3

Timophanes borrowed, did not always repay, he bullied, had fits
of rage, but young men admired his move against an older aristo,
Charaxus, son of Alcaeus, in an election for leadership of a running
club founded by no less than Periander. Timophanes disclaimed all
ambition, shouted for Alcaeus, even threatened, though followers

of both fought in the streets and were rebuked by the Council.

Charaxus was elected, weeping at the honour, embracing his beloved Timophanes. Shortly afterwards, however, in his absence, he was ousted by a sudden vote and Timophanes successfully claimed the presidency. To much spiteful applause, he presented Charaxus with a grey, artificial beard and a mouldy crutch.

Corinthians are children of laughter-loving Aphrodite but all Hellenes crave laughter, once joining in mirth when Pisistratos, in exile, had again bid for the Lordship of Athens. He hired a large girl, put on her a crested helm, placed a spear in her hand and drove into Athens with her standing beside him, the awed citizens believing her the city's patron, Athene. On realising the deception, people laughed even louder, gladly submitting to grim-intentioned Pisistratos.

'The gods', Timophanes, on training now for the Isthmian Games, grinned at Charaxus' discomfiture, 'help mortals to help themselves.' Lolling on a couch, he now sat opposite Timodemos, a jug of wine, a platter of fish between them, Timo on a stool, keeping quiet.

Timodemos had news. 'There's a new High King in Macedon. Philip. The Council heard it this morning. They say he's a warrior.'

Timophanes shrugged. 'If he's a big snout, we'll have to push it in. Macedon!' His irritable face, broad, fleshy, was like ham. The talk, as always, was of politics. In the last turmoil, provoked by a levy, a youth had been blinded, then killed, left to the kites. Disregarding, or unaware of, tension, Timodemos drank. His head, grey, squarish, lifted again. 'This violence, trying to intimidate the Council . . . there's something new, perhaps dangerous. I've been born and bred in Corinth. . . .'

But Timophanes interrupted. Impatience broke over him, he had perhaps drunk too much. Neither man remembered Timo almost hidden as shadows lowered, the light fading on Timodemos' face, as if he were weakening. Timophanes remained young, untamed, ruddy in the last lights.

'Violence? Messy, and, in the wrong hands . . . but how else did Father Zeus win Olympus? He certainly wasn't born and bred there. Though some of us think that expression is always followed by something silly.' He laughed, affecting a joke. Timodemos remained grave. When he spoke he resumed earlier talk of the Great War.

'Blunder of blunders. The gods stung us to madness. Twenty-seven years of massacre, plundered altars, sickness. It could yet be the death-rattle of Hellas. Athens went down, crushed by Sparta, Syracuse and her own greed. Temples in dust, Empire lost. Yet we too made it all possible, here in Corinth. Wanting to triumph without fighting. The jackal part. We backed Sparta, Sparta won, and in our cleverness to weaken her we broke pledges, restored our hand to Athens. Athens! Wounded but unforgiving. Sparta ruined herself through pride and cruelty. Thebes, reckless and crazed, let loose Spartan slaves to tear up all Hellas. Pain is retribution. Our policy has lost us honour, lost us credit. And after all the killing, who won? Tell me that?'

Timophanes uttered another laugh, but was mirthless, fretful, anger barely in check. 'Corinth won, with barely a scratch. But your stick-in-the-mud Council threw it away. Showed too much honour, not getting even a cabbage. They should have leaped on Athenian markets, got Sparta and Thebes to destroy themselves. They're old, played out, they get in the way. Had I been in command, I'd have butchered the lot of them.' Panting, gulping, he gave a stamp. Now he too was in shadow.

Timodemos remained quiet, appeasing. 'My son, Persia won. The peace was mostly of Persian doing, Persian subsidies. Her half-promises, half-threats make our wars easy. We settle our teeth in each other while Persia and Carthage grow higher. In the Great War she fought alongside ourselves and Sparta. When Sparta destroyed the Long Walls of Athens, Persia rebuilt them, playing us all like draughts.'

'Persia!' Timophanes' tone was frightful. Afraid to stir, to remind them of his presence, Timo felt turned to stone. 'Persia! An effete monster, more bloated than Athens ever was. Carthage! A race of savages. But we need something new. Men are around, good as ever. Thebes threw up the right sort . . . Epaminondas, Pelopides urged people beyond themselves, showed the way. But were betrayed by your men of restraint, civilian stay-at-homes, the men of honour! Ordinary people . . . but people can be too ordinary and usually are. Born and bred, of course, like most of us.'

Quick as a lapwing, the night changed. All was brutal, Timophanes in the gloom raising both hands like a boxer, then crashing them down on the table. 'I'm right. We need a sort of forgetting. All that muck about Troy . . . a pack of brigands squabbling about dishonest trade. Hellas . . . stupid little cities hating each other more than they ever hated Persia. Macedon waiting like a pariah-dog. Athens, stuffed with quack fancies and big lies. Ionia, where Persians mince up and down with gold in one scented hand, a whip in the other. It's all too old, collapsing. Such places have no future. Alcibiades laughing as he turned traitor, there's the truth of it. The cities will never choose to unite to free Ionia, rescue Sicily from bandits, refight Marathon. Hellas needs a master. He may never come.'

The lamps remain unlit. Timodemos in outline looked frail, and at last Timo realised that his father was old. His brother was master of the family. Timodemos, however, was still talking, as it were, upright.

'Son, beware of your passions. You demand that the whole should be more than its parts. Like Babylon and Egypt, like Persia. But the parts, our cities, which go back to the gods, are jewels. Even Macedon may one day shine. Surrender their independence and you will shrivel into a mere flapping in the wind. Persia has many gifts. The Fire God's chosen. She knows little conflict within herself. Each knows his place, is obedient to someone higher. The Great King speaks, his words are rushed down the imperial highways, the satraps hear and obey. All is well. Yet, behind everything is the executioner with the cord, the axe, the hook. To despise others can be impious, but the world knows that, in Persia, even to think can be treason, and to think aloud. . . .' Tidomemos paused, as if made awkward by his own convictions, though, arresting a retort, he said mildly: 'The master of united Hellas will cease to be a Hellene.'

Timophanes was panting again, as if after a race. 'What supports you and your rickety Council? Legal riff-raff, male matrons, a pack of has-been generals. Gabble here and everywhere, no one knowing his place. Factions screaming. Niggling pedants. That crew would have denounced Achilles for trespass, sued Odysseus for adultery, issued writs against Zeus himself. . . .' His words sputtered, lost themselves, vehemently regathered. Raw. 'But none of us wants a Great King with his band of soprano nannies. No, Father, think again. Most of our honourable heroes ended in failure. But they showed the way. In Syracuse, King Dionysius . . . his glance went everywhere, he struggled and won, half the Middle Sea lands cringed before him. Year after year. In old age he mismanaged his lot, fell foul of stinking Carthage. But with a city

like Syracuse, our own colony. . . . Its Corinthian blood killed and
enslaved the Athenian invaders. And what's happened since? In
Syracuse the mob and the bloodsucker continually change places
and call it government. Carthage may gobble her up, and her
stomach won't feel any better afterwards. But our idlers here in
Corinth should learn the lesson.'

Somewhere in the house, Demariste would already be sleeping,
amongst the women. Suppose she were listening, then wrote a
poem? What would it be about? But Timophanes had risen, unsteadi-
ly, like a champion, a son of Ares hesitating before a deep pool
crusted with thin ice or duckweed. Father had dwindled to a shadow.

'New tactics,' Timophanes rumbled, 'new blood. Perhaps new
gods.'

Timo pitied his father but was tempted by a fresh identity,
brother of a master of Hellas. Would Hermes be at their side and in
what guise?

4

'All these farewells . . . something's breaking.'

'Yes. But certain people . . . forerunners, to put it so . . .'

'All Hellas has long ears . . . Corinthians are longer than
any. . . . Not only their ears.'

'Indeed. The record belongs to . . . well, I don't care to say. But
his girl gave birth in record time. Suffice! As for forerunners, I've
heard . . .'

'*He* wouldn't care to hear it.'

'You're right. And sometimes I . . . I myself don't see as clearly
as before. I walk abroad with caution. I'm unsettled.'

Voices at the Zeus and Ganymede Tavern were dandified, as if
perfumed, but the young faces were strained, apt to glance around
as if anxious not to be observed. The talk hurriedly changed,
debating the various natures of Aphrodite: Aphrodite Pandemos,

patron of boy lovers, Aphrodite Ourance, who preferred girls, Aphrodite something or other who desired both. Aphrodite of the Beautiful Buttocks. They all sniggered. Languid Aphrodite, of so many names, so many offers.

Never, the Council insisted, had Corinth been so opulent. Resplendent suppliants arrived daily, though in secret conclaves elderly men counted misfortunes. In Attica, death flourished like poppies: famine, infanticide, abortion. Plague stalked where she willed. Persia dominated Ionia, Carthage, with her vile gods and debt-ridden clients, was inexorably completing an exchange ring to monopolise maritime commerce. Sicily was in turmoil. King Dionysius had left a degenerate son, Dionysius II, to grapple with a harsh and austere general, Dion, son of Hipparinus. Carthaginian troops and colonists had invaded, no saviour leaped from the sky. Up in Macedon, High King Philip was shackling the clans.

Corinth was unperturbed, cheerfully relying on imported food, craving luxuries financed by loans and mortgages. Banks and alien usurers were supplanting workshops. Glazed bricks, sealed jars, silks were baled with cords made in Carthage. A craze for Memphian statuettes trebled the price of even poor quality alabaster. The Council attempted forced loans, raised levies on ships being built elsewhere. A poet won applause, particularly from the wealthy:

> We are a summer people, charming and idle,
> The autumn gales will blow us away.

Never had the colonnades been so crowded with millionaires, with slaves, sometimes called 'indentured property'. Mysteriously, profits rose, but there was less to buy. Some warehouses were transformed into brothels and baths, clustered with boys and girls more grasping, more unscrupulous, and gamblers with new and frantic recklessness. They wagered farms, slaves, ships on the fall of a leaf, the direction of a seagull. At brilliant, barely nameable odds a drunken youth lost all, betting that tomorrow's sun would not rise. He too became indentured labour. To bribe Apollo was conceivable but improbable, like the Pyramids dancing to Orpheus.

Word had spread through rival ports that voyages to Corinth by no means enriched all who sailed.

Summer people pretended not to see the rind, dung, mouldy

bread piling up in streets, kites swooping more fearlessly, packs of dogs multiplying, even in opulent thoroughfares setting on children, forcing them to carry clubs.

Rumours began, stealthy but insistent, of conspiracy against the old men, the useless generals, the Council, the growth of 'Homage to Cronos', a proscribed slave association, planning a revolt, protected by Cronos, the deposed father of Zeus. More obvious were the clever, fluent Sophists, teaching not from love of truth, but, imagine it, for money! Another import, they never lingered long enough to observe the effect of their lessons. They revered the Athenian stonemason, Socrates, executed as a public nuisance, and reduced morals, duties, gods to market-place logic. Gods were not perfect, heroes were unheroic, the wicked deserved pleas, the Furies were mere lawyers, philosophy was fluent clowning. A joke could save the soul from demons.

'If gods exist, we do not.' Well-dressed youngsters were glad to feel themselves leaders of thought, then gaily buffeted each other to prove they were alive.

Corinth was drifting; feeble hands at the wheel, mast askew, timbers in bad repair. Factions were more ferocious, each under some colour, maiming, robbing, yelling against the fat oligarchs who betrayed the Peace Settlements.

The gods love balance. Reaction was starting against the lords, against the Homage to Cronos. This was encouraged by the prizes won in the Isthmian Games by a rising young man – Timophanes, son of Timodemos.

The Games, founded by King Theseus, remained part of the Fourfold Offering, along with those of Nemea, Pythia, Olympia. Prizes had become ornate, the betting extravagant, and the attendant puppetries, necromancers, abortionists sensationally overpriced. Timophanes' triumphs were popular, since, almost alone, he had disdained such profiteering and had not become professional. This eased his way further into politics. He now led young aristocratic horsemen styling themselves the Myrmidons. Only winners have respect in Corinth.

Councillors found themselves shouted down in assemblies, their edicts disregarded, their doorways fouled. They began lending money to the young men and not demanding repayment. Timodemos, like certain of his friends, had retired. His eyes were failing, his movements slowing. In his place now sat, with doubtful legality, Timophanes, eager under red-gold hair. 'Our Timophanes,' the people said, 'he has luck.'

For a general orator, even actor, luck was necessary, though none could explain its nature. Divine whim? An error of Fate? Caprice of physique? But even slaves repeated: 'Our Timophanes has luck.'

Butcher-boy son of Timodemos. You could not readily imagine him alone, bereft of Myrmidons and girls, praying, reading a lyric or tragedy. To him, the Agora wits jested, making love, making a table, making a row, were identical.

Unexpectedly, he rose in Council: burly, commanding. He spoke, he spoke at length, inelegant but resolute, allowing no interruptions, with well-timed pauses for applause, granted him by the younger men, trained like a singer's claque.

He announced 'the Programme' dedicated to Corinthian gods. Peace Settlements were barren; tear them up. Slaves and aliens were outnumbering the citizens; expel some, discipline others. Many were avoiding military service; flog most, enslave a few.

Much followed. Times were gay. Festivals for the Programme, garlands, sacrifices, Homeric odes chanted on the Acrocorinthus by children's choirs. All Corinth laughed at a Great War veteran who grumbled at the expense. A youth, very pretty, accosted him, soft face awash with smiles, then, very politely, begged to examine his well-famed sword. Affably, the old man handed it over and promptly received it back, in his belly. A Sophist had then composed an epigram, brief and indecent, calling it the simplicity of occasion, which all applauded, repeated and misunderstood.

No doubts were heard. Corinth was to be renewed, not by Asiatic star magic, or jabber about perfect shapes, mystical numbers, atoms which no one could see. Nor by Ionian steam and wind mechanics. No. But by the joys of right living, the pure lines of unity. Exquisite phrasing, the Council agreed, lovely comments.

Timophanes drove life like a chariot, his smiles more eloquent than any rhetor, his appeal direct as song, his swagger well earned, his words illustrious, in their peremptory, boyish, excitable way.

'We don't want to become a chatter place, like Athens.' All agreed. 'Nor a barracks like Sparta.' None dissented. Thebes would be taught her place, Syracuse reminded of her filial obligations. 'I see.' Timophanes' sparkle faded, his mouth was displeased. 'Too many warm baths.' At once some lesser Myrmidons,

swabbers of reputation, former boxers and swordsmen, hastened
to smash them. 'Too much gambling.' And various houses were
raided, the slave police standing aloof. 'We need no loungers.' Led
by the Myrmidons, all were at once stiff as spears. Boys wore too
many clothes, they hastened to strip. Women had too many; they
smiled, they assented, but did nothing.

The Myrmidons followed him everywhere. Paid from where,
none cared to inquire, few minded. Corinthian supremacy was
assured. Spartan webs, spun as far as Persian, were entangling
Spartan wits, never very polished. Athens was prattling the virtues
of Demos, the People, but in Corinth not even the People applauded these, perhaps unable to discern them.

Timophanes enjoyed quoting the words of Haemon to King
Creon. *No true city belongs to mortals alone.* This appeared to answer
everything: enticing, if ambiguous.

Civic offices, accustomed to rotate amongst the old families, were
now being assumed by the unseasoned, sometimes unknown,
with protests dismissed as *Factionalism.* 'Job-lot politicos,'
Timophanes reasoned. 'We must let in the light.' Gifts arrived,
from the grateful, the ambitious, the artful. Corinthians enjoy
giving: even more, Timophanes was boisterous, they enjoy taking.
They must not, he would say, be like the old time Cretans, *scared of
something happening.* This made life very thrilling. Familiar faces
were disappearing, sinking into the infinite recesses of evening.
'Nestors needing rest.'

Citizens welcomed new freedoms: the perpetual round of
voting, administering, jury service, was wearisome. They had
more time now for the processions, some spiteful comedy or licen-
tious satyr play. A poet announced that failure to show sympathy
angers the gods. This was understood to mean support for the
Programme, itself part of the light to be caught on a shield or
jewelled ring. Some armed youths, seemingly licensed, agitated
against aliens and plundered their houses, a process nicknamed
Redistribution of Property.

Timophanes with his intimate, Dinos, an overweight youth now
being called Drunkard Extraordinary and thus popular, many feeling him one of themselves, and in a resplendently crested helmet,
was seen everywhere, treating the crowds like a lover. He knew
how to make them laugh, a weapon feared even by gods. When a
wealthy sail-maker protested against the Redistribution of Prop-

erty, Timophanes jumped up as if from nowhere and exclaimed that no man with so dreadful a squint could see the truth. Though the sail-maker had no such squint, all laughed helplessly, forgot the debate, and forever afterwards hailed him as 'Squinter'. 'Corinth needs muscle,' Timophanes said, and onlookers cheered, thinking this an epigram. Some began calling the Myrmidons 'the muscles of Corinth'.

New labour battalions were recruited from slave combines. Massive public works began: a canal, towers, a barracks, a temple to Artemis. Within the unexplained withdrawals and collapses, the proscription of certain oligarchs for subscribing to the outlawed Homage to Cronos, was the promise of renewed war. The Programme envisaged the larger Hellenic cities absorbing the smaller, a new league against Asia and Africa. None was surprised when Timophanes, still only twenty, against precedent, acceded to a plea from Dinos and a turbulent assembly and accepted command of a small campaign in the Western Gulf. This would be merely a display against malcontents accused of the most heinous of crimes, the arming of slaves. The skirmish, and subsequent executions, were recorded as a Corinthian triumph, embellished by Timophanes' own words: 'They ran like shit off a shovel.' That tiny word *like* performs more magic than most magicians. As Tidomemos had done long ago, he received ovations rising to split the sky. Though no arms had been found on slaves, and no slaves had fought, Timophanes declared that pre-emptive action had saved the City and scared off certain barbarians, whom he forgot to name. Connoisseurs were delighted by his phrases: 'dabblers in promises empty as a virgin's belly' . . . 'degenerates lounging in forgotten fields'. What finesse! What delicacy! Odysseus could have done no better.

To give orders, they say, though, in Sicily, is even better than making love.

5

Timophanes, whom admirers were calling Ajax, still condescended to sleep at home and was thereby much praised for humility. At dawn he departed, escorted by the mottle-faced Drunkard Extraordinary. Despite his joviality he was never off guard.

Secluded in the women's quarters, Tidomemos said little. Though once a general, he cherished what he had called the massive powers of restraint, at this time not very evident.

Timo would soon be taking the oath to respect the gods, the City, the laws, then receiving the sword and spear of manhood. He felt himself a pale swimmer in a golden sea, for he excelled at nothing. He was not a champion, though this was less desirable than formerly: a champion charioteer often meant part ownership of a chariot raced by a professional. And not for him the ecstasy of Spartan boys competing to be thrashed, in utter silence, before the blood-drenched altar of Artemis. He could sing passably, come second in a race, but was no Ajax. When he did win a prize – for calligraphy, a lyric – he kept silent at home. Timophanes would not praise him.

The Programme might soon be reconstructing his school. Homer and Hesiod were still taught, though most boys and probably the master preferred love lyrics and the newer, swifter dance measures and flute trills, imitations of Timotheus of Athens. Old folk would be shocked by the classes. Ordered to recite the names of King Priam's sons, Nikias had giggled, then lisped thirty Arabian scents, the master barely repressing his amusement. He permitted lovers to ogle each other, allowed pet cats into the lessons, and only smiled when Konnos, son of one of Timophanes' richest supporters, placed on the reading table a monkey, which behaved badly and refused to recite Hesiod.

With desires flowing freer, Timo too enjoyed love lyrics, though no brother of Timophanes could fail to recognise that Corinth still needed heroes. Even a slave like Miron Clean-about-the-House, let alone old Sikinnos knew that. Dion, Epaminondas, Agesileus of Sparta. Timophanes too was no soft-speaking girl-boy, and indeed was governing the City.

Very occasionally, the great man addressed him, with a warning against dancers or flute players, or with a question about things overheard in the street. Timo dared not tell him that most people felt joy at the thought of 'Ajax' but now hated Dinos.

Isis, the Immaculate, once told Lord Poseidon that Zeus always supports an elder brother. Of course. But, part of the family Name, he himself was being sought by boys who had once ignored him, though he was less ready to join in the games of ball or knuckle-bone. Sometimes he was drowsy, inclined to hesitate, to linger; sometimes passionate to run to the shore, to the cave or to the summit of the Acrocorinthus, to gaze at the wide world. Sometimes a muffled pain in the soul, indescribable, sometimes a strange pride. Hermes might interpret, but he had not yet done so.

Then Konnos, very strong, very rough, began following him, awaiting him, watching him strip for wrestling. Rather clumsily, he presented him with a delicate oil-flask, a request for love. This must be rejected, and, probably afraid of Timophanes, Konnos pretended not to be angry.

Soon, however, even the Programme could be forgotten, for prayer moved Hermes' compassion and, out of sunspots, Kallias, who no longer attended school, at last turned his head.

The seventh day of the month was always a holiday. The momentous was simple. Tall, dark, quietly elegant, Kallias stepped from a dusty grove. 'Let us be friends.' Swiftly they were together. The kiss, the embrace, the small, delicious shudder. They pledged themselves to dance together in the spring festival where boys, with their protectors, danced naked, for Zeus and Apollo, to odes devised by Orpheus, then performing martial drill. The new Council had forbidden the customary drunken clowning led by a favourite actor impersonating Dionysos.

They met daily, alive to each other's touch, talking, talking, while around them, barely observed, Corinth seethed and jostled, astir with the Programme. Kallias' mother still had the alabaster chair, the black cook, though his father had died unexpectedly in some distant city.

Their voices crossed, Kallias' deep and slow, untroubled as a champion's should be, Timo's eager. Could Hector have escaped Fate? No. Should they swim? Yes. They argued, they laughed, wept, strove for the masteries of love. Kallias was beautiful. He said nothing memorable, revealed no surprises, but had grace of being, of gait, a hesitant, rather tender smile which Agamemnon could have envied. When he murmured his feelings, he often used words by somebody else, believing them those of Anacreon of Theos, and, if not, no matter. His dark liquid eyes were depthless, they were his true language. Alone at night, Timo murmured:

> 'Plucking flowers for a crown
> I chanced on urchin love among roses.
> Grabbing his wings I thrust him into the wine
> And swallowed him –
> His wings now caress my heart.'

They read Xenophon aloud, in alternate passages: *While the others departed to dine, Cyrus remained amongst the wounded with his aides and physicians, not caring to leave them unattended.*

At this, Timo was silent. Not even to wondrous Kallias could he confide his pang of disloyalty, his knowledge that Timophanes would have departed to dine.

Through the summer their talk flowed easy. Kallias was skilful with embraces, versed in unobtrusive magic.

'Magicians are lazy. The best have to hide in wild places. Demons tempt them. If they submit' – Kallias' face, smooth, browned, creased uneasily, the lustred eyes lowered – 'then their spells become hateful. To others. To themselves. But no gentleman needs magicians. They're only tradesmen!' He smiled softly, and they both thought of some ruined Athenian grandees, exiled but styling themselves 'Gentlemen', affecting contempt for the Corinthian tradesmen who protected them.

Timo smiled. Yes, one needed no spells, at best an occasional nudge from the unseen.

They stood together above the City, beneath the Temple of Aphrodite, its heavy reds, browns and whites rich in late afternoon sun, the clamour of streets and quays rising. Pilgrims, officials, loungers, glimmered vaguely behind them, white gulls swooped above the brilliant sea, the light, sun-streaked, intense, reaching to Helicon and Parnassus, casting gold over Attica, glittering against Arcadian woods, warming the stone lions of Mycenae, dropping into the north, the frontiers, the wild horsemen, mad dancers whirling for Pan and Dionysos. All Hellas lay inert in the hour of suspense, the elation of the day balanced by evening's promise.

Near them, in a small, tired garden, amongst ilex and rose, a nymph, a fillet binding her dark hair, was holding a basket of fluttering, sacrificial doves. Wide, neglected bowls of myrtle and thistle almost concealed the last grey stumps of the Sisypheum, where lizards ran between crevices and a faded purple stain covered a square stone. Somewhere a body lay buried and, in lurid underworld light, the ghost of King Sisyphus unendingly toiled.

Timo and Kallias saw the nymph regarding them, smiling at them, yet somehow pretending not to. Each knew that one day they would have to mount such a girl. But not yet.

Earlier they had swum, afterwards discussing girls. Kallias spoke more quickly. 'They've creepy-crawlies inside them. Snakes are afraid of them. . . .'

Both remembered the cherry tree dying at Artemis' touch.

'My brother says. . . .' Most of Timophanes' remarks about girls need not be repeated, but he had asserted that they could dream only in daylight. 'They don't think like us at all. Only in rhymes and songs. They live in music.'

Kallias' dark brows contracted, his eyes flickering not with knowledge but with an odd perplexity. 'Until they get babies. Then the babies steal the songs. Mothers' brains get smaller. In a sort of mud.'

They were silent, watching the white immensity of Corinth, the summer people, a thick blue and red merchantman rising and falling far out. Kallias pointed at it. 'She may reach the Euxine. Past Troy and the ghosts. Early men called it the Sea of Many Perils, but that would have damaged trade. So now it's the Hospitable Sea. Much better!'

They smiled, strolling down through trees, arm in arm, into the darkening streets, the day's riches contenting them. At a gateway they were obstructed by tavern-boys amusing themselves by kicking chained dogs: yelps and growls, frantic dodges, broken teeth, blood. Last week they had burned a live cat.

Pushing away, the two paused again, inspecting the latest wall graffito. Chalked very crudely above the scrawled invitations and obscenities were a dripping sword and tattered cap.

Kallias sounded very much the elder. 'The Homage to Cronos. It still appears everywhere. You know, Timo, that slaves have secret societies, with special passwords and hand-signs? They mark gates and fences. Each mark is an instruction or warning.'

It was difficult to imagine Sikinnos and the others behaving like that. Yet Timophanes had exposed the plot to arm slaves and criminals, and spoke venomously about disloyal oaths to Cronos.

Unexpectedly, Timo knew that Kallias had tensed as if before a leap. 'Your brother . . . that brute Dinos. . . .' He was indistinct.

The evening chilled, the squalid smells of alley and pit were stronger. As if from a gorgon's stare sprang the possibility that Dinos had had a hand in the death of Kallias' father. The ground became precarious, stricken, too thin for a sudden movement. Kallias, however, was smiling again, they were soon in a garden, twilight hanging from the Acrocorinthus. Pale clouds lay motionless on a dark-blue sky. Young men sat around them with their boys, drinking under lamps of burning lamb fat, a few wandering disconsolately and solitary between bushes. Soft stirs, sighs, small laughs, murmurs, while a dim glow showed the moon about to rise over the sea. The holiday had been precious; flowers had been plucked for a crown. Love was whatever began when the song ceased.

6

With head shorn, vows taken, weapons presented, Timo, son of Timodemos, became a man, despite his brother's scoffs about dreamy schoolboys asleep in stories. At the rites he learned that Titans, huge, painted white, had once slain a divine child, a crime which tainted all life, causing savagery and war.

In autumn he would serve in some colonial barracks, an unwelcome prospect, far from the City, probably far from Kallias.

He was now tall, but without the carved, glistening face and commanding gaze of Timophanes: his hair was more straw than gold, his nose blunt. But he knew from Kallias that he was less ugly than he supposed. 'In your face . . .' Kallias began, but then could only smile admiringly, without words. This was sufficient.

Admiring heroes, he seldom felt heroic. Formerly, to cast away one's shield was shameful, but Corinth was whistling a new song, vainly forbidden by the Council, joking about a certain Diaphantos, who had deserted during battle. One line, *better five lost shields than one lost sandal*, was explained by Kallias. The sandal signified a girl's gate of pleasure, recently opened to them both in the back room of a tavern.

Afterwards, they agreed that girls were for wet days. The girl they had shared, a tired Helen of the Ditches, had been glum, perhaps cursed, not one of those who besieged Timophanes.

Always in a hurry, Timophanes had not yet married. Boasting many lovers, he belonged to none. He was more than Ajax, he was Prometheus, the fire-bringer. Fire gladdens. Also, he enjoyed threatening, it purges. Myrmidons' axes then suppressed an unrest amongst Isthmian artisans so swiftly that some asserted that, again, they had succeeded before any outbreak had actually occurred.

A tame Sophist now wrote his speeches. 'The sun is not divided, it shines on all Hellas, like a leader.' None cared to remind him that it shone also on Persia and Carthage, turning barbarians black, yellow and doubtless green.

Timophanes now had his own mansion on the Acrocorinthus. At home, Timodemos was seldom seen: a thin shadow, he no longer saw his 'Particular Lady'. Old friends ceased to call, though Timo scarcely noticed. His relation with Kallias was acknowledged, even, somewhat grudgingly, by Timophanes, on his rare visits.

Follow your nature, Hermes advised. Those quicksilver feet, crooked smiles were glimpsed in a Gulf wind, on glinting waves, or sensed in the air.

Timophanes had offered his brother no occupation, merely told him to practise weaponry and obedience, so, ignoring the future, Timo still roamed the City, sometimes with Kallias, sometimes alone. He saw that streets were quieter, markets less thronged, many taverns and family houses were closed. Voices often ceased at his approach, brother of the all-powerful. His moods changed like clouds, as though the heights and depths of Hellas invested his soul, ploughed by many hands, fought over by spirits, touched by the dead. One day could be long as the Trojan War, another brief as a gnat's hour. Superbly happy, in Elysium's sunlit, dew-wet meadows sung by Pindar, he was ambushed by tears, which overwhelmed him like locusts in corn. Then a stranger's smile, the sight of waves, Kallias' admiring eyes, restored him.

He had tiny adventures. Blood enlivens ghosts, and in the hills he found an abandoned sheep. He had but to draw his knife, offer its blood to a ghost, who could then answer questions about the House of Shades. He killed the sheep, stood waiting in high, blue air under the spendthrift sun, but though he soon felt chilled, slightly unsteady, he could not be certain that any ghost was at hand.

He counted the famed dead. Achilles had preferred a short, outstanding life than to reign over shadows. Odysseus had restored the balance necessary for life. Heracles had begun badly but, unlike Jason and Theseus, ended in glory. Yet in the colonnades, Sophists, undeterred by the latest regulations, were pertly explaining that heroes were actually exhalations of mortal discontent, symbols of motion. However, unorthodoxies had ceased, with the forbidding of Factions. Too many flashing tongues meant that brother fought brother, to the glee of evil-wishers. Citizens must learn to love each other as they did the City. An exciting police force had been devised, the Children of the Goddess, spying on suspects, denouncing malcontents and babblers, waylaying messengers. Accidents occurred – on cliffs, hilltops, roofs and at crossways. The torn throat, the fly-ridden body. Parnyssos, son of Dorax, a public letter writer, had turned a corner and was never seen again. Some villagers were said to have been changed into crows.

People took refuge in riddles, ostensibly harmless. 'Which is more beautiful, fire or flood?' A market-place witticism was: 'They see to it that they are seen no more.' Slaves and immigrants suffered. Timo saw a head roll from a doorway and lie like a hedgehog curled against danger. People learned not from what they heard but from what they did not. The silence of Corinth. A listlessness, as of plague or famine.

Timo and Kallias avoided politics, continuing to talk of a newly discovered Homeric poem, lights on the sea, an ill-tempered rhetor. Occasionally Kallias, his face and bearing usually composed, slightly awry, looked as if he were striving to disclose something unusual, even dangerous, but he always forebore. No rift divided them, but moments of unease, of timidity could overshadow gaiety hitherto unforced.

Could Kallias be reluctantly accusing him? He was brother of the man now throughout Hellas abused as Despot of Corinth. He would have liked them to discuss the nature of despotism, which might lie not with a Timophanes but with uncontrollable webs and fluctuations of the universe. Gods in the sky, Titans in the blood. The whims of the unseen. A bandit was favoured, a wise man blinded. Dogs growled viciously at one twin, graciously licked the other. The star-gazer, Thales of Miletus, could date future comets, appearing like actors on cue, yet he had not discerned the fate of Miletus herself. Protesting bravely at Persian occupation of Ionia, she had been sacked, her survivors enslaved by Persia and Macedon.

Timophanes had fortune, the smile of Fate. He himself, Timo, probably did not. Timophanes crushed others like beetles, but, like Heracles, laboured for the public good, prosecuting extortionists, fraudulent ship combines, neglectful priests. Whatever Kallias might be thinking. Timophanes, though not Dinos and the Myrmidons, deserved praise. Timo, despite intermittent misgivings, knew that he was hoping to be selected for the Myrmidons himself, to be promoted to the Council, help build the Programme, stand alongside Timophanes, sharing the Name.

Must devotion to Timophanes be disloyalty to Kallias? Probably none in Corinth was haunted by a dilemma so tragic. Perhaps he was honoured, perhaps doomed.

Corinth herself, despite the Programme, the resplendent future and the beat of exciting government, was still nervy. Awaiting what? The more vigorously the young men in power bestrode the City, the more resonant the expectations. Exciting government feeds on success, or hopes of success. Anything might happen. Tidal wave, collision of stars, a nameless fleet in the Gulf with gifts for all, a dream of the moon drinking the sea.

'It's so difficult to explain. I think . . . but my thoughts scatter like butterflies. Yet perhaps . . . very soon. . . .'

Very soon. Soon indeed the Despot ordered a force to engage against the Argives of Clene who had reneged on a debt, itself trifling, and delivered instead an insulting message. A general requested that this should be read aloud, but Dinos said that it had already been destroyed, its language blasphemous, thus liable to provoke sickness.

Preparations began at once. Some believed the Despot jealous of the young Philip, High King of Macedon, who was beginning to be talked about, in the race towards a united Hellas. A half-barbarian.

Timo's age group was conscripted, girdles broadened into sword belts. Sorrowful about parting from Kallias, serving elsewhere, he welcomed action. He would have preferred to fight Sparta and her aristocratic war machine which, when slaves were deemed too numerous and powerful, hunted them down. Too young for politics, too old for playgrounds, never wholly absorbed by races, dances, songs, he too surrendered to *very soon*.

Father emerged, very weak, now blind, and kissed him, Sikinnos quavered that Zeus' gifts are various. Timo prayed to Hermes, who probably did not hear. But for once Timophanes paused and actually adjusted his brother's belt. 'Yes' – he gazed past Timo's head as if suspecting some intruder – 'you'll at least learn what use a draughts-board or quoit are against real men. Or,' – his meaty face, with the thickening jaw, animal teeth, contemptuous eyes, deigned an intimate grin – 'sweet smiles and soft buttocks you've enjoyed too long. Don't disgrace me.'

The armed recruits paraded in the theatres for the Dance of Ares, to over-quickening flutes and trumpets dodging, feinting, crouching, aiming, doing all but retreat. Dinos, grimly helmeted, metal masked, watched from a scaffold but said nothing.

Next day the populace massed on streets, at gates. *Euoi Timophanes* was everywhere, though never *Euoi Dinos*. Small, oblique gestures were made against misfortune, unnecessary though these were. A few shouted *Euoi Corinth*.

Several thousands marched out, mostly the foot-soldiers, hoplites, joined by Timophanes and Myrmidons with cavalry in the van, Dinos in the rear, ready to ensnare runaways. Mutters about a dispute between the two were disregarded. Young men were enthusiastic, pleased with each other, determined not to cast aside shields.

The first day was uneventful. Hours of descent and climb, bracken and thyme, midges and bees under a dense summer sun. The usual scurrilous songs, jokes, jovial sensations of irresponsibility and freedom enforced rather than suppressed by the discipline. By next noon the terrain changed to a plateau, unsown, dry, brown-green, gradually lifting towards grey heights long despoiled save for scrub, cut by steep ravines. The hoplites straggled in wide, irregular lines, shedding the strict columns. Timo's group was now closer to the cavalry.

They neared the foothills, the scrub and bush taller than they had seemed. Without warning, all was clash and alarum. Ambush. A trumpet shriek. Flashing cuts, sudden gleams and spurts, brief faces, red mist, instinct, a slogging affair, disorderly and savage. The attack had been too swift and headlong for orders. Timo rushed forward blindly, sword ready, as if into brazen fires, all sparks and glitter. He glimpsed Timophanes' plume ahead, still above struggling Myrmidons, many unhorsed, some toppling. Spears were on all sides, a bloody medley, but, still unharmed, already breathless, beginning to stagger, Timo felt queerly immune, even exhilarated, felling an inexpert spearman, almost a boy, half-naked, now smashed. Through a gap, over an appalled, still breathing heap, he saw the unthinkable. Timophanes aloft, besieged, glancing back, soundless, irresolute, stricken by fear, even panic. Before the yelling Argives closed in, Timo and several others had reached him, slashing wildly as if with a third arm. All was delirium: terror and blood, splitting noises . . . a hiss, a whirr, a crunch, a scream, an agonised neigh . . . atrocious heat, until, almost at the last, battle order was restored by Dinos, whose charge from the rear broke the Argive spears, not, as was then revealed, very many, over-relying on surprise.

Only at nightfall could Timo recognise his own feat. Scalded with sweat, he had reached Timophanes, a gigantic shadow, erect, wild, then falling, his horse speared. He lay stunned, Argives about to dispatch him, maddened by the soiled, torn plume, but themselves exhausted, thinking that they had already won. Reckless of darts and blades, Timo and the rest plunged into them, covering the prone Timophanes with Dinos' riders already at the rescue. Choking, dazed, groaning, but barely scratched, Timo leaned on a spear filched from a dying Argive and could see the uproar was subsiding, the battle splintering into separate duels, flights, pursuits. No Dance of Ares had rehearsed this: the salty stench, greedy flies blackening the lopped and gashed. His body had obeyed orders he had not given and not heard. He was one of the fortunate, perhaps chosen.

Timophanes recovered before the end, was seen swirling up, monstrous and glaring, as he set on the last fleeing Argives. Honour stole back to the befouled day. Amongst the corpses was Dinos, a sword between his shoulders.

7

Freed from the hateful Dinos, the City acclaimed Timophanes, ritually adorning him as First Servant. He enjoyed referring to the famed Periander, son of Cypselus, descendant of Heracles, whose heart would have rejoiced at the Programme. 'Hellas', he assured Council and assembly, 'is a rotten old warehouse, waiting to be kicked in. We know who will rebuild it.'

Prospects were unlimited. With old rivals depleted, Corinth would warn off the brutal Illyrians and Macedonians, counter the Great King, even break the ring of Carthaginian monopolists.

Acclamation replaced administration, and Timophanes was adept at the commonplaces of statecraft, stoking up hereditary feuds, exploiting old obligations, rewarding supporters.

He had not rewarded Timo. No thanks, no promotion. To him, all was unchanged. A brother was a nuisance, a spy, a danger. Timo too was wary. Receiving nothing he now expected danger. That instant of fear on Timophanes' face could have brought them closer and had reinforced his desire to stand with him. He had sworn by sun and sky, sea and river, Earth and Hades, of all oaths the most sacred, to honour his kin. Simultaneously he was freer, more himself. In battle he had not run: jabbing at a deranged face, heaving towards Timophanes, he had felt protected. By Hermes? Or were Hermes and himself bound by Fate? Hermes, though slippery, might be less capricious, more scheming, than most gods.

Kallias too was different. Not aloof, but reticent, at times unseen, on unexplained business, perhaps not always sleeping at home, and avoiding all but the most public of thoroughfares. People still fell from windows, were found lifeless under a wall, or, with the Council totally unopposed, fled abroad. He still seemed as though nerving himself for a momentous disclosure. His embraces were over-hurried or over-emphatic. His fine eyes had cooled, his skin very slightly coarsened. He had a secret.

Timodemos' death at first aroused no popular interest. Teeth in the belly, neighbours' children laughed. Long silent, his deeds forgotten, he was merely kin to his mighty son, who at once, however, proclaimed public mourning, a civic funeral.

Demariste remained secluded. Timo dreamed of sacred Eleusis, a child screaming in a fire, a saviour holding corn, and blocked a hole in the wall to prevent the dream escaping, distracting others.

Streets, long hushed, were raucous; soldiers everywhere, musicians, flowery priests, dusty rustics, Timophanes in golden armour tramping ahead. Roofs, balconies, streets were packed. Processions marched through a high, prolonged keen of lamentation, dirges, invocations. People stood in misshapen attitudes of loss.

Timodemos, in golden straps inscribed with antique instructions for the soul on its dread journey, was hoisted on to a pyre on the Acrocorinthus, to flare before all Hellas, slaves brandishing whips against demons and scattering dust and wine. Surely gods too were watching. The flames leaped and crackled, then dwindled, and against the roseate sky, from Aphrodite's temple, golden Timophanes, First Servant of Corinth, looked down on a populace awed not by death but as if at some unearthly birth.

His voice was never melodious but, strong as a bull's, it clanged vast and universal, yet, by some trick of feeling, confiding in each blank, upturned face. For him, his Sophist had ransacked traditional screeds, long-familiar orations. 'Mortals are made great by deeds. The deeds of Timodemos. . . .'

What else? None cared; annalists would later add words less stale. A true Hellene, Timophanes, drunk with his own spirit, was born adrift by sonorities, insensate music, the splendid promise. Listeners were dwarfed, scarcely any were aware of armed soldiery under column and statue, and by gates.

Timophanes' voice changed. Words hardened, no longer music but nails.

'Dying, my father saw, written on a cloud, words that dazzled, despite his blindness and weariness. The prophecy of the crown and mantle of Hellas.'

Applause was as if from the heavy sea, the guards ground spears, all were swamped in the largesse of feeling, the divine dispensation of Corinth, until the spirit became visible, first wispy, then gaining cohesion. Greenish, slightly spectral, mist was rising, not from the Gulf but as if from cracks in walls, pavings, soil, from statues, from the stupendous crowd itself. An omen? Of course. But of what? No matter. Timophanes unfurled the miraculous, reviving tales of heroes vanishing in clouds, marrying the sky, ascending to Heaven.

Priests of Apollo, priestesses of Aphrodite, all manner of sooth-sayers agreed. The Greek dusk actually confirmed a prophecy, hitherto kept secret, of the mighty destiny of Corinth seen in his final breath by the hero Timodemos.

Timo faced his brother, grown slightly paunchy, now affronted, eyes reddish, barely controlled, throat tight, face as if polished. Man of the hour, he stared across at Timo.

'Father said nothing. He saw nothing. You never came – you hadn't come for weeks. You used him like a street cry.'

Timophanes was incredulous.

'You young prig! Kallias should have raised you better. Taught you men's work. But for our Name, you'd be a common singer. This may help you dance.'

The swiftness of the blow gave no time to dodge. Timo fell across the table stung with pain, a laugh still sounding after the door had slammed.

8

The Programme was discussed throughout the Middle Seaboards. With or without Thebes, Corinth was on the move. Voices chattered, the conversation of dogs. People remembered the words of Pericles of Athens, many convinced that he had stolen most of them from marvellous Timophanes, he of the remarkable phrase 'mortals are made great by action'. Blessed language. *Athenians must grant their homeland the passions of a lover. Whoever ignores public affairs cannot merely be called quiet. We call him useless.*

Pericles had gone, Athens had lost stature, not least at the hands of Syracuse, daughter of Corinth, and was left to artists and scoffers. The crown, nay indeed the mantle, of Athens, of Sparta, lay in the dust, awaiting rescue. The Hellenic genius could crush Persia, reach India.

Rumours crept through Corinth. An oracle foretold a flowering tree, scarcely sensational. Then talk of a new war tax, a possible alliance with, of all cities, Carthage. Timophanes the sensationalist retained his flair to astonish. Could the Programme restore golden days when animals spoke and a wave prophesied wonders? Assuredly. Meanwhile, an afterthought, a shortage of bread and prosecutions for tainted wine.

His spies were brisk. Occasionally they dared report a mutinous face, a clenched fist, a silence, tiny stirs on a flat sea, which a skilled helmsman should fear.

By autumn, much of the Programme had been realised. The temple, the towers, though slaves still toiled on the canal, the purpose which was disputable and covertly disputed. But the watchers saw that Timophanes was dissatisfied. Overweight, he spoke less, his mouth set in a grim line, his face flared, his eyes somehow accusing. Few were surprised when he discovered a plot. Secret stores of arms had been impounded. Cities were again breaking faith. Sparta would attack in the spring. Consulting none, he had already hired four hundred mercenaries, garrisoned in an unnamed place.

Saved from disaster, the City gave thanks, wondered a little, braced herself for the war tax. Timo, unimportant, without much to do, avoided by those who adored Timophanes and, more markedly, by those who did not, knew that his brother, for all his array, was doomed. He had flinched in battle, Hermes disregarded him, statue and wave told him no stories. Such knowledge endangered Timo as though he were an alien spy. His hand seldom strayed from his dagger, he avoided windows and the cliffs of the Acrocorinthus.

Timophanes thought him ordinary, less than a slave. This was insupportable: without pride, a Hellene sinks into the barbarian ant-heap. Yet an appeal from Timophanes, the charioteer, even a smile, would restore almost all.

These would not come. Winter was at hand. All was on the verge, a leopard was about to spring. Following the execution of several treacherous generals Kallias revealed his secret.

They met on the shore at nightfall, the waves scudding white-topped under a harsh wind. They were almost as before, their embrace sacred as a gift, but Kallias was pale, his chiton stained and creased. All glow had departed. He was urgent, clutching his friend's arm. Against the dark sky and sea his voice trembled, no longer leading.

'Timo. They need you. Your turn has come.' The words, so drably uttered, startled.

'With your Name you're essential. Please listen. Listen carefully. . . .' In something like his old, amused tone, Kallias said: 'Only a madman dreams of India.'

Timo was astonished. The neat, composed Kallias, so adept, so little hurried, so beautiful, was a conspirator, was already risking torture and death. He was telling of some inner Corinth. The four hundred mercenaries were imaginary. Timophanes, even in Council, was stupefied by wines. The Programme was archaic prattle. Hegemony, Persia, India, Carthage . . . nothing at all, mere theatrical posture: the ornamental poverty of a knavish god.

Timophanes had made two irreconcilable enemies: his brother-in-law Aeschylus, and the wealthy Satyrus. They had a plan. Unable to resist Kallias, Timo agreed to hear it. He felt dullness overlaid with pain.

Aeschylus was small, eyes bright, darting with malice, with capable hands. Satyrus, large and bearded, spoke little. He had reputed powers of divination, was known to have foretold that Corinth would be grateful to a blind man. This had been interpreted as a tribute to Timodemos for siring the First Servant. Kallias soon left them.

Aeschylus spoke rapidly, without preliminaries. Unguarded, on foot, aping the ways of Demos, Timophanes, on the last day of the month, attended Aphrodite's temple, ostensibly to report news of the City to the goddess. The workings of the Programme. Here he could be accosted, pleaded with, praised. A crowd had now been chosen, sworn, primed, collected without difficulty, for underground opposition to the Programme was running fierce. Backed by these supporters, by the honour of Timo, son of Timodemos, an appeal would be made to halt the war levy. All would be very public. Corinthians love such confrontations, pack theatres to see them.

Drearily, Timo assented. Assuredly his brother was now lunatic, afflicted, out of balance, due for destruction, but not by hired crowds and vague divinations. For himself, though, it was a challenge, a test of manhood. Father would understand. Scarcely speaking, he joined the pair, standing over a bowl and swearing support for each other, united in love for the Genius of Corinth. Afterwards, alone, he recalled solemn lines: *Often, indeed, Hermes bestows benefits, yet in the darkness of/light he can deceive mortals beyond measure.*

The darkness of light. Timo shuddered.

To show good faith he decided to face Timophanes unarmed, but, preparing to depart, he heard Hermes whisper 'Dagger'.

That he was risking his life meant little. Life is a maze. Agamemnon in glory was lurching towards the underworld, Odysseus wins through, then the poet is silent. The more indistinct the Programme, the louder it is praised for its benefits. Now, his accomplices – the word was unlucky – on either side, he was climbing the Acrocorinthus, between mossy walls, olive trees, ferns, under a rough blue sky. He was in the stupor of some sacrificial beast, condemned on behalf of the City. Blood was due, against Fate he was unprevailing. The others said nothing but appeared resolute. Hermes was grinning.

Around the temple the crowd was thicker than usual but standing unnaturally still, as if posed. Above the grey, towering citadel beyond, a gull hung in motionless scrawl, as if nailed. He was recognised. As if on orders, a spontaneous chant: 'Timo . . . Timo. . . .' Already, in queer surprise, he saw Timophanes quite close, on the temple steps, in yellow cloak, unpleasantly resembling the porcine ex-athletes he so despised. His tufted hair, now thinning, had lost lustre, sore spots disfigured the mouth, his face contained too much blood. Puzzled by the crowd's greeting, 'Timo', he was watchful, blinking against the sunlight, then hurriedly refocusing, common life ranked before him, a priest behind, lank and pallid, a yellow-wigged skull above a flat strip of linen, seeming to hover slightly above the tessellated stone.

Hundreds waited, trained on the five: the hero, the suppliants, the priest. Timophanes gazed at his brother, refusing recognition, stolid in pugilistic security. Then he spoke, jeeringly: 'An embassy from Fishmongers' Alley!'

Unperturbed, Aeschylus, as planned, began: 'The liberties and privileges of our citizens. . . .'

Timo heard almost nothing, feeling Timophanes' stare,
affronted, now ragged with anger, land on him with the numbing
impact not of a blow but a drug. . . . His throat was parched,
dumb as stone. Aeschylus' lips were still moving; Timophanes was
no longer a boxer but a bull, about to charge. But, like intimations
of earthquake, the surroundings moved: feet stamped, stepped
forward, the priest dissolved, perhaps had been only a wraith
issuing from a smoking urn, columns and portico quivered,
Timophanes was vast, enraged, solitary; unexpectedly youthful,
he was shouting. Timo hated him, the hatred uncoiling, rising. He
felt himself pushed, though none stood behind him. As if of its
own, the knife was in his hand, part of a crazed exultation, the
howl of Titans. He had struck, his arm was sticky, hideously red,
Timophanes' face swayed incredulously, the sightless body very
slowly collapsing, like a heap of red granite mysteriously dribbling,
other bodies now closing around it.

9

At last he awoke, in the temple of Hermes, rushed there for
sanctuary. Greenish effigies gazed with identical expressions,
slanted, impudent, careless. Dozens of supporters guarded him,
kneeling, holding jars, fruits, caressing his forehead. A restlessness like heavy waters penetrated from without.

The day filtered through him, disjointed, in constant false starts.
Dazedly he learned that Aeschylus and Satyrus had fled, all gates
open to them, with shouts wishing them well. He also heard that
Demariste had forbidden all utterance of his name. In ritual
phrases almost forgotten she evoked the Furies – not the 'ladies of
a certain distinction' but the antique avengers, winged and black-
robed. For her, he would be less than a slave; he was forsworn and
defiled.

He wanted Kallias, but amongst the smiling, concerned faces, continually ebbing, slowly reviving, not always complete, he could not yet recognise him and felt too weary to ask. From splintered faces, swelling mouths, faint voices dropped praises.

'You have saved the City . . . your statue will stand for ever . . .'

'In your greatness of soul you hated crime . . .'

'Your Name demanded restitution . . . justice. . . .'

His vision cleared. Kallias had not come, none mentioned him. He was perhaps dead. Next day Timo saw priests' awed concern lapsing into uneasy forbearance. Amongst those around him, all strangers, fingers were surreptitiously crossed against a murderer's shadow. He knew himself poisoned by his brother's dying breath. Rich life oozing into rich meat, tossed to a ditch, a scarlet lattice, all else scooped out.

Assured of protection, he decided to leave the temple and find Kallias. Without family, he might have lost the Name. Had Hermes counselled or deceived him? Despite attentive hands and obliging offers he knew himself alone. Should he starve himself to death, he might appease Father, even Timophanes, wrathful in Hades. Meanwhile, he must risk the streets.

Escorted by a long procession, ostentatiously armed, he slowly descended the Acrocorinthus in ritual attitude of grief. It was also sincere. The shrouded head, the dust on his hands. Immense crowds waited, at first silent, then noisily welcoming, with shouts of gratitude, denunciations of the Programme, cries for Old Times, the younger Hellas, acclaim for the Best of All, though he had died on no field. *Euoi.* He contrived a secret smile, reflecting that none could now accuse him of being *idiot*, unconcerned with City politics. *Euoi.*

He was given a small room near the Agora, while Magistrates deliberated and men fell to their thoughts. Visitors dwindled, an old woman brought him food. He awaited a sign from Heaven, reassurance that he had not committed what Sophocles called a remedy too powerful for the disease. Corinth's stars might have been jolted from their harmonious precision, their smooth dance, Fate herself bearing down like Demariste with noxious visage. At his window he then sensed changes, an unhealthy stillness settling over Corinth. Messages of comfort arrived, delivered by slaves, but otherwise he was secluded, probably avoided. Passers-by quickened pace at his door and made the sign against malevolence. He remembered from childhood that man in the market-place, polluted, the people averting themselves as if from stench. From Kallias, nothing. *Adrasteia*, Inescapable Nemesis, punishes the animal and wanton, though he still scarcely credited his own deed. The piercing, dripping hand, the shock of bone, sensations not yet fathomable.

In certain quarters, he would hear, a joke was about that Timo, flummoxed with unwatered wine, had believed himself a Macedonian, for in that garbage backyard to be acknowledged as a man you had to split open a boar.

Word came that he must attend before the Archons and a jury of leading citizens in a public assembly, on an evening of full moon, serene above the vast, phosphorescent sea.

Refusing assistance, he prepared, very clumsily, his defence. Proceedings were in the open, in the forecourt of Apollo's temple on a cliff overhanging the Isthmus. This would permit the largest gathering, but also in the fresh wind of the Gulf dispel the aura of murder.

He had ascended alone and without goodwill or curse. The long ranks were mute, all feelings hidden. Nothing was certain. Timophanes' friends still held positions, Factions were reappearing, though cautiously, and Demos repressed libertine urges.

Fumbling with his tablets, facing the wide crescent of judges, Timo received a shock, as though an actor had in mid-speech removed his great mask. Amongst the jury, gazing as if into some ultimate recess of air, sat Kallias, and his blood told him he was doomed.

In set phrases recited as if from a play, speakers stepped forward to praise him, winning steady claps and cheers. He had made the supreme decision, choosing the liberties of Corinth above private love. He was brave, he was public spirited, he was judicious. He began to believe it himself, nourishing his spirit on eloquence, save that Kallias still sat, a stranger, very clean, as if purged, very thoughtful, like some onlooker strayed from Ionia or Thebes, attending out of well-mannered curiosity.

An old Archon invited Timo to speak. He was nervous, he dropped his tablets, rousing a few unfriendly laughs. His tongue was clamped, finally releasing a few muffled words. He began again. The judges were impassive, a row of white slabs, the massed onlookers craned forward. A ripple of impatience, memories of the dead Timophanes raking them with effects still undecided. Timo stumbled on. No stories came, no pictures to enthral a multitude. He had followed Timophanes, had opposed him, then . . . he stood speechless, finished.

There followed a nervy silence. His flesh stilled unpleasantly. Kallias' treachery could be serving justice, Zeus the lawgiver. A bird cawed from a dusty tree, as if in disapproval and at once, as if sensing tidal change, a cousin, crony of Timophanes, a suspect in the killing of Dinos, stood up. A closed, pouched face, suspicious at mouth and eye, bald, flaccid crown, the sourness of lost ambition, the voice thin, but very distinct:

'On behalf of Themis, the law who dwells in Zeus himself, and the Furies who punish violence, I demand the ancient law of Corinth. That the murderer be hurled from the Cliff of the Fratricide. In the words of Euripides of Salamis, you must hurl yourself from that dreadful height and fall, and break your neck, surrender life, be pitied by none.'

The stillness regathered from the cliff itself. Stricken by the enormity, the horror, many felt dizzy, overcome by dread sensations of falling, by childhood tales of ageing kings hurled to the rocks, saving the land from blight.

Timo, hopeless, bereft, observed that his guards had moved further from him. The jury was already conferring, Kallias smiling at the air. From somewhere a cry of disgust, a shout at the judges. He was like those whom the gods hated and transformed to stone. Through waves of sound perhaps inaudible to all others, he heard with indifference words intoned on behalf of the indignant Genius of Corinth.

'A black ewe and white ram shall be sacrificed to the shade of Timophanes, First Servant of the City. The slayer shall forfeit all goods to Artemis, Judge of Wrongs, to Apollo, Hater of Iniquity, to Zeus, the Preserver. With breast bared to the arrow or blade, cudgelled by black Necessity, hated by Heaven and Earth, he shall, at midnight, depart from the City for ever.'

PART TWO

The Wilderness

1

The dark, matted head on the straw bundle they shared was always changing, never wholly still and entire. Now the dark-brown eyes, tumbling hair, dry lips were scarcely human, now they were oriental, but always alien. She could be much the elder, passing through perpetual phases, by day often companionable but at night powerful, even dangerous. Her name she never disclosed, and his questions angered her. She served some unpronounceable goddess in ways concealed. She could be a girl, running with panther agility amongst streams and boulders, no Nausiciaa, but coarse-skinned and tall, sometimes laughing, sometimes weeping, more often silent, locked in herself. Her body would seek his own with passion, his fair head, his smoothness, enraptured her, but her love mutters were to herself, not to him. He sensed her oppression by a dim rock inscription of a child or animal impaled. To himself he called her Moira, a primitive name of Aphrodite, though she might be a Pelasgian, from days before the goddess's birth, when the Fates were young. She might be a daughter of Rhea, distant mother of Zeus. She could be crafty as a spider, then simple, easily pleased or angered, eager for the bed. Sometimes she sang, tuneless, brooding, incantatory, archaic, only to wilt into drowsiness, fretfulness, unexplained resentments, or withdrawing altogether, returning only after several days, without sound or gesture.

At full moon she denied him her body. At her throat she wore a lump of coral which he was forbidden to touch. Their dark matings were like those of foxes, her cries no endearments but battle-calls. Her bites were angry, she desired him wounded. He too was joyless, merely completing the day. Occasionally glimpsing her blood he thought only of Timophanes. She caressed his cone like a toy or a sacred snake, fought it like an enemy, gazed at it in wonder as it dwindled and curled, endlessly reviving. But no love would come. Love was affliction, the chilling eyes of Kallias, the impurities of Timophanes, to be disciplined by song, politics, dance, even war.

Her language was ugly and barbarian, though he detected certain words akin to those of farm-hands at home. She seemed living in metaphor: his drawings of a tusk, horn, wing were more real to her than the live reality. He was learning that when she grunted *red* she meant 'danger'; when she whispered, it was 'sun'. Black could be 'peril', but sometimes 'joy', occasionally 'safety'. *Stag* was linked to her goddess. Certain hand movements were untranslatable: he learned more from her eyes.

She might cook a meal, then refuse to eat, though contemplating it with satisfied intensity; drop dirt in her wine, swallow it greedily, or throw it untasted at that impaled figure.

At first he had slept outside the hut, but one moonless night she beckoned him in. In the bed, more a byre than a shelter, her nakedness could alarm: it possessed Titan currents, striving to master him. The body's ancient sea, the ageless struggle. In bright morning, back in Corinthian time, he repeated lines about Medea, the witch maiden:

> 'For, but a few instants ago, I saw
> her glare, as a bull glares'

then remembered Timophanes.

Their hut, far above the stony plains, held the strong tang of goats, thyme, gorse, wild lavender, dung. They hunted together, he taught her words though learning few. Her duties, if duties they were, remained unexplained. Occasionally she killed a goat, sprinkled it with honey over a huge ochred jar, then apparently cursed the knife. She was forbidden to wear knots, often entwined crocus or violet in her hair and at such times her speech was more lucid. Close to earth, water, rock, she would arrange stones in groups of nine which she would finger cautiously, as though watched. When he traced letters in dust she angrily smudged them, seeming to believe them a trap. He would find her standing before a boulder with deep-cut crevices or markings which he thought might map the region as seen from the sky. At this place she always appeared unaware of him and always those brown, slightly irregular eyes, somehow charred, never looked directly at him, always around him.

Villagers below avoided her and wore garlic ringlets against evil. Yet furtive offerings of milk, bread, cherries would be left, seven paces from the hut.

These wild hills were remote from towns. Coins, by which Ionia had transformed society, meant only the uncanny. Tiny faces, weapons, numbers. The existence behind him, of festivals and games, boasting, debate, the jeering rhymes and passionate bargainings, were as foreign here as a trireme or the Great King's painted, jewelled courtiers. He wondered how she explained death.

She had found him, a winter ago, lying senseless by water, almost dead from wounds and starvation. Through a soiled gaze he had seen a shape, seemingly mortal but neither man nor woman, bending over him, in long-sleeved, vulture-yellow cloth, a knife glinting at her waist.

Recovering, he realised that by queer powers she had divined his unpurged blood guilt. Even when she could understand some of his words she asked no questions, as if these were forbidden, by the nameless goddess, or the shadows of the high peaks rearing aloft. He remembered tales of a distant, fish-tailed goddess, fettered by a golden chain in some Arcadian temple opened but once a year.

Education, Sikinnos had quoted Xenophon, resides in a question, but even a simple question asked of Moira would be a hopeless and dangerous siege: in this green and black desolation, *Xenophon* was a password to the bright but by now imaginary. He too was in metaphor, sometimes trance. He was neither in shelter nor outside it, was in a void between madness and despair. He had no word for her: friend, wife, Particular Lady, whore. None fitted. *Friend* was a sickening reminder of Kallias.

Bare-breasted, hunting, strained to the utmost, she could be

Persephone, the spring, beloved of Demeter, leaping, running, scrambling in constant fluidity. As from powerful musk, he felt a tinge of the unearthly: the killer eagle avoided her domain, she could fondle snakes. Her limbs flickered with light, her silences were those of a chasm. Moods crossed her like clouds, stormy or sunlit. She would devour a bird or mend its wing with the same deliberation. Her laugh was inhuman, very high, very clear. She appeared sterile, dedicated to the goddess alone, a moon girl. With a dog or horse he would have been closer, more able to share, and provoke love or hate.

Knowledge other than of *Xenophon* was needed. The dance of bees, communicating the direction of food; one bird adding snakeskin to its nest, another a scrap of finery. The appeasement of ghosts. From massive, still wooded crags sounds were hollow but dense with menace.

Awakening before dawn, in wolf light, he would see her standing naked in cold dew, as if from a frieze, great poppies behind her slowly regaining colour as the cicadas began.

Moons waned. She disappeared, she returned. He too was free to depart but scarcely considered it. A ring of fears debarred him from men and cities. Entrusting her his sleeping body he did not always expect to survive the night.

Incapable of love, he was absorbed in her mystery. Creature of the unknown she was perhaps an Amazon, and indeed *Theseus* evoked a dark gleam of mistrust, even hatred. Or a few Trojans might have fled to such places, clutching stricken gods, glad even of ghosts.

She knew plants to cure eye and joint, blain and ache, could feel a storm behind untroubled blue, descry signs in the moon.

By now, learning his words more rapidly, she sang less, and, remembering his lyre, he himself regathered distant songs and tales. She listened, head down, unmoving but perhaps not unmoved. *Tell our stories.* Plaintive lyrics of love and deception, stories of heroes betrayed and betraying. In his wanderings he had tamed tribesmen by stories, having then to repeat them, exactly, without deviation, for a misplaced word, inconstant rhythm, would jar more than the story, like a fault in a statue wounding the model.

He told her of Epaminandos and Pisistratos, indifferent to how much she understood; of Jason and Orestes. Occasionally he suspected that she had heard such tales, but differently, her silence reserving other versions, unpropitious, even vile. At the descent of Orpheus she seemed to awaken, shaking her head for him to desist.

She now prepared him brews in which floated tamarisk stems, fungoid and brittle, and in the sleep that followed he looked down on the moon, flew aloft to the great city of Syracuse, heard dim acclamations, his heart now racing, now languid, as he clove the sky.

He was forgetting not his crime but his Name, standing amongst mountains like petrified Titans, intent upon a shape suspended blackly ominous above a fretted peak, or examining the plain, still but alive. Occasionally, he thought he heard a bell, very faint, impossible to locate, as if from outside the air. He never mentioned it: in such regions bells were magic, sometimes kindly, often malevolent, like Moira herself. Here honour was meaningless, Moira was claimed by no kin, perhaps claimed no name, was free to live, to kill.

Unexpectedly knowing himself watched, he turned. She was standing within the rocks, almost smiling, though not at him. Cold to the bone, he knew that here might be a Fury. Fate had jeered at his birth.

2

Crossing the Gulf, bare-footed, in thin, sleeveless chiton and beggar's cloak, in a boat manned with black sails, he would let his life be extinguished, without resistance, if Fate so decreed. He envied Odysseus, who met Death at his most gentle, from the sea. Outcast, he must tempt fever, ambush, slavers. Hating himself, he repeated famous lines: *Of those who are honourable, more survive than perish, but from fugitives comes neither glory nor help.* Hermes had vanished at the leprous glow of pollution: keen-eyed, he dodged from light to shadow, giving life savour, denying it convictions. No favouring sign lay on leaf or stone, birds flew low with irregular wing-beats. Ill-omened.

That schoolboy lexicon had given the great too few faults. Odysseus, Achilles had grim flaws. Zeus the Father can swiftly change to Zeus of the Black Cloud; Athene's eyes, cool and level, to pitiless rage; fresh, glowing Artemis withers to savagery like sky or ocean; the loving wiles of Aphrodite, torture. Against such, a mortal must toughen his soul.

Time alters the past. Timophanes the Cruel will become the saviour piteously and unnaturally slain, Best of All. Trudging the earth, Timo realised further that his guilt was deepening, his own flaw more gruesome. That plunging, crimson instant of murder had not been wholly ugly, like battle itself. In flux of mindless anger he had felt release, like lust with Kallias. He might seek it again, a bloody Fleece, at one with Ares, god born in foul air.

Avoiding roads, he limped into Megara, though determined to reach the north, the Thracian head-hunters, the crazed Macedonian highlanders with their black, magical Orpheus, giant bears, their High Kings without Programmes. A beggar, without lyre or purse, he belonged only to aching precipices of wild cat and lion and the lurking Furies. Sophists had honed them to tolerant old 'ladies of a certain distinction', their black blood refined to gold, their tearing claws to shapely beringed fingers, but here, beneath swarthy skies and famished moons, they remained primitive and ruthless. From tight, parched skin, their eyes dripped bloodily as they swore vengeance. Snakes rose from their heads, their wings made dry clatter. Hecate's brood, they were most fearful amid stones and aridity; lit by dreadful torches, lowering, they sought blood for blood.

Gods too changed. In lonely defile, abandoned hamlet, Apollo was no Light-bearer but Lord of Groans, Artemis the implacable slayer. Arrows of retribution. He laboured towards Boeotia, cow country, under low, grey cloud. Villagers knew without words that he was a violater. Most fled from his shadow as though his face were blotched red. All men know that a lion selects a victim by staring, so that the rest of the herd abandon it. He was such a one, chosen by the implacable. Once, however, awaking under a broken wall, he found a handful of dried figs beside him and devoured them recklessly, suspecting poison, ready to die. A child showed him a half-filled wine-jar and, his thirst intolerable, he emptied it on to the earth, to placate Timophanes.

Until purified, he was forbidden homes and rites. He should have sold himself as a slave to Sparta or Persia.

Onwards, on steep tracks between huge shapes propping the sky, jagged torsos, sickening ravines.

He had yearned to make famous his Name, and, by the sardonic will of Fate, the three-in-one, had done so.

Landscapes tilted as if at random, impoverished realms of the mare-headed goddess of terror-dreams. Sometimes, to avert malice, he feigned lunacy, easy for a mind divided. Dully he seemed to recognise what he had never seen, the desolate Phthiotisian sweep where gods had fought Titans, then he awoke on a thyme-scented hill. Such hills were residue of Old Times; masked lords towering on high heels, praying before felling a tree, conversing with centaurs.

Challenging death, he entered a mountain cave, having heard of it as the abode of a snake-nymph. It was empty, so, dislodging a great stone, he trapped himself within and lay down for ever. After a frozen night he heard voices and stolid woodcutters dug him out, shared their scanty meal, grunted unsmilingly as he departed.

Partly reassured, to retain memory, he would now recount rhymed lists of the Fates, Hours, Graces, Muses, even Furies; of the Argonauts, and the heroes of Corinth.

Sometimes he blundered northwards, sometimes retreated without knowing it. Thorn bushes by the rushing Asopus, nooses sacred to Artemis hanging from Boeotian pines, the pungent smell of boar. He slept on stones, on broom, in regions where men are descended from ants and worship none but smiths. He saw the dreary field where Sparta broke Athens in the Great War, and Plataea where, in an instant of unity, Hellas repulsed the Great King. Such places, like Marathon, have spectral, muddy shades. Further on, above fields depopulated, left to marsh, no habitation visible, a massive gate stood starkly isolated yet well oiled. Weakened by hunger, he saw boulders dissolve, trees bend on a windless day. He traversed valleys hung with frozen snow where small, ill-nourished clansmen used bronze tools, clumsy and antique. Once, from within a smooth, dirty green mound, sounded stamps and wild cries. Again, his blood knew gods.

Sometimes he could forget his poisoned existence, interested to discover that even in the derelict acres a network of feud and obligation was drawn across the land, trapping the unwary. All was necessity, the veins of Hellas. Apollo and Artemis, like quails, must vanish east in winter, return in the spring. One summer he was hailed by satyrs escorting a column of cracked wood, acclaiming it as the Great Goddess: oafs in shabby pelts with swollen, artificial cones straining towards her. They threatened to offer her his blood, then, very drunk, abandoned him.

The north. Unfinished shapes and shades, wild Boreas shaking the forests, the Archer still engraved serene above misty night skies. By marshes overhung with fever flies the scanty tribesmen were listless. Reconciled to survival he persisted, grateful for a crust after guarding oxen; convinced that in one famished week he became an animal, four-footed and rooting: ambushed, by song he astonished the marauders into dropping their weapons. He taught ignorant villages that a spear could be used for vaulting, be thrown from horseback. He supervised a circle of threshing mules, sold querns at a wayside market, trod grapes, rubbed salt and fennel into a ploughshare for luck. In snow-bound Thessaly he organised a torch race between cliff villages, was driven by thunderous winds from Hyperborea, the edge of the world where Apollo dwells in winter and Perseus slew the gorgon. Twice he was surprised by a glimpse of mighty Olympus, oaks black against snow, its falls and gorges concealing barbarous Macedonia, where roamed horse-lords with huge swords and blood-painted spears, escorting the mules packed with gold from Macedon's only soul, the mines of Pangaeum. Still he repeated stories, names, genealogies, striving to retain a self. He related stories to shapes, shapes to numbers, to opposites, and found that he could entrance not only by song. Women, charcoal-burners, shepherds would laugh themselves drunk by his old tales of bribery, deception, betrayal, of queens who stored treasure, returned from the underworld, who stood naked for the king's friends. Lean, ravaged, he urged himself into whatever direction offered itself, and still, in darkened glens, cavernous slopes, his burden seemed mysteriously known. Sometimes he was expelled with stones and curses; sometimes, fear or anger were stilled by Zeus Xenias, protector of strangers, though almost never was he allowed to cross thresholds. In savage Thesprotha he heard of an ageing oak-king slain by a double axe. When? A few moons ago? At the beginning of time? Last week?

None knew. There, granted bread and wine, he was addressed, with both fear and compassion, as Pentheus, the suffering king. Later, deep in the night, glimmered the ghost of unforgiving Timophanes, two staring eyes amongst giant ferns, mute but hating. In the morning he was fed, given a few coins, ordered on, to meet, almost at once, as if stationed for himself alone, a pillar on a treeless heath, topped with Hermes, god of travellers, with erect cone and encouraging smile. Boundary stones adjoined it and he stepped cautiously. Here was neither Corinth nor Athens. Such stones held powers; to move one might provoke blood feud and stabbings.

Another spring, yet not lifting the low cloud, the oppressive loneliness. A reddish barn on a gaunt hill did unexpectedly shine out, abnormally bright, as if it had sucked all richness from the soil, but faded at his approach.

At damp Thermion under a cold sun he hired himself as a runner in local Games. Bribed to lose he strove to win: near starving, he lost, was rewarded and feasted, none suspecting his pollution. The dark wind lapsed, the sun gained vigour, he watched a Festival of Return, where wraiths clustered in walnut groves and one corner of a barley field was left uncut, 'for the Lord', though faces were strained or fearful. Few of the dead love the living. That summer he was induced, indeed compelled, to marry thin Irus, nervous and unwanted. They were given a mouldy hut, lived contentedly enough, though she died later, producing a dead son, doubtless cursed by Timophanes. The townsfolk, however, decided he had an evil eye and demanded to blind him, to save the sunlight from contagion. Again the cries of 'unclean'. He fled to Maenad lands, untamed Edonia and Bolben swamps, then turned towards Thrace, to Orpheus, son of an apple king. The borders were unpropitious. Leather phalli hung from stakes, black wooden triangles amongst them; horse-masks and skulls were nailed on trees and doors; kites pecked a dead child suspended on a cross. He had encroached on the rites of Dionysos Orthox, Lord of the Rising Phallus. None questioned him, all were drunken, bemused by distant throbbing, sharing little toadwart cakes and dried mushrooms born from lightning, the god's flesh. The throbbings increased, then tinklings and clangs and all were dancing, pushing blood to its limits in toxic caperings, now fierce in enthralling speed, now languid and soothing. Timo surrendered to urges formless but violent, insensate freedoms in which they would all collapse, gasping, moaning, joined to vast stars, and, despite their inert bodies, treading a maze, ascending to Hades, descending to Heaven, in delirious reversal. He plucked a fish from a mountain-top, particles of snow from the sun.

Next day the sun itself had vanished, rain scourged the valleys and, awaking, the celebrants sought strangers to blame. Lately they had drowned a mule-seller for attempting to count the clan, and Timo was swiftly away, far on a rocky slope. In bad light a lean shadow barred him, a spearman ragged bearded, stooping but strong, in grey skins. Surely a Lycurgus, Thracian wolf-man, de-scendant of a king who had tried to kill the child Dionysos, and, driven mad by Zeus, had hacked down his own son, believing he was reaping the vine.

'Friend, who invites you to barren lands? Your name? Your kin?'

The voice was drily hostile, like the chipped fingers curled round the spear, the heavy, bearded cheeks like ramparts, above which eyes were sentries. At the belt glinted a knife, its old-gold blade and ivory horse-head handle like Timodemos' Scythian dagger. The skins had carrion stink.

The two were inescapably confronted, amongst dark copses, shadowy hills: hub of a limitless twilight. Timo gave ritual reply. 'I am Timo, son of Timodemos. I am a stranger and beggar, thus son of Zeus.'

The wolf-man's grin revealed only mockery, as he completed the exchange. 'And to them a gift, however small, is precious also to the giver. So how shall he enrich himself?' His speech was unex-pectedly precise and melodious, at odds with the garbage clothing and bare, filthy legs, disorderly hair, leathery, sprouting features. Timo tried a smile on this figure: neither old nor young, he seemed by no means brutish but not wholly human, with a grin spread unpleasantly under the fierce eyes. 'How can I believe in any Timodemos, trust any stranger? We once had gods on earth pass-ing themselves off as minstrels, cowherds . . . but, if you are no god, your speech suggests Corinth.' He motioned Timo nearer, then pulled out a loaf. 'Harvests are gifts of the dead.' His laugh was caustic. 'The dead tempt me more than Corinth.'

They shared the bread while he mentioned further names, test-ing for blood feuds. Evidently satisfied, he then produced a wine-jar. 'I am Theodotos, son of no one in particular. Grey of visage, grey of speech. I can show you a live joke.'

He loped expertly through the dark to a shack, lopsided as if lamed, lit by a few lamps. Stumbling, Timo saw a dog in messed straw amid several pups, all dead, her eyes glazed, her paws mournfully fondling some scraps of cloth. She ignored the two men.

'It's a good joke. One of my many treasures.' His thumb jerked at a stool, a heap of jars, a palliasse, the rickety walls. 'The brood was born dead. She took it badly, refused all food. My neighbour, a randy young runaway from deep in the scrub, came in, carrying her baby, born perhaps from a passing lynx. The dog eyed the baby, howled louder than Niobe, never much of a song, then began sorting straw into a sort of crib, licking that bundle of cloth. Comic old rot.'

His laugh was mirthless. He thought, then, after a prolonged, threatening silence, laughed again, now graciously. Timo accepted more wine, then a clap on the shoulder. He sat down, nodding at the dog, herself too preoccupied to notice. The thick shadows implied utter trust, or irrevocable danger. Knowing it, Theodotos spoke: 'You can sleep here. If we both kill each other, I can leave the race to you. My own spirit got lost, won't ever reach Hades.'

Beneath dirt, bristle, fatigue, his bent frame and appearance of frost, he was still young. Men grow strange shapes, remembered in tales.

They shared many days, hunting, drinking, quarrelling, storytelling, with elaborate, jesting reconciliations and pact makings, Theodotos using laughter now as sword, now as shield, probably always as mask. Timo learned, without always being told, that he had been lamp-maker, wheelwright, mercenary captain, probably much else. He could quote Homer in two versions, and, between those desert-wind gusts of laughter enjoyed repeating: *For of all that breathes and crawls upon earth, man is the most wretched*. He made it sound a tavern witticism.

At times he was his wolf-self: surly, hungry, absorbed in the hunt, displaying skills scarcely definable. Once, at supper, gnawing bones, chewing a bluish hunk of boar, Timo thought of Timophanes, that brutal frown, raw-meat visage, and Theodotos' voice abruptly accosted him, like a mast breaking: 'You're thinking of blood brotherhood.' Again, the bar-garden jest, but Timo shuddered. Only then did he realise that this lonesome fellow had occasionally answered questions before they were asked. On furthest scree, most dreary outcrop, Theodotos would abruptly halt, sniff, peer forward, grunt approval, set a course surely unlikely, but unerringly find game, water, home, on paths impeccably straight. 'I was buggered by Pan.' His wink was caustic, but for animals he had an aura fitfully Panlike. In certain moods he would sit smiling distantly behind the unkempt beard and rocky features, and savage dogs, lynxes, wild cats would emerge from trees, whimpering, pleading, licking his feet.

Without change of expression he would be the gentleman, soft, mannered, almost ingratiating, then the yokel, vigorous, fierce, urged from within into the deepest current, the grimmest canyon.

After a long day of charged, sparkling air, of unison left mostly unspoken, they reclined, tired, pleased, well fed, so that Timo, by now seldom surprised, was startled at the voice from the gloom.

'Tomorrow you'll be going.' The tone was casual, or apathetic. 'We'll be meeting again. Your noise will reach me.' Then he curled up for sleep. It was final.

On parting, Theodotos showed his usual stance, midway between an embrace and assault. He did neither, merely frowned unpleasantly. No partaking of *Xenia*, exchange of gifts, oaths, embraces, blood. Instead, more frowns. 'A joke, to speed your travels. A Great King ordered his annalist to write the story of all the world. Far too long, kings have time only for war and fucking and too many meals. The annalist sighed, and shortened the lot. Three words were enough.'

Theodotos' grin looked deadly as a mantrap: his laugh was manic. '*Birth. Suffering. Death.* Dreary snivellers.'

3

Not purged but revived, he tramped Hellas, still aimless but convinced that fortune was with him, Hermes within call. Conscripted into a blood feud more violent than expected, he rallied, then led the pack, burning a farmstead, gathering sorry spoils, and later lay drunk after feasting. Praise he accepted gladly yet ruefully. His gifts were not those of song and stories but for mauling. Theodotos must have scented it. A zest for blood. The curse unlifted.

When he told them he must leave them, the squalid troop held a wake, groaning at loss or danger, once vowing to kill him, to retain something of his spirit. Yet he left unharmed, all avoiding his touch, without farewell.

One autumn, after drought under a scalding sun, the Archer at his most pitiless, rain fell seven days until, overnight, huge crocuses, saffron and sun-swamped, covered the brown earth, shrunken carobs were green, the cisterns shining. The strong light recalled no Dionysiac frenzy but the choral dancers of boyhood, golden, simple as leaves, and the torch races at nightfall, though in dreams the lithe bodies could lie withered and pocked, the blood dried, after hideous maimings.

He missed Theodotos. There had been some love: love with twisted face and jeering throat. Then, somewhere, ambush had left him naked and senseless, left to Moira. Once, in the night, he was woken by a harsh, shaking noise, laughter. His own. Moira, beside him, stirred, imagining he wanted her, or wine, but he had dreamed of the snivellers.

Now Moira herself was thinking of him, while watching a lizard sunning itself on a flat stone. She still had a morning's journey before rejoining him. She would soon be alone again. It had always been so. From the near came voices, from the far, occasional strangers were sent: a stag, a man, for the Goddess. Vengeance was demanded on a world now averted from her. Timo had emerged as if from burial, his blood restored and fresh; to cleave further to him was dangerous, and to release him might doom herself. Yet he was accursed, dispatched to her because all others rejected him. Perhaps even the Goddess would scorn blood so impure.

He was undoubtedly one of those outlanders who had come from the sea under a black moon, settling the land, insulting the Goddess, building impious cities, driving the gods from caves and hills into the sky. Yet to gaze at him obsessed her. His height, his thick hair, greying since his arrival, touched by their common life, his clumsy gait, had power. Covered by him, possessed, she was stung by secrets and left trembling, unbelievably sad, in hues not fruitful but arid.

She had counted the moons since their first bedding. Within her, she felt the Goddess's anger. She had risked all and must let him escape.

The lizard twitched, the light broadened, deepened, bullfrogs choked and gurgled. She felt the call of her own ground.

PART THREE

The Return

1

Light of step, again entrusting himself to the god of roads, Timo felt himself Odysseus released from Circe. *Endure my heart.* . . . His purpose was now clear. He had endured enough to risk offering himself to the Mystery of Eleusis, no Dark Goddess but Bright Mother and Child. Already he had found in his sandal a dried corn ear, emblem of Demeter. Expiation had been in some measure earned. A brief dance of wind must contain Hermes.

Pericles had advised people to await Time, wisest of counsellors. Time cures all.

These journeys had unlocked the world. Empty Mycenaean castles, vast stone lions were questions not yet answered. Bandits of Mount Oeta, mercenaries who had killed their general, the rustle of oak leaves at Dodona where Zeus lives among men, all spoke to him. He was awaking. In horse-loving Colonus he had taught words to a village, words finely tooled, dew fresh, burrowing into meaning. A child's face had grappled with a sentence, was suddenly radiant. 'I've opened it!'

He was moving south, already joining a baggage train, all glad of new sun, high clouds, as they lumbered through Attica, where sacred bands propitiated the last trees. Over cypress groves he had seen Athens, red and white against the taut blue line of the sea, though, unpurged, he could not enter. He had passed Thebes, old and grim amongst peaks, seen flocks driven high on Kythaeron, had stood above the world on Parnassus, where steep slopes reached towards sacred Delphi, the world's centre. Myrtle, laurel, pine held breath when he neared the crossways where Oedipus, son of Laius, encountered Fate. Purged, he might venture onwards for ever: through Persia and her elaborate, drowsy officialdom, to Ethiopia, where death was unknown, to India whose heroes recruited monkeys in wars against evil.

On a detour alone, he met an image of Hades, enemy of fig-loving Demeter, hateful to Eleusis. Daring, exuberant, he plucked the pebbles from the eye-sockets, threw them on to a cairn dedicated to Hermes, built by stones dropped by each traveller. At once his blood thrilled as if verily struck by a prankish youth in a blue cloak amused by mortals.

Kingfisher days. Beehives rimmed with light, shrubs thick with red berries, gorse, wild poppies, lemon tree, fiery as the clouds parted, oleander and quince in sharp leaf, almond foaming into pink and white within the pungency of thyme. A region can be judged by its barns: they can be holed and shattered, barred or open, and here they were well roofed and secure. In one he was invited to sleep, and brought wine. Very tired, he dreamed of a sea-bound island city joined to the mainland by a causeway. A naked girl was pursued by a man, almost caught on the shore. She became a fountain and at once he was riding through streets jammed with waving crowds.

This was propitious, and he found fortune continuing. A hawk dipped over him, three goose feathers lay in a circle of dust. Life was unconquerable as the vine which flowers, is harvested, and then crushed to a fine juice. The hidden processes of existence which, deeply, Moira must have known.

Apollo himself, at Delphi, had told Croesus, son of Alyattes, that Fate, once decreed, cannot be escaped, even by a god. But she can seldom be known by men, who must persist as if she were not. Only partially serious, Timo examined his hand, as so often before. Like his head, it was now patchy and discoloured but the deep lines were clear. They might presage gold or sudden death, but were long, promising more years yet.

On a wall, under bulky, bee-swarming Hymettus, where rocks jutted like half-buried elbows, waited a graciously carved Demeter, small Persephone in her arms, corn stacked around her, and, above, a boy driving a dragon-born chariot and holding a sceptre.

Here pilgrims were assembling. At sight of him, they cheered, for they had been told to expect a tall, grey-headed man. 'You must lead us to Eleusis. The goddess respects grey hairs.'

Remembering those lifelines, he laughed and assented. His limbs still served well enough. Calendars are inventions of priests, are slippery and can be shapeless. His years of exile should be weighed, not counted. For the dying, a day is briefer than a lover's wink, a week in a besieged citadel longer than forty nights in a brothel. One horse of Achilles was immortal, for the other a particular day promised death.

In this month, 'Running for Help', the flea-ridden pilgrims rejoiced with sun and expectation, blowing reed-pipes, swapping lies, self-importantly reciting hallowed sayings, preparing for the Mysteries.

'Hateful as Hades' gate is whoever thinks something and utters the opposite.'

'An exception to that, friend. Never confide all to your wife. Indeed, tell her the one and hide the other.'

Loggy with cheap wine they sought the attention of their greybeard uncle with the oddly powerful shoulders and calm demeanour.

'Evil deeds do not prosper . . . the slow overtake the swift . . .'

'I wouldn't wager that at the Games.'

Behind such chatter, much appeared unchanged: the Great War ravages, the Factions, depopulated estates, overcrowded cities, roaming bandit soldiers. Throat cuttings, rippings.

Eleusis. Let Demeter wash away stains, free seekers from hauntings.

2

Imagine Eleusis amongst softly luminous poplars, rebuilt by Pericles after the Persian sack. Her grove of white aspen, ever quivering in memory of Heracles, led here by King Theseus, begging expiation for his massacre of centaurs.

Ponder Heracles himself, son of the Father, on a mountain, his young sap in tumult, tempted towards despotism, revolting against Zeus, then dedicating himself to overcoming monstrous dangers to Hellas: draining, ditching, building, then, watched by helpless followers, meeting atrocious death. Then earthquake, and divine ascension in a cloud from Mount Oeta. His spirit lingered here, reminding Timo of hopes lost long ago.

An aged priest, head like a peach stone, white smear over his left cheek, expressionless, both men locked in a grilled cell, where little light penetrated, had heard his story.

'You killed your brother in hatred?'

'Yes.'

'You solemnly repent?'

'Yes.'

Timo suddenly felt a third present, though unseen. A shadow shifted. A strict silence followed.

'You seek admittance to the Sacred Pair?'

'Yes.'

Light oozed more clearly from unseen lamps. The priest's tone was unexpectedly younger, his eyes more intimate.

'You cracked the divine order, yet perhaps were the instrument, not the begetter. You have suffered in freeing others. The world knows that inordinate passion mocks the gods, the Goddess may decide that Timophanes doomed himself. You may go forward. When initiated, you may prosper, in ways to surprise you.'

The door opened as if by no human hand and he was swiftly back with the others.

Candidates must fast three days, then, carried by mules to the shore, pray to Demeter, Persephone, Dionysos, and bathe, transferring sin to the wholesome waves.

Several hundred, naked by tumbling waters in golden light, chanted: 'We swear by the Ten Foremost to hold all in this holy place secret until death, and after death.'

The temple, walled above the small, shining town, glimmered within gardens heavy with pomegranates. More pomegranates were carved on wells, fountains and pediments, and painted on tiles. The outer courtyard centred on a cypress, tree of rebirth, the inner on a floor mosaic of three joyful Cretan shepherds adoring infant Zeus, of the Mother and Daughter, of tiny Dionysos threatened by Titans. A wide terrace was engraved with maze lines, on which dancers would mime the soul's last journey. In the forbidden sanctum lay Zeus Meilichios in the guise of a black snake.

In the outer court, all drank mint and barley in water from the Callicoran spring, near the cave which led to dark Hades. They abased themselves, foreheads touching soil, then a voice spoke, apparently from the unseen: 'Oaths taken here, if broken, visit upon you damnation.' At once priests were bestowing little cakes shaped as triangles and pentacles, then myrtle coronels. A novice escorted them down to a crypt fumy with sulphur. Between short pillars a hierophant, his long, yellow and white sleeves ovalled as he upheld a small silver snake, bowed, then in a deep, monotonous voice, chilling, even marmoreal, spoke words of Sophocles, son of Sophilius:

> 'Nor did I then believe that a mortal
> Could by a breath extinguish or override
> The unchanging, unwritten laws of Zeus,
> Laws not of Now or of Then
> But eternal, children of the unknowable.'

That third night, after drinking poppy juice, chewing bay-leaves, they were swiftly asleep in long, underground dormitories. Timo slept deep, seeing men glistening like honey, like panthers, wheels revolving in a windless sky, a thick, green sea crumbling into corn.

Later that night, or perhaps after several nights, gongs awoke them, into rims of hushed, greenish light. Each was handed Little Foxes, raw, fiery mushrooms begotten by lightning. They descended to an indistinct hall, empty save for corn sheaves on a round altar. From thence into clammy darkness, fumbling blindly in procession, as if abandoned, misled by closed alleys, complex windings, sometimes slipping on stones, always slanting downwards, shivering in weird chills, some cried out. Bare feet had sensations of the slithering and creeping. Fetid, intense, the darkness was infernal, the domain of Hades, until, sudden as an alarm, the night was drawn apart, a voice sang, echoing in triumphant purity, light flowed from all sides, from meadows now near, now barely visible, where dancers approached, mingled, receded in hues endlessly changing. The song ceased, the dancers faded, five white-robed hierophants, each radiant, sat in a circle. A nymph cross-legged in golden smock by a fountain was playing a double flute, the sounds merging with other instruments, unseen, unknown, the sounds nameless, quivering like thin silver rods in a breeze.

One hierophant murmured from between fat cheeks painted with black scrawls: 'You are still lame.'

'Assuredly.'

'Look not to the left. Gods themselves shudder at the vaults of death and corruption. . . .'

A shadow was darkening all, spreading, unstoppable: sterility, disease: the left. Though no walls were evident, the initiates yet felt imprisoned, a bondage of flesh and spirit.

A white staff lifted, some power seeming to pull the priest's hand after it. All eyes closed. When opened, they saw in light now flimsy, hazed, an icon of the goddess, a mass of dark, converging lines assembling features simultaneously of Virgin, Mother, Crone. The lines diminished, vanished, now Demeter in black, trailing gown was ranging wasted fields, distraught, hands outstretched, pleading for her lost daughter. The congregation sighed, lamented. Timo perforce shed tears. Distant fires gleamed, a singer intoned *Iakchos*, for Hades, Ocean, Olympus. A voice from the earth. From a velvety pall of mist brilliant details shone, were at once gone: a red-tipped ivory oblong, a purple buskin, a pale-blue sky, inducing the tensions before battle, when weapons are aimed, horses pack for the charge. Now in utter darkness the hymn soared: 'Fasting . . . renouncing magic . . . the barley mead . . . ascent. . . .'

A girl's face glimmered, perfecting a sad smile, changing to a silver bowl topping a wispy spiral. Coloured lights played on a void, flutes sounded harsh discords, the soul splintering to its elements. The bowl reappeared, dwindled to a small chalice, then spread, was a pool shimmering beneath vines and pomegranates. 'The Showing Forth', the voices sang. At once all was glittering as a trumpet call, corn was sprouting, Mother and Daughter embraced, harvest mantled the earth, senses awake. *Iakchos*. White radiance, then golden, a mass of dazzling atoms. Each candidate felt crowned, soaring, aloft, meshed above the seasons in the fierce particles of the universe, liberated from the swirling flux of existence.

3

The hamlet overlooked the Ionian Sea. Cicadas chirped, summer light smote the cliffs, fishing-craft dipped and swayed. As if in harper's land, the small port promised calm: old, patient men, smiling women, children laying violets for Hera.

Eleusis had stilled all fevers, appeased hungers. To be Best of All was contemptible, akin to Timophanes' lust for applause, to lead the charge, sport the garland. Here, far from the world's gaze, Timo smiled at Polydamus' words to Hector: People are assigned different gifts: *one can fight, another dance or sing, or play the flute and to yet another Zeus allows wisdom*. His own gifts he had dropped in dust. He was content, gazing at the incessant quicksilver topping the waves. No triremes arrived from the Maeostian with Baltic amber or news of cities, demagogues ranting for cancellation of debts, profits heaping up as Hellas declined, small farmers surrendering to usurers, wagers on chariots, Sophists belabouring reputations, a mob sacking a temple famed for research into the powers of numbers, thus endangering stars. He had rid himself of the dust and clamour. In politics angers change, anger does not. Welcomed here as a man of peace, he concerned himself with the folk's petty concerns. A marriage, a fire, an eclipse sent, the priest explained, to rebuke the fish. He drank in the tavern, told a few stories, joined the singings, learned to mend nets, badly. He was awaiting nothing, expecting nothing, complete in himself. The gulls, the sands, white upon light blue, gold upon green. *Zeus is breath of nature, sweep of the tireless flame*. He had endured. Without future, he might be a slave. He might also be favoured by daytime gods.

Days, weeks, anchorage in summer. Happiness, nevertheless, is briefer than sorrow and, in late season, the alarm bell rang. Fire? A raid from the hills? No. Look: far out, cutting shorewards, all sails cresting, a warship, shields bright, swords doubtless bared, the wake – oars swinging as one – pale on the dark-blue waters, straight as the hair of Artemis. The villagers ran to arms; grabbing their children, the women huddled indoors. Timo stood with older men, club in hand, waiting. Death from the sea. Avengers seeking only himself, to settle all, as at Eleusis his prayers had demanded.

All were silent. The warm air quivered. The port was too shallow for a vessel so heavy and several men in civilian robes were embarking in a skiff, landing, already ascending the steep path.

Four men were following a fifth, himself bearing the maple staff of authority. They halted before Timo, made respectful salutations, repeated by the puzzled villagers, amongst whom the women had reappeared, inquisitive children already capering, starting songs and, excited, leaving them unfinished.

The leader was broad, his black hair and beard touched with white, his bright, grey eyes young on features lined and jowled.

'I am Apelles, son of Podakos. We have sailed from the Gulf, a deputation to the son of Timodemos. The gods be with you, Timo.'

That night, alone with Apelles, he must listen. Apelles was gruff but lucid. Since Timophanes, a moderate oligarchy had ruled Corinth, grappling with the dispossessed farmers, aliens and slaves, the spendthrift leagues and alliances. Sparta's urchin love of mindlessness, lampooned in every Hellenic backstreet, was rusting, but the Great War had not expelled the lure of Ares so hateful to Zeus. The mainland was restless, ready to fight again, to recover colonial monopolies and Ionian footholds, relieve unemployment, enlustre each City Genius. Persian pensions remained readily offered, her gem-cutters working busily on bribes and gifts.

Persia . . . so clever, so ceremonious, where torture was a fine art, a refinement of pain: slow impalings to stately music, disembowellings by expert Asiatic dancers. Slow ripples of Persia, to Babylonia, Assyria, Bactria, India: over Phoenicia and Ionia, blocked only by implacable Carthage, but, in Hellas, tempting an Alcibiades, even a Xenophon. Persian meddling had no limit. Furthermore, undeterred by southern threats, encouraged by lying oracles and giddy youths, Macedon still hovered. King Philip had married a young witch, raised in Thebes, apt to change herself into a snake, no asset in marriage. He had absorbed the warrior skills of Pelopidas, the inspired resolution of Epaminondas. His land was barbaric, but its mines were attracting hundreds of jobless men, able not only to scour for minerals but hurl a javelin, juggle a shield. Discontented with his frontiers, watching the disunity of

Hellas, he too had agents with fat purses, specious promises. Already a fine harbour had succumbed to 'respectful donations', a city, besieged, had surrendered too swiftly.

Apelles waited a little, drank, gave his short but friendly smile, then resumed. All this was background, familiar through both their lives. Now Corinth, unscathed by the Great War, had prospered, revoking the aggressive Programme. Nothing, however, remains still. Imperceptibly the light ebbs, leaving the well in shadow.

He leaned forward, jabbing one finger on the stained table as he might on a map. Rough, doubtless unlettered, he was sturdy, independent, probably trustworthy. He said, very emphatically, 'Syracuse'.

Here could be something new. Timo had known little of this, colonised by Corinth, chief city of Sicily after the high days of King Dionysius I, lawgiver, despoiler, prize-winning Olympic dramatist. Since his death Syracuse had endured revolution, counter-revolution, criss-crossing between his son, Dionysius II, and his harsh, austere brother-in-law, Dion, murdered for his severity. Syracuse now languished under Dionysius II, a perfumed sophisticate, one of those sceptics or atheists who, to control Demos, build temples and punish blasphemy. Sicily was now derelict, riven by old feuds, gruesome vendettas and colonial expansion from Carthage. Night was enveloping the sunlit isle. Backed by the colossal overseas republic, Carthaginian settlers were continually encroaching, encouraged by a local king, the half-Hellenic Hicetas of Leontini, ever jealous of Corinthian Syracuse, and summoning Sicilian patriotism against her, though visibly in Carthaginian pay.

Syracuse was already under siege, the African republic ostentatiously neutral, while her colonists and mercenaries officered a Sicilian army pretending to take orders from Hicetas. Already it had invested most of the countryside around Syracuse, though her citadel was rated impregnable. 'Like Troy,' the wits said.

Exiled by Dionysius II, some Syracusan nobles and financiers had appealed to the Mother City to dispatch an overseas expedition to restore Hellenic supremacy in Sicily, restrain the alien settlers, relieve Syracuse. Amongst the deputation, disguised, was a messenger from none other than Hicetas, ever the timid gambler, the double-dealer, promising secret support for the 'Foremost Champion of Hellenic Liberties'. More substantial was the offer of another Hellenic chieftain, Andromachus of Taormina. Scared of Carthage, threatened by his own Sicilians, he offered his city to Corinth in return for support.

Apelles gave that mature, agreeable smile, another signal of youth refuting the tufted brows, streaked beard, the grooved forehead and a somewhat sententious manner.

'The House of Timodemos is not forgotten in Corinth. The Name survives.'

The Archons had scrutinised the appeal from Syracuse. Deliberations were brief. For an impressive jumble of mixed motives, not all disclosed, backed by Demos at its most raucous and deplorable, the expedition was sanctioned. But who was to command? Of late years, Corinthian policies had been only commercial, covert assistance to shadowy leagues, intrigues conducted beneath elegant conference, elaborate embassies, at Hellenic Games and Festivals.

The Archons and oligarchs, grandly submitting to popular will, had regathered in public, on the terrace of Aphrodite, above the assembled populace. Each was to enscribe a nominee on a tablet, then drop it into the urn. Before they began, however, a voice yelled from the seething mass, cheerful but menacing, echoing around the tall, scarred columns and vestibules, assailing the affronted rulers in their pomp: 'There is but one choice. Whoever opposes it is hateful to the gods and the City. Save yourselves from our wrath and submit. The people demand one who is hidden but known to you all, the Best of All. Timo son of Timodemos. Timo the Liberator.'

4

Childhood glister rimmed the towering Acrocorinthus, the red roofs, the dash of waves in the Gulf, the masts. *Euoi*, sang the crowds, waving from porches, balustrades, streets. Some might recall that foolish prophecy of mantle and crown. All had known that, despite Timophanes' cruel proscriptions, the family house was barred to the killer, as against a stinking pi-dog. Demariste had died, obdurate, unforgiving.

Mortals must pay dearly for much they never intended.

In a pageant of return he had driven through the City, upright in an antique chariot. *Euoi*. Garlanded, acclaimed, he had simultaneously felt himself rising from the dirt, the multitudes, the din, into a bright headland of cloud, from which he saw again the tomb of King Sisyphus on the Isthmus, the small, pale temple by blue water, the gardens and groves of Aphrodite and Apollo.

Euoi. The chariot swayed, all was dizzy, the crowds a blur from which a child's grin, a solder's belt were suddenly distinct. *Euoi*. Waving, smiling, he was undeceived. Hellenic loyalties are rootless. They had been yielded to Father, to Timophanes and the Programme – tomorrow, perhaps, to the Great King – with the fervour of a wealthy Sophist condemning the iniquities of wealth.

As precaution against secret curses, poisoned fealties, he had entered the ritual bath, been anointed with fumigating myrtle and bay, stood naked before Zeus, offering libations, until, as he lacked wife or concubine, he was robed by a slave, obeying the laws of gods, and of his own being. He had destroyed, therefore he must create.

At once the days were packed with strangers, discussions, plans, though only when alone did he escape loneliness. With Apelles beside him he sat in Council, praised, deferred to, saying little, keeping his back protected. Already a message had come from Kroton the Rope-maker, once a general, a lover of Timophanes, hinting at vengeance. Furies, clansmen, even victims, can forgive murder more easily than they do any rejoicing or profit resulting from it. Killing had allures almost sensual. Timophanes knew this better than most.

Distant relatives greeted him with suspect delight, recalling occasions usually imaginary, and assuring him that he must marry.

He wanted no wife. Silence, Sophocles had taught, gives women true grace, but few Corinthian ladies are silent. Nevertheless, when they brought him a cousin, Aigle, daughter of Konnos, he consented. Their child would maintain the Name. Also, as cousin, she would help erase the kin-curse.

Aigle, stupid as a Phrygian, very young, very frightened, very docile, glad of an Ephesian scent-bottle, glad of a night's inexpert mating, in equal measure, gladder still to glide away to linen press and shuttle and the compliments of slaves. Almost at once he knew that the Name would be disappointed; Aigle the shining would bear only daughters.

Hastily, amid planning the Expedition, imposing decisions on a Council still suspicious and reluctant, still cautious of Demos, always less excited by mortgage and collateral than by triumphant armies at a safe distance, and learning from Apelles, Timo had by fortune acquired a Particular Lady, Ismene, dwelling in fashionable quarters above the Isthmus. Her trained gestures and grave smiles, her restraint which implied much and asserted little, were soothing after the boasting, thrusting overstatements of contractors, officials, officers.

His wanderings were unabated. Striving towards the boy he once had been, the boy with lyre and singing voice and taste for stories, he stole time for streets, quays, hills and shore, back with the quickfire disputes, whiplash repartee, voices like rubbed flints. The beloved cave remained undisturbed: the cracked walls, King Sisyphus almost obliterated by spray but still fondling a tiny sun, the hum and dazzle of waves.

Had Kallias survived? Timo grimaced contemptuously at the sea.

Summer darkened, rain fell, autumn came early. Ships had been lost to Carthage, harvest was poor. No expedition this year, more time for preparations. Mercenaries abounded: sold-up landowners, runaway Ionians, hard-fisted Celts, Illyrians, Etruscans, from threatened homelands. Apelles enrolled a few, despite Timo's doubts, then dismissed them. Such fellows followed only the purse.

No advantages of a surprise attack on Syracuse had been lost. There were no secrets in Hellas. The citadel would probably hold out until spring. Neither Dionysius II nor Hicetas were warriors. Both would offer terms, or pretend to. Carthage would not waste money on a winter campaign.

While Apelles supervised shipyards, quartermasters' offices, recruiting booths, Timo studied Xenophon's mastery of discipline, strategy, hygiene, his respect for Sparta. He also learned all he could of Sicily, helped by Ismene, who had lived there.

The island had seldom known stability since the long past

aristocratic despotisms of Gelon and Heiron. The prodigious kingship of Dionysius I had for years awed the Middle Sea. Etruria
collapsed, Celts plundered Rome, but Dionysius remained victorious until in old age overreaching himself with Carthage. Thereafter, interludes of democratic agitators, the 'severe moderation' of
Dion who had ejected Dionysius II, effete scribbler, erstwhile pupil
of Plato of Athens, whose quarrels with his royal father were
celebrated. The proudest and loftiest despot is 729 times more
unhappy than the humblest philosopher, Plato had boasted to his
angry host. Plato had been mentor of Dion, outlining the Perfect
State, based on schools, universities, lawcourts, presided over by
Harmonia, goddess of unity, staffed by those who through wisdom are virtuous, with the dissidents and unruly expelled. Dion
had been in too great a hurry to achieve this. A slave revolt
followed his murder, then petered out.

The Great War left all Sicily open to bandits giving Carthage
chances to intervene. Twice King Dionysius II had received Plato,
only to dismiss him in rage. He would not long resist Corinth,
unless Carthage forestalled her. His father had allowed him wealth
and comforts but mocked his writings, cursed his companions as
grubs and panders, refused him political training, though from
whatever purpose or jest, allowing him to inherit. He was soon
famous for a drinking bout lasting ninety days. He was proud of
his verse and inscribed it on vases for his favourites:

> If you seek nonsense which most of us do
> Pronounce, very loudly, 'Fate'.
> The rest will follow – on a plate.

Timo discovered that Dionysius had already sought help from
the Great King but jibbed at a perpetual Persian overlordship and
annual tribute.

Cat-loving, jewel-caressing Persians in scented pavilions, so unthinkable in the small stone cities of Hellas, might well be Dionysius' final refuge, but Sicily had once been great, could be so again.
Gelon had slain the Carthaginian war-lords at Himera, Dionysius I
had trounced an immense Carthaginian invasion, further assisted
by plague, the result of a prayer devised by himself, kept very
secret. With the spoils he had raised the awesome Citadel, then
New Hades, a black granite prison, always well filled with those

reserved from the fatal quarries where an Athenian army had perished.

Carthage never forgives defeats. Timo's interest deepened. He was glad of Apelles, down in the barracks. The ultimate threat to Syracuse was not Macedon or Persia but the Sacred Republic, black sun of Africa, crouching to devour all Spain, Corsica, Sicily, subjugate the entire Middle Seaboard. Plato had urged young Dionysius to rearm while he had yet time. He giggled, agreed, grew bored, yawned, was barely civil, composed another verse, then, to his annoyance, forgot it. Dion was now being praised by those who had killed him.

Timo heard that Dionysius II insisted that his cooks be adepts in astrology and architecture. Corinthians were chortling that his father had built in marble, he himself in cake, his army dependent on the latest supper. A late autumn attack on Syracuse might thus be feasible, but Timo and Apelles were looking beyond that. Syracuse was a step towards the inescapable collision with Carthage.

Nights could be spent with Ismene, the long, calculating hours dissolving in that coloured room, a considered pattern of balances: the yellow bed on blue and green tiles, glazed Minyan jars red against white walls, crimson petals above a black bowl, Ismene's green robe matching that of Athene above the arch.

With Ismene, quiet, reflective, affectionate, he evaded politics and, at last, confided, found warmth. She led him from the ivory gates of illusion and phantasmagora back to fruitful earth. He brought her his problems. Kroton the Rope-maker remained unappeased. His threats reached Timo, had been heard by Ismene herself. Under a mat they found a drawing of a coiled snake; a box was delivered, holding a dagger daubed red.

Should Kroton be attended to? Ismene's grey, appraising eyes gazed over the waters before she replied. Timo stared, then laughed. 'Such tactics, Ismene, are those of Athene, perhaps better. They could muzzle Cerberus, stop Heracles in full surge. I shall discover how well I can perform, then return to you either crowned or bespattered.'

Next day, unattended, he arrived at Kroton's sheds, begging admission. Kroton was meagre, grudging, rank with suspicion and a little fear.

Timo smiled, apparently open-hearted, apparently modest.

'I shall not insult you, cousin Kroton, by attempting to buy off your anger, taint your honour, overlook your undisputed bruises. Certainly not. A man's spirit is unaffected by gifts . . . though a trifle may well be reaching you, the tribute one cousin owes another.' Surprised by his own guile, his unsuspected fluency, Timo saw that Kroton was already disconcerted, then baffled. 'No, Kroton. As one famous for transgression, folly and ignorance, I am come pleading and begging not only forgiveness from a blood relation, but, on behalf of the City, aid from the foremost rope-master in Corinth. You are known far, you are known wide, for your skills. You, and all the world, know that in the spring we sail to deliver Syracuse. Our ships, Corinth, Hellas herself, depend on rope, rope alone, nothing but rope. You, you above all, rope-master-in-chief, must wear the garlands, superintend the fleet's necessities.

'Corinth.' Timo, grey and erect, spoke with some grandeur. 'Corinth waits. On her knees.'

To win without fighting, Ismene agreed later, is the best of bargains. There would be no more snakes, no more daggers. They lifted goblets to Athene, watching them, while dusk drooped over waves now opalesque, now blank.

'She stands not above but behind us. Sometimes beside us.' Her voice was always friendly, slightly amused, a little teasing, likely to say the unexpected but with a graciousness that, however professional, implied that she was reminding him only of what he had long known. She gave him confidence, stature, as they talked through the night: Babylon and Persia, high-stationed gossip, changing fashions in decoration, the custom, curious and distasteful, of circumcision, seen in Egypt by nosy Herodotus of Halicarnassus, son of Lyxes.

Their embraces were shared pleasantries, she knew his wants intuitively, neither ever needed explanations. Both were un-afflicted by passion. Love deceived only others; shimmering, elusive, it was somewhat ludicrous, like a triton. Much older, he yet felt himself the younger, a pupil, being taught without pedantry by an ally against market passions.

Ismene rose. A white hand touched the long, brown-gold tresses, her small, restrained smile completing the movement.

'Dear Athene! Through her we see long, long consequences. So very long! In pride, we forget her, she does not forget us. I could tell you of a girl so presumptuous as to believe her body more beautiful than is allowed on earth. She was punished!'

She sighed, then returned to him, her eyes lively, and touched his rough cheek. 'Should we not be as generous to ourselves as we are to others?'

In quiet pleasures, their nights were identical. The finest wine watered from a blue Persian krater, one handle scarlet, the other gold, the juiciest olives, strips of pastry so thin that, they agreed, a lover's letter could be read through them.

Cressets were lit in the street below. Ships vanished, the night hum rose from the City. They talked on. The Expedition, the latest poet, the failing repute of Oracles.

'Yet they want you to go to Delphi.'

'It may help the venture. The priests will have agents in Syracuse. Their reports should bless us.'

He might perish, he might for a while push the wheel of existence. The Sicilian Expedition might slip into the great tales, the Odes of Hellas. Spartans at Thermopylae, Persians routed at Marathon, at Salamis, the Theban Band, manned only by lovers, dedicated to Heracles and Iolus, the passionate friends.

'Sometimes, Timo, you speak as if your fate is already prescribed. But it is the onus of us both to behave as if it were not.' She looked at him unobstrusively, affectionate. 'At their best, so seldom, alas . . . the gods are seldom magnanimous, but often ironical.'

As always, she was no teacher, but fellow-pupil, sharing discoveries. Cribs, minor injustices, small jokes.

He left at dawn and at once was startled by a touch on his shoulder. His weapon-hand leaped, was instantly thrust aside.

'Passion is fiery, friend Timo, but it cooks no fish.'

Shaggy, soiled, all but his eyes smeared with grime: Theodotos.

5

Winter passed. All Corinth cheered when the embassy returned
from Delphi, assured of Apollo's goodwill. Then a native priestess
dreamed of Demeter herself preparing for a sea voyage. Just what
was needed and Timo, her adopted son, at once renamed his
flagship, bought by popular subscription, the *Mother and Daughter*.
Near Sisyphus' tomb, sacrifices were offered to Galena, Lady of
Clear Skies and Quiet Seas. All feuds were forsworn, all quarrels
forgiven, or said to be.

The fleet would sail to Rhegium, opposite Sicily, best suited for
invasion. Before embarkation, a letter reached the Council from
Hicetas of Leontini, master of crooked counsels. He begged his
illustrious friends, the nobles and gentlemen of divine Corinth, not
to deign notice of feeble Sicily. He himself was already uprooting
craven Dionysius on their behalf. Should, however, the impossible
occur and his love be rejected, he would be forced, nay impelled,
to transfer his affections to the Sacred Republic of Carthage.

The laughter was prolonged. None thought a reply necessary.
Reassuring news came from Andromachus of Taormina. Seven
thousand volunteers stepped aboard from Corinth, from Corcyra,
from Leucas, like Theodotos, from the wilds; veterans of the desperate to retrieve position, feckless adventurers, all shrewdly
selected by Apelles, none of them mercenaries with their fly-by-
night loyalties and demands for plunder. Syracuse, a Hellenic city,
must be preserved, for the reconquest, for the Hellenic Idea.

Timo stood watching, Apelles and Theodotos beside him, with
the staff, the Equals, most of them Magistrates and landowners,
with scant military experience but steady supporters of Timo's
claims and the Name of Timodemos. Timo himself was burdened
with an extravagant title, *Somatrophylax*, which nobody used, certainly not himself. 'Our Timo,' the men cheered. Remembering
Xenophon's maxims, he set himself to learn their names, persona-
lities, this man's weakness for girls, that man's swagger, another's
recklessness, after ruin by dice.

Aigle had wept as a wife should. Ismene remained very calm,

yet bade farewell as though not parting but sharing another mood, a further dialogue accepting his gifts with a small adroit shrug, his embrace with a gesture of understanding, a refusal to lament.

She would have heard the City's plaudits, the toasts and wagers, as the masts unfurled against the flushed sky, the oars lowered, rose, dripping silver. That night the prow of *Mother and Daughter*, leading towards Italy, gleamed throughout, lit by no human hands. Lord Timo, Eleusian initiate, favoured by Apollo at Delphi, was fated for triumph in Sicily, island of Demeter and Persephone. Indeed, resolved to restore the tormented land, he was serving the divine pair.

Seas were calmed. At Rhegium they were greeted respectfully but quietly, the citizens nervous of Carthage. They would remain some days for rest and repairs. On the third morning the commanders were roused by a bright-eyed subaltern. 'Sirs. . . .' Three foreign ships were sailing into port, heavily armed. Soon a delegation, purple-cloaked, gold-helmeted, besashed, was standing before Timo, Theodotos, Apelles, and a wide crescent of Equals. Not Carthaginians, only Leontines.

On the quay, watched by curious locals, their spokesman bowed to Timo, to Apelles, stared insolently at slapdash comedian Theodotos who, as someone must bow, did so himself without interest. Some onlookers tittered.

'Great Lords of Corinth, we bear propitious news. Your friend and ally, Hicetas the Great, has defeated the unworthy Dionysius outside Syracuse. He is crouching in his absurd Citadel. Our fleet, graciously assisted by the Sacred Republic, blocks all entrances to Syracuse and watches the coast.'

Theodotos belched, his narrow face sharpening unpleasantly. The rest stood silent, few caring to assess fully tidings so unpropitious.

'My lords, there is more. Royal Hicetas, as you have known, seeks no enmity with beloved Corinth, especially with Excellency Timo, favoured by the word of Delphi. He wishes to spare blood. He commands all Sicily. You need do no more than disband your small flotilla, accept his safe conduct home and thank the gods. You, Lord Timo, are welcome to sail to Sicily alone, welcomed by Hicetas, Hicetas *himself*. Our finest vessel will shelter you, every man will be at your behest. Hicetas will receive you as brother and adviser.'

After the Leontines' withdrawal, the Equals sat disconsolate. One speaker spread his hands as if opening a fan. Their forces were no match for Hicetas and Carthage. These Leontine warships were heavier, more powerful, perhaps swifter, than the Corinthian galleys. Others agreed. Theodotos examined his dirty fingernails, as though counting the weeds. Apelles sat silent, huddled in his frayed green cloak, waiting. Voices trailed away as Timo stood up, though only to order the Leontinians' recall.

They stood, disdainful, smiling, in full military rig. Feathers, engraved breastplates, ornate belts, metallic buckles, slaves holding the polished, circular shields. At a long, tense silence the smiles slowly evaporated, like water cooling.

Timo, still seated, was unhurried. From his wanderings, from Ismene, from his performance with Kroton, he had learned that the craft of survival is in endlessly surprising oneself.

At a tiny nod from Theodotos, otherwise unobserved, he finally addressed them, not bothering to leave his stool, secretly entertained not only by the grandiloquent delegates but the distress of his supporters.

'Hicetas, your employer, speaks as all would expect of a warrior so courageous, a deceiver so smooth, a gambler so forthright. None would dare address him as anything less. Tell him how gladly we acknowledge proposals so honourable. To be brother of Hicetas, what ambition! Adviser, what glory! I of tarnished Name and few resources . . . Leontini is mighty, Carthage does not lack resources . . . I am nothing!'

He smiled pleasantly, deferring to the Equals' incredulous bewilderment, Apelles' stricken eyes, the fat smiles and taunting stares of the Leontines. Theodotos, suppressing laughs, seemed to have detected undergrowth beneath a thumbnail.

Timo, story-teller, was braced by new self-confidence, a precious ichor of spirit. His words dropped with leisurely fluency, as if enscrolled before him on the air.

'And yet . . . and yet. . . .' He hesitated, as if suffering grievous disappointment, recoiling from bereavement. 'My very good friends. . . .' The sudden smile on the weathered, storm-tossed face would have melted that vaunted Citadel of Syracuse. 'All must be seemly, lest those far away be told that I consent through fear, through hateful ambition, through greed for the favour of wondrous Hicetas. We must abide by formalities, the requisites of diplomacy, our famed Hellenic grace. I must honour Heaven-born Hicetas with fitting ceremony. Pledges are best made before honourable witnesses, the gods themselves do likewise. The citizens of powerful Rhegium stand neutral between us, respectful to gods who delight in harmony. Let us summon them, in their majesty, and swear our swearings before them all, that earth and sky may acknowledge the powers of Hicetas of Leontini.'

Understanding flickered on Apelles' eyes as the envoys inclined, very gracious, very generous. Yes, witnesses were useful, yes and indeed: essential. Corinth was wise, her lords' words were leaves of Parnassus, envied by the Muses.

That night Timo conferred with Theodotos alone. To deal with the Leontines was simple: Theodotos began to plan, Timo completed it, the two sat back, enjoying the joke. Hicetas! Theodotos retold the story of that paragon, masterpiece of nature, mellifluously welcoming the fugitive wife and sister of murdered Dion, then unobtrusively drowning them. A royal joke, Theodotos showed teeth, but a bad one. 'One day we'll make him eat it. Meanwhile, our own joke. Quiet as a thrush's blink.'

Relieved of threat of war, Rhegium, feeling herself in history, was quickly astir, fighting for the best views. There, on a balustrade, draped purple and gold, sat the respectful Corinthians, Timo in grey tunic and leggings, on a humble bench in the background, almost alone. Theodotos, Apelles, most of the Equals, were missing, but Rhegium was excited by the panoply of Leontine, the magnificent intimates of Hicetas, Light of Sicily, Hope of the World, Tutor of Ares, deigning to give terms. Rhegian civic dignitaries sat with them, disposing of Middle Sea fortunes.

The Leontines seated themselves on crimson stools, with much bowing and deferring, murmuring compliments, patting shoulders, occasionally allowing a nod to Timo, harassed and unfortunate without supporters, so far beneath them. The crowds were already shouting, as if at a comedy, swigging, devouring little cakes, holding up children to see the great men. Many thought Timo a slave, probably a scribe.

A Rhegian stilled the clamour, to give formal welcome. He spoke well, he spoke lengthily under a noonday sun. All, he declared twice, was halcyon. Yes, halcyon, happy word! He lowered his head as if in respect to himself for having invented it. Then he continued, more slowly. This far-famed city did not love her

neighbours but respected strangers. He praised Hicetas, he must
mention Corinth, more than once. He explained that, to honour
the illustrious guests, the gates, shops, taverns had been closed.
That is to say, shut. Indeed, emptied. A Festival indeed! Earlier, a
cobbler had halted him, though of course respectfully, to remind
him of the majesty of none other than Hicetas, merciful and just.
Just and merciful. Mercifully just. Justly merciful. Just so. Between
friends, all is equal, all is sacred, that is, holy – that is, the opposite
of impiety.

Timo joined in applause. A dazzling Leontine began rising, had
already opened his mouth. But no, the priest of great Zeus must
first have his say, and he said it, in prolonged, eloquent sentences,
sometimes repeating them in rustic dialect for the benefit of the
unschooled. For an occasion so momentous, the temples too were
closed, locked, that is to say, shut. About to reseat himself, and
with Hicetas' plenipotentiary again rising in full pomp, he smiled
reassuringly and resumed, one hand upheld in minor blessing.
Listen. That very morning a fishmonger had accosted him and,
respectfully of course, praised the serene magnanimity of no less
than Hicetas, bright son of the morning.

Resigned, perspiring in their grandeur, the Leontines submitted
to further orations. Praise for themselves, their sea captains, their
gods. Verily, their condescension to exist on earth deserved the
gratitude of the earth.

People were noticing, however, that Timo was uncomfortable.
Broken by terms too onerous, ashamed before all men, abject at the
desertion of his officers? A cowskin fellow needing pity, perhaps a
public subscription? No. At last laughs began, winks, grins of
fellow-feeling. During a florid peroration, Timo, almost obsequiously, pleadingly, pointed to his belly, patted his stool and,
amiably cheered, stepped down and vanished. The best of men
have natural needs, but he was probably shaken by nerves, even
fear. He would return in improved condition.

Actually, he did not. Speeches continued. In brocaded gowns,
metal sheaths, the Leontines sat on while, screened by hired Rhe-
gians, let pass by bribed gatekeepers, Timo was speeding to the
harbour.

On board, setting sail, the Corinthians heard songs starting in
Rhegium, very loud, very bawdy – Zeus' leonine cock, Hicetas'
ducklike rear, Dionysos' imagination – enveloping the miserable

deputation of Hicetas, to echo overseas to Persia, where the Great King's stiff, painted features momentarily quivered, and the annalists hastened to record his words that would live for ever, that Excellency Timo was indeed a Greekling. Was he yet on the pay-roll?

PART FOUR

Syracuse

1

At night the ships anchored under starlight. Timo drank briefly with the watch, retired early, to lie at one with the stillness of the little cabin, the quiet rock of the tide, the creaks and murmurs.

All Hellas had sniggered at his display at Rhegium; the pledge from Delphi had delighted his men, but he himself lay oppressed, as if sea-mist oozed through him, or a curse from Moira had begun to work. O Ismene. Without her, his thoughts were footsteps sounding in a city built for the dead. Or tainted by Delphi.

Everything, Thales taught, is full of gods. Places exist, numinous, taut as a lyre, vibrations never wholly subsiding. Perfection of balance, fateful stillness. Dodona, where Zeus dwells with a consort older than Hera, perhaps Moira's goddess, where suns are tiny and the primeval oak, flecked with doves, is hung with brazen cups whose clangour gives messages to a withered priestess, though sacredness is not in them but in the sudden rustling of leaves in a windless noon. From a hidden valley, voices had sung, plaintive, slowly echoing between rocks as if seeking rest from sorrow. He never found the valley, only a small tribe, all blind, eerily neat and assured, like guardians, their pots polished like mirrors. Around them the motionless air was stiff, resisting, he had to strain against it to reach them, but they were silent and aloof, slowly withdrawing, as if by suction. Parnassus remains holy, where an image of Rhea fell from the sky, and Mount Lykain, birthplace of Zeus, where the temple remains barred, though not empty, intruders lose their shadows and die within the year. Sacrificial meat, sometimes human, if devoured by a thief, transforms him to a wolf. Had Theodotos been an incautious thief?

Timo had journeyed to Delphi only at the Council's behest, no guilt-ridden candidate but bearing treasures, without need to remember that Apollo was vengeful, and that even his glittering love could be fatal.

Beneath the Council's staid prayers was a necessity to aid recruitment, influence Sicilian waverers. Oracles themselves, though capable of twists of truth, were seldom a safe insurance. Nikias the clove merchant had been warned by Delphi against water: thereafter he avoided ships and rivers, but died in the Baths of a seizure. A Spartan general had received, after due payments, the advice: 'His Excellency must depart for war while not forgetting the advantages of remaining at home.'

The Sacred Way gave a sharp instant of awe. The Corinthian cavalcade climbed through fern and pine, wound through craggy defiles under the snowed heights, valleys widening beneath. Silvery groves mottled the reddish soil, sea winds cooled against the precipice, Zeus' eagles circled the double peaks. Then, at another turn, above dense laurel and oleander, the long, gleaming terraces cut from slopes black with caves. The roofs and columns, the golden bees, of Delphi. Then noseless, cracked, bearing scales and a broken jar, a statue, of Fate, of Law, older than Lord Apollo, older than Zeus, touched with the uncanny.

Timo muttered a prayer, bent his head under the renowned portal. *Know thyself. Measure is best.*

His reverence soon chilled. Apollo had left Delphi to priests, self-important and supercilious. The great river of Hellas, the Idea, had shrunk to a trickle. Whoever presided at Delphi had but one craving. Coin. In the Great War, whatever Apollo's feelings, Delphi had backed none but Persia, where the treasury was largest.

Forecourts were as crowded as those of Eleusis but differently. Youths sporting soiled garlands junketed around towering stone phalli, themselves wreathed, chipping them for luck. Water-carriers, muleteers, labourers unable to afford a sacrifice, whining for charity, quarrelled with dagger-tongued guides, each anxious to show wealthier clients the stream where Apollo slew the python, often grabbing their arms and forcing them to notice,

while boys who sold wreaths or the breath of snakes, sacred but
torpid, fluttered their painted eyes, whispering that for a little
more cash, the merest glimmer of silver, a bow could be made to
Pindar's throne, to the bronze head of Homer, to the flame burning
without fuel on Hera's sacred hearth. Meanwhile, escorted by
armed brutes, ornate boxes were vanishing within, the tribute of
cities, corporations, monarchs. Bullion of corruption. Altars were
piled with cheap statuettes, amulets against plague, herbs against
old age sold by the decrepit. The Vestibule of the Seven Ages was
stifling with sulphur, burnt laurel, aromatic thyme. Timo, treated
with deference, chose a goat for sacrifice. 'Ah!' The priest was
unctuous, smelling like a catamite. 'See! It trembles. The god is
present.' He half glimpsed a figure, heavily veiled, crouched above
yellow fumes issuing from a crack in the centre of the world: a low
tortured moan, then words muffled and incomprehensible. Afterwards he was handed a tablet.

> *Light leads to Dark; Dark supresses Light:*
> *Darkness must pay: Light in its turn reveals Nothing and All.*

After accepting this concoction, Timo found his baggage stolen,
at best an ironic gesture from Hermes, god of thieves, messengers,
journeys, which might have entertained Ismene. Grinning, a slave
demanded a tip to remove a leaf from his path.

Alone in the cabin, Timo had uneasy premonitions. Again he felt
himself ill-fated, perhaps endangering the Expedition. All were
heading for a murderous isle, already blockaded, under the fearsome shadow of Carthage. Few were trustworthy. 'Trust none of
us,' Theodotos had smiled spikily. 'Each man has too many faces
and a thousand eyes.'

By morning his dejection had gone. The sky was brilliant silk
from a heavy sun, golden darts penetrated a sea soothed by
Mother and Daughter, or Galena. Notos, the South Wind, sped
them easily forward, the rowers' spirit cheered by a flute-player,
who performed so lustily that he had long blown away most of his
brains.

Apelles maintained a constant look-out. In a general's decorated
cloak, chin sunk on breast, he stood like a crested, dignified water-
bird assessing immediate prospects. Gummed skins protected the
bulwarks. Leontines might heave into sight, or worse. Athens

boasted success over pirates but more probably colluded with them against rivals.

Theodotos stood with Timo in the bows. He was trimmer now, his beard well oiled, sallow cheeks clean, the thin eyes bright, even merry. At first professionally cautious, Apelles now accepted him as a versatile brother officer, perhaps useful with the men. Timo made himself conspicuous and accessible: *Somatrophylax*. His cloak embroidered with lions flashed and rippled, his silver buskins shone. Between the small, crowded ships dolphins leaped. Gulls screamed above the call of the Cretan balanced above the oarsmen, bawling the rhythm. Now they were singing, crushing the flute with rhymes lavish with quayside filth.

Green sails, scarlet and yellow sails, brazen beaks, victory wreaths on masts. Last night a captain had dreamed of pelicans, hastily interpreted by Theodotos as enemy disunity.

The singing ceased, not from fear of Leontine masts but at dark Etna now looming ahead, giantlike, swarthy, smoking, scorching a hole in the sky.

The blockade was bluff, perhaps confined to Syracuse. The empty sea caused some unease. A trap? Apelles gave warning, the Equals stood silent, Theodotos pointed carelessly at Timo. Commanders have ready answers. 'A trap? What else is life itself?' Everyone laughed, without knowing why, and they soon beached near Taormina. The shore was unguarded, though on the hills was an armed squad, gold earrings and bracelets flashing, before speeding away. Leontines, scouts from Dionysius or Sicilian clansmen who hated Carthage and Hellas alike. Not Taorminians. Soon the camp was receiving carts, horses, provender from loyal Andromachus. Embraces, libations, reports. The Leontine discomfiture at Rhegium had already grown in the telling. Men joked that Timo of Corinth, shown a secret path to Hades by a quarryman, had recruited Ajax, Achilles and the rest against Dionysius and his besieger Hicetas, only Odysseus crying off.

Other news was graver. The Sacred Republic of Carthage had promulgated an Inescapable Edict, promising support for Hicetas, the plunder of Syracuse, the submission of Sicily.

'Our Timo,' the Corinthians said, sometimes sang, unloading the barley bread and onions, figs and wine, the weapons, examining baggage mules and Andromachus' horses. Apelles kept them too busy to exchange misgivings. Few knew Sicily, known for its flaming mountain, for bats and snakes, for orchards, for Demeter robbed of Persephone, for aboriginals, formerly giants, now meagre, darkened by fumes of Etna, beneath which Titans groaned for deliverance. Sicilians were secretive, flitting between villages to steal, to poison, clasping runic blades forged by the infernal. Not far away was Kyane, where Hades had raped Persephone, dragging her below.

Apelles was more encouraging, speaking of enchanted places of lemon and grape, and a spring of eternal youth. Almost all fancied the lemon and grape, few credited the eternal youth, belied by Apelles' own face, respected, obeyed, not greatly loved. A bright tumble of butterflies was explained by a Coan wiseacre as the souls of the first Corinthian invaders wishing them fortune. Men laughed and felt better.

Sentries were stationed, pig's fat was offered to Zeus and Ares. Theodotos was already showing competence, supervising storage, wax rubbing of javelins, encouraging boastfulness. He was popular, had reassuring style: when the men spat, against misfortune, he sneezed, apparently at will, to reinforce it.

At dusk, small fires glowed along the shore, wine was broached, men lay on dune and couch-grass, and at moonrise, when the moths flew, Timo, who, like his father, knew how to delegate, strolled amongst them with an ivory-handled, twelve-stringed lyre, recovering childhood skill, quick, precise, as he sang verses from Anyte of Tegea.

> 'Shrill locust, seen no more by Apollo,
> Singer in the rich mansion of Alkis,
> For now you fly to the Clymenusan meadows,
> To the wet flowers of Golden Persephone.'

They crowded round him. In the firelight, against the glimmering sea, he was larger, lordlier; the slow gentle words and pluckings were largesse, pledges of victory.

Much had to be done, Apelles forwent sleep, worked, planned, seldom leaving his tent, while Timo continued mingling with the troopers, praising, repeating jokes he had not known he possessed, making showy allusions to his youthful fights which he now half believed.

These lumps, mostly unconcerned with causes, enjoyed war as

they did games and first love. He himself, adopted of Hermes, preferred overcoming by ruse, feint, even witticism. These might outrange Dionysius, but not the larger enemy.

The island was mountainous, the only road looped the coast, much of it between Taormina and Syracuse controlled by Mamercus of Catana, to whom messengers had at once been dispatched. Others were sent to Selinus, Megasa, Hyblaea: spies must reconnoitre Hicetas' forces and the situation at Syracuse. Hicetas must be driven out, Dionysius be disposed of, swiftly, before Carthage acted upon the Inescapable Edict.

After two days, few recruits had appeared. Villagers had fled. Leaving Apelles and the Equals to follow, Timo and Theodotos rode forward to Taormina. Timo disliked riding – Theodotos compared him to a half-empty sack – but had secured a sound horse, Black Cloud, his thighs were still strong, and he managed well enough, goaded by Theodotos' casual perfection.

Andromachus was friendly. He was more: childless, old, eyes tired but wily, sunk in a bony, depleted head, with his lands threatened, he was obviously relieved. Corinth in arms. Furthermore, he was honoured that the two generals had come unguarded, trustingly. Too old for fighting, with a blood feud against Hicetas, he would produce further horses, provisions, a battalion of swordsmen. Feasting his guests, he was garrulous but explicit.

'The Leontines . . . they've numbers, little else. A careless lot. They've still got most of Syracuse, but anyone but young Dionysius could sweep them away. They resent Hicetas, always biding his time, avoiding action. There are rhymes of his cowardice all over Sicily. As for Dionysius, he's locked in that monstrous Citadel, barred from sea and land. Meanwhile, you need not fear Mamercus. If you spare Catana he'll leave the coast undefended. When you take Syracuse, he'll rush to clasp your knees.'

A fresh report was delivered. Hicetas, remaining in safe quarters, was sending five thousand men to reinforce those investing Syracuse, and to overawe the hill towns. Men laughed at Theodotos' assurance that two of Hicetas' feet were cloven.

Andromachus was unperturbed, but warned against overconfidence. Too many cities since Heiron and Gelon had welcomed mainland liberators, only to sink into treachery, factional intrigue, corrupt speculation. As yet, only one city had declared for the Corinthians. Adrantum, south-west of Etna, sacred to a fire-god,

Andranus, whose temple was guarded only by emasculating
dreams. Powerful, perhaps not powerful enough.

Next morning they heard that the Carthaginian colonists had
placed themselves under Hicetas' protection, swearing an alliance
to endure throughout eternity.

Timo and Theodotos looked at each other. Andromachus suggested immediate advance on Syracuse, to intercept the five
thousand and win sufficiently to impress both waverers and opponents. Timo agreed, though resolving to dispatch a force to reas-
sure Andrantum, where, though, from Theodotos' invention, a
trumpet had already sounded from a cloud and one of the temple's
distressing dreams had travelled far enough to thwart Hicetas in a
critical situation.

The two rode back to camp. Heat, failing water, grumbles,
disputes, gnats, a wounding. Etna had rumbled, its fires more
blatant. Songs were listless, but Theodotos' tale of Hicetas and the
sight of Timo quickly restored good cheer, and Apelles agreed that
lack of water need not impede the distribution of wine.

'History', Theodotos said, at the Equals' supper board, 'enters
on silent foot, Clio's tongue is bandaged. How happy the absence
of portents!'

True indeed. No eagle had actually alighted on bald Andromachus, or snapped off the plumes of the mighty *Somatrophylax*,
leader of men: not one baby, he continued, was reported gnawed
by a griffin, no girl ravished by a centaur or metamorphosed into a
swallow, nor had too many snakes arrived, fleeing from the Royal
Macedonian bed.

'To Syracuse!' the ranks were soon shouting, none apparently
worried about the Leontines, for already in lusty chorus they were
singing to all Sicily:

> 'King Dionysius, light canary
> All aflutter, see him scary.'

2

Syracuse was now three fortified cities united by thick walls. Two, called the New Towns, with tall mansions, colonnaded avenues, wide gardens, were linked to the island Ortygia by a causeway over reedy marshes. On this was Old Town where the great marble Citadel, with fierce ramparts and massive towers – some jokers insisted, now packed with poets – creation of renowned Dionysius I, lover of mathematics and engineering, reared white and red above the houses.

Silence pervaded, the silence of blockade and hunger. Many suburbs were captured by the Leontines, themselves ill-provisioned. The Grand Harbour was almost empty, with Dionysius' fleet destroyed by fireships. The Lesser Harbour was bright with enemy troopships and native fishing-smacks.

Leontines cowed the New Towns, where citizens, hating Dionysius up there in the Citadel, feared Hicetas' arrogant soldiery and possessive quartermasters. Beyond the outer defences, the Achridina Wall where, in the Great War, Athenian generals had been captured and executed after a grandiose attempt of invasion, the vital stone quarries were being worked by doomed slaves, Syracusan conscripts. Surrounded by pine, cypress, and the sea, sacred to all Sicily, was the fountain of Arethusa, who, fleeing from Alpheus the river god, had miraculously changed to water, mingling with the mystical, underground flow, a swig of which, blessed by Orpheus himself, gives sensation of plunging into Aphrodite's lap, hearing the strains of planets and being drenched with the jewelled spray of Poseidon. Despite constant upheavals, royal, oligarchic, democratic, despotic, the women wailed every spring for Adonis the Lord, whose flowered effigy they cast to the waves before rejoicing in his triumphant return.

The Leontines themselves were cautious. All knew that gods had been seen, stepping over the waves, deserting Syracuse; nevertheless, both the Citadel and New Hades, the prison, were reckoned to be stacked with sulphur, pyrotechnic gum, catapults, and Hicetas had not yet sent the promised siege-machines and rams. The atmosphere was more sullen than resolute, not assuaged by news of the Corinthian landing, the defection of Andromachus, the silence of Mamercus, the apparent occupation of Andrantum by the Greekling. Wooded cliffs might conceal danger, the blue, irregular crescent of sea be less deserted than it appeared.

Within the Citadel, the hush is not due to events outside or to the famine, and the water now rotting in the cisterns. Despot Dionysius dislikes all noise louder than a murmured lyric or softly plucked string, a whispered epigram or invitation. Lulled by colour and perfume, the air of the royal apartments is of subterfuge and illusion through which figures dimmed by absence of windows, glide rather than stride, afraid to disturb the man within the deepest recess, even by a frown. A shot – even more, a groan – is unthinkable. One treads like a conspirator, bare-footed. Tiny giggles are muffled by the thick, carpeted walls and heavy doors which, repulsing the summer lights, fashioned another and abnormal season without sun or tide, without night or wind. Dionysius shrinks from stone walls, preferring his elaborately tasselled tent, so that his most private sanctuary is decorated to resemble it. The domed ceilings, painted tassels, the triple folds of Tyrian silk, long and glistening. Sometimes he speaks of retiring to Egyptian deserts where people darken their skin by brooding on complex gods.

Shadow of Apollo, Beloved of Adonis, Foster Son of Zeus, Dionysius has not for some weeks felt himself any of these manifestations. The monotony is oppressive.

Still young, not perhaps very youthful, he rises late, his night companion usually dismissed before midnight. To lie naked, completed, in candlelight under the blue Syrian coverlet, reliving the deft, fluttering hand-play, the small struggles and inveiglings, the tidal flow, until they merge in brief, startling dreams, reduces the tedium of the day ahead. Privacies are ecstatic, Priapus' treasures.

Favourites succeeded each other like days, needing no names, acquiring no abiding aura. The Orphic wheel of rebirths. He might have loved that solemn young fisher-boy stooping over a coracle, that girl brooding by a fountain, but such miracles appear only at a distance, like gods. They have become statues, needing but a single glance to remain for ever.

The day is already curving ahead, to be savoured, flattered, caressed, deceived. He can complete the lewd poem about Hera ever renewing virginity in a lustral bath and twist it into a symbol of Hellas revived. Hellas, the mighty heart of neighbourly malice. He must insert that line, beat the verses into submission.

Lines glow, brilliant butterflies, phalli that grew bodies.

Plato quacked at poets as disruptive liars. *All that deceives may be said to enchant.* Such a tone poisoned the fruit of existence. He had wished impiety proscribed, to induce order, even if the gods were imaginary. Well, Zeus, if doubtfully a truth, was indisputably a phenomenon. Plato, your move.

Caskets need renewing, this wearisome siege is halting supplies. Yet these apartments hold sufficiency. He can see Orpheus, who rejected all bloodshed: close eyes, and the figure crumbles into a pattern of meaning within chaos. The live and the inanimate fuse in that block of onyx endlessly changing shape and colour. A Cretan gem displays a divine trinity, six hands reaching for crossed axes. Around the shell-clustered bed are mosaics of cypresses, intricate as spray, curled like scimitars, distinct as . . . oh, them-selves: glistening lilies, deep, convoluted roses so easily trans-muted into bodies sprawling on clouds. Such bodies, cut so neatly from the stock of vulgar flesh, refined to so many exquisite depths, outlined so richly against gold-dust bronze. The black horse of lust can be a guide, wise as Cheiron, breaking moulds, ranging towards incredible light in regions scarcely conceived.

Syracuse's fall will be revenge on Father, the war-god, hero, tamer of horses. At a glance from Father, love wilted, lust retired from the Presence. From the first, Father had drugged him with scents, wines, arts, but, volcano with a grievance, had sneered at his writings, his talks with Plato, his requests for political instruc-tion. Now, in this hopeless war, the war-god is useless, even his plays were forgotten. Politics are the last chance: the art, Father declared, of gambling on short memories, a sort of forgetting.

The Peace Council can no longer be kept waiting. He need not disclose that a rascally Ephesian has sold him information of *the highest importance*: that Ethiopians are ruled, doubtless very sensi-bly, by a dog. A dog, if well-spoken, would be welcome in this quicksand Syracuse.

The Peace Council deliberates under lamps shaped like grape-clusters, behind a crescent table, installed on pearwood stools according to rank. The long, white robes, the pink sashes render them doll-like. They have been searched for arms, or should have been. The faces are set, unforgiving. One is conscious of one's

weak eyes, slack jaw; one wears a scented, corn-coloured wig
crowned with a scarlet comb, pinned by green bira, adorned with a
red ring. One lolls in scarlet cloak, green slippers spotted with
gold, on a couch above them, facing their cold eyes, their barely
concealed distaste, treachery quivering, about to break surface.
Bawds, the lot of them, without spice, without gravy.

Behind him, arms folded, immobile, a chamberlain stands.
Father had on such occasions carried a small mirror to defend his
back. So do I!

'Approach us, Athene, and guide our heads.' His amused tone
causes offence, though none stirs. King Dionysius II condescends
to address them. Conversational, glad to share the joke.

'You remember those fellows at Delos? They began calling themselves priests and invented a god, managing to induce the locals to
build them a temple at considerable expense. All went well, they
were living more than well, until one day, to their embarrassment,
the god spoke, rather pointedly!'

Obscured, somehow disused, in the artificial light, travesty of
the shining heat without, the weasel faces remain still. In the
mirror, a star tips the chamberlain's rod.

Disappointed, Dionysius yawns. Beneath formal courtesies are
barbarities gross as those of Macedonian head-hunters, though
comedy can be extracted by fostering rivalries, playing alarmed
apologies, elegant insinuation. To retain power one must have
powers to baffle.

'Honoured excellencies, you will remember what our departed
friend Plato, the ever and only good, told me when he first saw me
drunk? He advised, he *opined*, that my best cure must be a mirror.
See, I carry it still! We might, perhaps, dispatch a mirror to this
Hicetas. Yet no, his smile might blotch it. As for the Fratricide. . . .
But I was regaling you with Plato. He had eyebrows like shells,
always high, curved, disapproving, like his nostril, the smaller
one.'

'Nevertheless, sir, the Hellenic genius. . . .'

Ah, that again. Gygos speaking, whose own genius corners wool-
markets, smuggles goods to Carthage and calls it public spirit.

From outside dully penetrates the tramp and mutter of sentries,
the cry at the random arrow or brand discharged from the causeway. These tedious proceedings are at least quieter than the forthcoming War Council. The news would be worse than usual. That

patch of slime, Hicetas, has sent reinforcements already said to be intercepted by the Corinthians, and battered, despite absurd odds.

Gygos is droning on about Hellas. He must be stopped before all teeth crack.

'Gygos, my dear friend, there's nothing very special about the genius of Hellas except a desire to hurt each other as nastily as possible and find eloquent reasons for it. A barrel of gold, to hire mercenaries, from Persia, is called Civic Enterprise, and so on. Some of you look slightly uncomfortable. Much Hellenism is like slavery, a matter of accident or blood, inferior or otherwise, or disposition, loosely pronounced as divine order or favouritism. We've a flair for hating each other more than we do the barbarians, like those alarmingly verbose Celts. We box ourselves into our big-named hen-coops, furnish them well, but forget the fox. You'll agree that here in Syracuse we're beset not by these puny Leontines but by our own vague yearnings for catastrophe which multiply like cranes in Africa. Prayers of course get answered, usually by jokers. You will remind me of Euripides' Medea.'

In slow singsong he intones: *Lady of Cyprus, may you never launch at me passion-poisoned arrows from your golden bow, those arrows inescapable. May moderation content me, fairest of heaven's gifts!*

His face, plumpish, slightly tinctured, contrives a smile. 'My own policy!'

Strained, fretful, the royal advisers submit to a discourse on Aphrodite's Temple at Eryx, where sacrificial stains miraculously vanish overnight, replaced by leaves bright with dew. 'You yourself', he flaps at a banker notoriously impotent, 'cherish *Heithe*, goddess who demands the most total lasciviousness. I demur, I content myself with Aphrodite *Kallipygos*, of the lovely bottom. Our trusted colleague', he stares at the Treasurer, not recently, employed to the limit, 'is celebrated for his fealty to Aphrodite *Tymborychos*, the Grave-digger. The theology is impressive.'

Glances are disquietened. Skirmishes will have begun at low tide. Assault will not open the Citadel, but bribes seldom fail. Dionysius hitches his robe, eases his scented limbs. 'We'll soon be welcoming the Corinthian. On his trip to Delphi, I hear, a wreath embroidered with crowns dropped on him. Very vulgar!'

The Council leaves him hungry. Duty completed, he orders a repast: honey, mullet, goat's cheese, sharp black olives, wines slightly rancid. These wretched times! But is not civilisation the cultivation of the preposterous? He drinks, then is distracted by a rebellious flake of sunlight and summons reluctant officers to adjust the draperies, ordering the youngest to remain: sipping, all smiles.

'Tell me, my lad, what has puzzled me.'

'Lord, I shall give you my life.'

'That is not necessary. I desire something more difficult.'

'Lord, speak.'

The youth's beardless face, downy, flushed, over-eager, too open and submissive, lacks appeal.

'Imagine a strawberry.'

'Lord, it is done.'

'Now, tell me, is it a fruit, vegetable or a nervous complaint?'

Clearly, it is not done. Dissatisfied, he retires to a secure turret for sleep. A painting hangs: pale grass on which Pan buggers a screaming nymph. Dropping to cushions he taps a gong, a Nubian mute drifts in with crystal flask on a red lacquer tray, yellow wine thickened with henbane. He lies back, awaiting nude figures which move through green daubs that slowly dwindle to sparks. Space empties, shakes, solidifies into a fat, jewelled tortoise, which shrinks in order to swell. A mountain, a smile merges into hands twisting, then a bird's eye bright amongst leaves. Dreams break time and events like bread, redistributing the fragments: Titans mate with Macedonian queens, Prometheus disputes with Socrates and Plato. Language has leaped from meaning to sensation: petals hidden deep in black earth are brilliant Olympus, a magnolia clump is a silver cord linking stars with spirit.

King Dionysius sleeps, nearby a praise-bard lightly strums a kithara, the sounds spreading like foliage. Fingertips are more powerful than javelins. He soon awakes, after a glimpse of Demeter at Pyrasus, gentle, suffering. The music has ended, but a sound from the threshold startles him. Uncle Dion, who drove him from this very turret, had died, murdered. Even the war-god feared the knife, allowing his barber to use only a hot coal. 'I fear the intelligent,' he had said, 'for they aspire more to rule than to obey.'

Syracusans all wish to rule, though most are mere fish nosing around a tank. Recently, they incited children against one of his supporters, a lame historian, pelting him until, bored, they slashed off his head.

Up here in the sky, encircled, he is unpleasantly alone. Guards still deign to keep watch but, significantly, informers no longer want secret audience. Once he had had twenty thousand troops, two hundred warships. They vanished when the alliance with Sparta and Thebes had withered.

He changes costume. Yellow and white for this cursed War Council. What could be said? No relieving banners will flout the skyline, no valiant promise be concealed in a loaf. Athens, Sparta, Thebes, god-almighty Corinth, are obsessed with Macedonian Philip, would-be Hellenic orator-in-chief, Zeus' rival for his wife's couch . . . what will emerge from these grotesque matings? A lion-headed dwarf? Last year's wonder had been a philosophic treatise, boring, but dictated by a duck.

Philip loves to go a-roving: hunched on top of the Pangaion mines he is the richest in Hellas.

Dionysius wanders, selecting a ring, a bracelet, to add sparkle to the fog of Council voices. They may propose surrender, on terms easy for all but himself. His preoccupation with failures may be fatal. Yet Cronos and Theseus, Alcibiades, Socrates . . . Xerxes . . . were more poetic than Hercules. Losing is more evocative than winning. Poets love defeated generals. There can be grace in surrender, overpowering victory is offensive to Zeus. Without awareness of squalor, beatific insights are shallow. Success inspires neither tragedy nor comedy, only farce, though of literary crafts this is the most difficult, yet daily, inescapably, on view, in the gyrations of busy men who need only watch themselves. Is a ghost, is a dream also a fact? Before his own murder, tiresome, lecturing Dion had seen a woman, vast and shadowy, sweeping his house. Small future in that.

Imagine Father struggling with a farce! His own tragedies were stiff but not despicable: his dry feelings for the laconic, his ear for an epigram, his juicy invective against Plato have shown that to be both civilised and professional, though rare, is possible.

The son contemplates an amethyst, sees blazing apples hanging in an instant of lucidity. Once, crouching from the war-god, he had shrunk from a ghost, mouthless amber afloat in violet dusk.

Dionysius II, Despot Supreme and Extraordinary, presides from a high stone chair with lion's feet. A slave fans him. The heat is oppressive though the War Council insists on meeting in the

Ariadne Hall, which has windows open seawards. He is in black wig streaked with silver. Beneath him a slave holds a scarlet platter on which lies a purple hat with green rims. To irritate the boiled veterans stationed below, each at his table, he sports a false beard curled red and black, too obviously Asiatic for those who remember his father, Architect of the Empire. As haughty concession to the occasion he wears the golden military anklets which periodically tinkle, usually during some important argument, to which they add the effect of a titter.

The Naval Secretary is speaking, very fluently, though he now lacked a fleet. The situation is, as usual, bad. The Corinthian advance, failure of supplies to break the blockade, sickness. He nods, occasionally smiles, once strategically coughs, but says nothing. What indeed is there to say? Some of these swanking louts would have backed the treacherous appeal to Corinth, all would rally to Hicetas if he could repulse the Corinthian. The gods may have drilled into them only stupid ambition: to invent mayfly alliances, control tides, restore Troy in order to knock her down again. They are incapable of envisaging a new word, a new letter, to win power more lasting than facts, handmaids of the unimaginative. They are the real slaves, for amongst legal slaves immense empires may be breeding in words unimaginable. The slave, a tragedian has written, is whoever cannot express himself. These fellows, however, have no self to express.

At the tables below, tempers are ragged, voices higher. On marble benches are flagons which none can approach save at his nod, and he still desists, inwardly grimacing at their impatience. They are barnacles, their resonant titles stolen after Father's death. In an alcove scribes sit writing, inventing history.

He strives to listen more intently but, through the limp, perfumed air, despite the unpleasant windows, words crawl, reaching him too late. If he stares long enough at that crisp, terraced hair, he might make it twitch, startling the talkative owner sitting beneath it like a tenant. Finally, at pronounced impatience from below, he forces himself to attend more firmly.

'Hicetas, sir, is scared of Corinth. He sent a deputation, including some Carthaginian settlers, to King Andromachus of Taormina, suggesting a treaty, on pain of his destruction.'

Dionysius interrupts. 'Yes, I've heard of that. The Carthaginian insulted the old fellow to his face. Not, I believe, a very impressive one. He stretched out a clenched fist, opened it, closed it. Not subtle. "Thus," he declared, in bad Greek, "we shall break Taormina. Into dust." Andromachus inclined courteously, the African sniggered, uttered various threats, which I spare you. Like all military men you are fastidious and clean-minded. Andromachus dismissed them. Right about turn!'

His chuckle is ill-received. A black-browed youth, careless of protocol, stands up, angrily. 'And, two days out of Taormina, moving like antelopes, the Corinthians killed or captured nine hundred Leontines. They are now besieging those who besiege us. And we sit doing nothing.' His sentences rush out, in eagerness perhaps genuine. 'Sir, you could lead a night break-out! It's downhill and you've done the Leontines the honour of calling their general a small-town ferret. They've no love of fighting, of Hicetas. The name Dionysius could be sufficient.'

It certainly will not. Perhaps if he leads the charge on stilts, covered with scarlet leaves and panther-skins he might win by sheer surprise, but only to reach the Corinthian camp, and Corinthians are too age-old to be surprised at anything. *To drop into Hades is the same everywhere.*

The speaker is clearly being insolent, does not merit a reply. The senior commander, all beard and bracelets, intervenes importantly. His contribution is indeed massive. 'One can hope, sir, that your men are still capable of ancestral virtues. Against Troy. . . .'

The magpie eyes, black and polished, are too large for the worried face and courtier's smile. His *your*, slightly over-emphasised, was significant, another stage towards betrayal. Glossy repudiation. To Hicetas or Timo. Well, devotees of Achilles himself yearn for his downfall. Such is mortal instinct. Excuse for sensation.

'You always make interesting suggestions, General. Mind, I've never quite believed most of the Trojan doings. That matter of an apple, the triple jealousy. I hope you are all as interested as I am in that other version, from which Homer averted whatever eyes he had. That tricksome Hera spirited Helen away to luxuriant Egypt. That Paris, never very bright, fell in love with a replica fashioned from star-dust. So all fought for an illusion! My father summed it up: *For a cloud, for nothing at all.*'

His yawn is elaborate, prolonged, seeming to spiral, then slowly fades like a moonlit flower. It is modelled on that of the actor, Milo of Phocis, famed for his rendering of a dancing fish. He closes his eyes against the intrusive light, preferring to imagine sunlight lying now flat, now deep, on petal and wave.

The General continues, throttling all dreams of light: one of those terrible engines of flesh who push you into war, howl at you to win it, then flee from the enormity of their own mistakes. Water has almost vanished, little wine remains. A deserter has been recaptured. A gross coward, already sentenced to hang.

Dionysius sits up, eyes wide between charcoal-black frames. The anklets give their faint, irreverent giggle. 'Send him back to his friends. At once.'

'But sir . . .'

'Send him back. We're not dealers in soft flesh. Remember the saying, that he who finds himself in the mouth of a lion will appeal for help even from the lion.'

But he will never shock this ponderous lumps into mirth, into dance, into heart skilling over its own beat. They dance only to strengthen muscles already ugly: they sing to develop their capacity to bawl stupid orders, despising the words of Odysseus: *None taught me. A god alone sowed in my soul the richness of song.* They will be thinking of the impudent song about a canary, wafted from the Corinthians.

The Council is over, though scarcely completed. Giddy with fatigue, Dionysius retires to his writing cell, tall, vaulted, sumptuous, hung with bloodstone red, supervised by a tilted Hermes, delightfully ithyphallic, lounging in a chestnut grove, a Milesian chlamys draped over one shoulder. An ordure of resin and camphor drifts from within, where guards probably sleep sound. Late afternoon always holds unofficial truce. Royal poet, poet royal of Syracuse, he is open to radiance, a meadow awaiting butterflies. His stylus is poised above a tablet. There it remains. A frown ripples over the powdered brow. He sighs. Military chatter disarrays his thought. Words flicker, short-cuts to the ends of the earth, like moonlight and as fleeting. Touching wax, they collapse into the outworn, the obvious. *Purple as Attic slopes, bright as the cap of Attis, Shepherd of Stars* . . . phrases mouldy and stinking.

Father's words had swarmed in battalions, at his command: he had marshalled them into plays, lyrics, epigrams at will. Yet as war-god he had relied upon grandeur, on a thousand archers paid regularly with cash stolen from temples, from Carthaginians.

They had not defended him from Plato's endless advice, encouraged by heavy Dion, boring as justice.

Advice about exchanging Dion's beauteous sister for a lady of mathematical genius and disgusting teeth which could have cracked a pillar and have probably done so; advice about war with Carthage; about government. Right knowledge produces right action. Knowledge is virtue. Nonsense, Father said, politely. I have right knowledge, more indeed than you, but am by no means virtuous. Educate people to virtue, thus to happiness, thus to justice – three follies in one, like Hecate, Father said, still polite, but seeking another quarrel. He himself had immense knowledge but little virtue, expelled Plato, perhaps plotted his death, though vainly. Plato had frozen all that he touched: he analysed love, calculated music, defined happiness. Zeus! How affronted Plato had been when Father interrupted his discourse on Poetry by, with dangerous courtesy, inviting him to observe the sharp, fractured light exposing a leaf's membrane after rippling across the inconstant sea!

Shown a painting of lovers growing wings, Plato deplored the set of a head, the geometrical proportion of limbs, ignoring the flesh tints, then quoting that ludicrous Pythagoras. He had compared Father's eloquence to cookery, told him that, with fortune, he would be accepted as an Idea! The body, with its inordinate hopes, unregularised passions, its scudding flights, was for Plato a mere cage for the cold, unblinking soul, which, on evidence, did not exist.

His stylus at last lowers. He gathers himself like a diver. He writes:

> Could it but be again, that marvellous instant,
> Could it be again what already was.

Neat. Unforgettable. But what does it mean? Father's face glimmers, suspicious, then raddled in contempt. 'Back to play, son. Your words are pitiful.' As though he were a tyro seer trying to extract the future from a flea's liver.

Father always had the last word, though last words are not always final. Yet the old man remembered what he wished to, the son what he has to. Meanwhile, contract time to a metaphor, reveal a familiar figure as a javelin, as a dish of colourless liquid.

Metaphor abolishes distance, rolls up the world. Timo of Carthage is perhaps a wasp. He himself is a mansion in which he can pace from room to room, now a dancer pivoting on brilliance of spirit, now a tragedian dreaming of Ithaca, now Alcibiades intoxicated by a world of flux.

Can his own future await him in Persia, in India? These squabbling little city-states are fetters, forcing life to be not art but duty. Life should not be, as Plato insisted, ringed with the discipline of virtuous magistrates and teachers but by the soaring caprice of those he wished to expel: actors, jokers, poets. He had rebuked Father for his poetry. The poet, of course, is a bandit, at home in the night, revoking order, institutions, convention, scorning limits, alert for the random, the inconsequential. The bright bee, sunlight on thyme, wind in full throat, a child's love for a bird, a brutal slave's care for a sterile tree . . . these are not poems but they can induce poetry.

Meanwhile, crisis. Tiny pictures of a canary are being scrawled in latrines, passages, slipped under his own cushions. Timo, hero from nowhere, could be more than some bandy-legged, carp-faced Theseus in search of a monster. Certainly more interesting than nail-biting Hicetas, Carthaginian toady. Timo appears to conquer by suffering, a new course for Hellas, a modern Prometheus. From reports, he has the dignity without style. I myself have only style. Hicetas has neither.

But how to stop Timo? Last week an assertive priest grandly placed on a tripod a silver plate engraved with the alphabet; over this he had swung a ring, which, while he muttered incantations, periodically halted over a letter, eventually composing a message. *OMIT*. What did it signify? Only *Timo*, spelt backwards, for which the incense-ridden shaveling demanded exorbitant reward.

A letter can probably reach Timo, but to what purpose? Aristocracy is as dead as a last year's treaty, though Timo perhaps does not realise it. Bribery, flattery will be useless, and how can one flatter a fratricide? Actually, no real difficulty; to murder a brother, if not original is scarcely conformist, though a trifle unsavoury. Yet . . . yet . . . the Corinthians are few, none has martial repute, only Timo any repute at all. There is difference between *I am a warrior* and *I have fought in a war*.

The worst is better than nothingness. Life is a mass of suggestion, at present suggesting little. He has no friends. Goaded by

Plato, Dion had turned his back, then turned rebel. He had been Plato in action, enforcing virtue by laws before being disposed of as a public disaster. Plato himself, after a quarrel, he had almost killed, as indeed had Father. Archytas of Tarentum had intervened, just in time. Mathematician, general, diplomat, praised even by jealous Father, Archytas could have resolved this dreary siege but had carelessly got himself drowned. A waste. Fishes gnaw his brain and learn very little.

A slave shuffles in with a platter of cake, a jar of wine, tasting both against poison. Does the fellow have a name or regard himself as *it*? With the cake was a list of tomorrow's arrangements. A teacher wishes to present a map of Hades, rather too aptly; a baby is to be exhibited, born with full-grown teeth, and a seer will decide whether this is propitious. People are thoughtless, exploring Hades, bearing freaks. A youth from Catana is begging a pension for being the youngest of seven live brothers, seven dead sisters. He should join the sisters.

Plato. Intolerant as a wife, he had envisaged Syracuse as the perfect state, factory of wisdom, a theatre of order, the State training the actors and audience and writing the play; an aristocracy of celibate sages dictating the *supreme science*, right government. A Spartan despotism of education, religion, art, hacking away the loose, the irregular, the odd. The Babylonian paradise, of utter stillness, common folk scarcely breathing. Plato could never understand that occasionally a slave must be comforted, a dog spoken to. Like a lawyer, he reduced life, seething and restless, to a text. Having measured him, Dionysius, and his rather skittish niece, in physique, in intellect, he had urged them to marry. Harmonious breeding! People should be grateful to himself and Father for saving them from the pernicious. The enterprise of imperfection is more enthralling than the still beauty of abstraction. The saving grace of gods is in their faults. That man craves only the beautiful and true is manifestly absurd. Repulsive Thersites can utter truth. Boredom can stimulate more often than eternal wisdom.

Dionysius gulps the wine. The fatiguing day floats away. More important, born on wind, distinct even beneath the screech of maltreated language and wailing notes of tavern singers, is chatter, vague but persisting, of 'the Arrival'. Whoever arrived, he would not be Plato or a Spartan saviour. Oafish Philip perhaps, or the Great King, or Timo the Wanderer. The Macedonian would blow strong air into ramshackle Hellas, some roughness to make people skip. The lure of barbarism. Athens had never been the same since the Spartan brigandage, and a very good thing too. Very few people, of course, actually exist, though a number make fair pretence of doing so. Plato had spoken of the world as a tarnished mirror which, for a butterfly moment, had clarified into a vision of purity, which only the wise remember. Or pretend to. Father had retorted that a search for grievance is an image as valid as any mirror or golden fleece.

'The Arrival'. No more, perhaps, than the conjuring of some Thracian shaman who, manipulating slants of light, secrets of colour, sickly fumes, by a peculiar stare or caress, then with a scatter of salts into a cauldron, transforms dust to pearls, a donkey into a charlatan hero. The true magician does more: he issues bubbles of wit, floating in marvellous shapes, dissolving at threat of completion.

A rhapsode is craving audience. With a new song? More likely with a reminder of unpaid fees. Dismiss him. No, give him this ring, worth little but ornate, and inscribed *To the Most Illustrious of the Living*. Evening is near, the Leontine attack is renewing. Distant thuds, a cry, running feet. Dionysius stops his ears. Plato had asserted that no matter is of serious importance, at which Father chuckled and reduced his pension. Plato failed to appreciate the joke. Yet the Athenian had charm, like music or scent: at his absence the war-god was sad, though swiftly stoking up fury on his return.

Footsteps. He tenses. A young officer parts the curtains, glistens in the archway, bearing the customary wreath of victory, requesting the night's password. He is slender, dark-eyed, attractive, but scarcely 'the Arrival'. Smiling, Dionysius, neither young nor old but a curious mingling of both, beckons him towards an ivory casket engraved with satyrs encircling a desperate boy, cocks straining to high Heaven as if about to burst moorings. The youth gazes politely but is evidently worried.

'But the password, sir?'

'Ah, yes. The password. Well, what do you suggest? Helen? Yes, that will do. Admirable. We've settled it between us. My gratitude is profuse.'

The youngster's flinch is amusing; virginal and incredulous at that name of ill-omen. He departs as if himself escaping satyrs.

Helen will protect no one. Understanding must be procured, not with guileful Hicetas and awful Carthage but with the Corinthians. Leontine victory would finish poor Dionysius. Few would die for him. In the taverns, supper clubs, markets, he is unpopular: everywhere hands raised two fingers at him, like horns, against the evil eye. Yet he has crucified none, tortured only a few, and those mostly women and an occasional child, has given them spectacles and processions, has written them a tragedy, effective enough, about Niobe, at which some oafs had laughed. He might rouse the Old Town, not with a charge downhill but with an oration, a blazing imitation of Homer, shouted through his new brazen tube which magnifies the voice tenfold. A crowd can be convinced that Zeus, for sensible purposes, turned himself into a swan, Syracuse might mistake his voice for a half-pay god's. But gods are less than they were, omens are unfashionable. Can he but escape this hideous Citadel – Father's taste, while building it, had been on holiday – he can wrangle a sinecure from some temple, perform as a rhetor, hire himself to Macedon to teach good manners.

He shivers. The troops here, fighting for him against usurper Uncle Dion, slaughtered hundreds throughout the Ortygia, tried to fire all Syracuse. Forgiveness is no Hellenic trait. To be fated to trust to mercy. . . . He feels tearful, soggy with confusions. Sophocles mentioned the immutable, unwritten laws of Heaven; let them remain unwritten, and, if possible, unknown.

Suddenly desirable are the diadems and yellow buskins of Persia, the scarlet cloaks and brilliant ostrich feathers, the flamboyant treasuries, the mighty highways radiating power unquestioned as a river. He needs bed, but anxiety and curiosity still struggle. Has 'the Arrival' really been promised, and by whom? An initiate of Athene's Mysteries, he knows that existence is a seamless skein unfolding in *aiones*, periodic Great Years, which climax unnumbered decades. A Great Year blossoms a hero . . . Dionysius, Heracles, Prometheus . . . redeemer of decay and impiety, before ascending to the beautiful, indifferent gods. Hellas, Persia, Carthage had already felt quivers, as if before an earthquake. Conceivably 'the Arrival' is at hand, to break the circle, a vast ship splicing the sea. A new Dionysos! Hapless Pentheus, the unbeliever, called the god an intoxicating spirit, a barbarian and expert wizard. How delicious! A morning of inconceivable promise, perilous ambiguity: the stamp of frenzied dancers scorched by black

Pelasgian flames. None of this quite suggests Timo.

He reaches for a flask. Night is all around, thickening over Syracuse, masking plots, conferences, dreams of blood and colour. An Egyptian, styling herself Princess, has been applying for his bed but, like all women proud of their independence, is exacting. Tonight he will sleep alone, refreshed by poppy juice, and dream of lounging with centaurs, exchanging sophistries with a dolphin, changing to gorse. That fraud Gygos extracted a thousand drachmas for a recipe to induce favourite dreams, not yet delivered.

He is safe under the silks, the air hot, swimming up from bluish depths a krater hangs before him, containing the world. On it a godling, naked, with neat penis but no mouth, somehow manages to smile. A trident, a bull's horn. A girl slain at the altar, a be-laurelled hero bleeding in the heel. Then, nothing but green, immaculate ether.

Dionysius II, Despot of Syracuse. The Canary, Most Illustrious of the Living.

3

Apelles had studied the tactics of the Thebans, Epaminondas and Pelopidas: strengthen one wing, weaken the other, reinforce the centre. Lighten the armour, train cavalry for hill-fighting, increase mobility. Improvisation from unexpected angles, feints and out-flankings, more effective than staged and massive frontal onslaughts. Philip of Macedon had studied them too, lengthening his spears, packing his battalions closer, replacing chariots by cavalry.

Before the Expedition started for Syracuse, well provided by Andromachus, another thousand had joined it, mostly ruined gentry. Deserters from Hicetas and Dionysius were rejected. News, however, speeds fast through Hellas and the small affair at Adrantum had swollen in the telling. Mercenary offers, though unwanted, were significant, a showing not of belief in a cause but in its chances. Some were eventually accepted; had not great Heracles been a mercenary?

Thracian swordsmen arrived, their torsos daubed dark blue with gorgons and cyclops, men useful in battle though unruly on the march. Theodotos would control them, knowing their ways. Horses landed, supplied by Corinth. Theodotos, proving as skilful with horses as with all animals, Thracians included and, by unspoken right, was training a cavalry wing. His laughs, usually misleading, encouraged the men, and a successful skirmish was now being called 'The Battle of Theodotos' Laughter'. When men cursed his rigorous discipline, his retorts, overwhelmingly foul, won respect. He retained that gait, loping, slightly menacing, as if seeking a dark lair. The men loved but also feared him. Unexpectedly, teasing or in anger perhaps inexplicable, certainly unexplained, he would utter words that made them flush or turn white, leaving them speechless, as if he had reached into their most ditchlike recesses.

Sicilian slaves, with ankle sores and scarred backs, sought the Corinthians. Freedom, for service. The Equals disputed. Aristocratic cavalry officers demanded that to accept slaves would antagonise the world order. Macedon and Carthage, Athens and Sparta, Persia and Rome would unite in terror against a slave army. Finally Timo accepted them. 'Slaves don't demand the destruction of property, they want some for themselves. Free them and they'll be our most strenuous supporters.'

These movements were irritating the Sacred Republic. Throughout her long years of conquest, Carthage had never captured Syracuse, essential for her maritime monopolies. Soon the Corinthians heard that Mago, Suffete of Carthage, was sailing to Sicily in a fleet commanded by the ever-victorious Hanno. Mago had threatened, Mago had landed, joining Hicetas, racing Timo to Syracuse. Corinthian ships had fled in panic from colossal Punic galleys.

Some of this, Timo admitted, might be true. At once a local priest, 'the Adopted of Heracles', offered a ritual curse on great Mago. Timo accepted, but promised payment only on the curse's success. The priest was displeased.

Slug-eyed Hicetas, insured by Carthage, dispatched heralds throughout Sicily. 'We hear that an ageing dwarf from fainthearted Corinth is prowling for the spoils left from conquest of Syracuse. Aided only by Andromachus' cast-offs, he is pollen already blighted, perishing at noon.'

The heralds usually found closed gates, taunts from the walls, references to faulty biology. Hicetas was a mere grasping usurer in lion's skin, Carthage was noxious. Dionysius had borrowed freely and repaid nothing. Neutrality was dangerous. As if signalling to all cities, as spring deepened into summer and the Leontines now had the full Corinthian army wedging them into the New Towns, Mamercus of Catana, though of untrustworthy repute, dispatched to Timo a train of mules laden with wineskins, breastplates and javelins, so successful in the Great War. A company of volunteer archers escorted the gifts. Their captain delivered the royal message.

'Son of Timodemos, understand that I, Mamercus, I myself, dislike sieges, but the gods favour me in battle. Syracuse will be yours, and when you confront the greater enemy, be assured of my presence beside you.'

The army cheered Timo, knowing him lucky, protected by well-disposed stars and lucky numbers. Cheers greeted Theodotos, who grimaced, as if to spit. A few cheers were even awarded Apelles, who appeared not to notice, staring into the vast, chipped sea as though calculating its weight.

Theodotos had Mamercus' gesture known everywhere, much exaggerating it. Provisions and loans then arrived daily, many, significantly, from goldsmiths, always quick to assess the times. Each gift, like an insult, must be accepted warily, repaid swiftly. From a Corinthian client city landed, without interference, a contingent of Syrian physicians, famous for skills with wounds.

The sun was unremitting, parching the soil, endangering the last wells of Dionysius. Etna hovered, sometimes far, sometimes near, but inescapable; above its charred groves, its summit gleamed like porpoise-skin.

Concerned with diplomacy, Timo was not with the army inexorably encircling the Leontines and Syracuse, but encamped midway between the City and Taormina. He summoned Theodotos, Apelles and experienced Equals for conference.

As always, he listened while others had their say. He was scarcely needed. Andromachus and Mamercus had brought over thirty cities. Even Apelles was cheerful. Dionysius, locked in his Citadel, had a court but no government. Leontine outposts were deserting.

Finally, Timo spoke: 'The occupation of Syracuse will begin in a week. Until then, cavalry will occupy all approaches. We'll let the youngsters, Eucleides and Telemachus, lead them. You may accuse me of idling in safety.' He gave them his smile, as always surprising them with its boyishness. 'You will be right. While the young are winning themselves garlands, I'll be scouring the pots and pans, supervised by Theodotos, who recognises dirt when he cares to.'

He made mock obeisance, which Theodotos parried, then croaked assent. The others laughed. 'Our Timo.' Eucleides and Telemachus, sleek and rich, were also courageous; the choice showed acumen. They should easily chase Leontine scuts to the sea. Some Equals were envious, none showing it save the banker volunteer, Deinarchus, who fancied his horsemanship. Brown as beech, mouth like a trap, he gazed at Timo through eyes like berries furiously ripening. Timo was unabashed.

'Yes. My tongue will be more useful than my weapon-hand and, for the taking of a city, Apelles' experience exceeds my own. At this stage we don't need commanders quarrelling like Athenian democrats. When the time comes, you will see me in battle, doing my best.'

Routine orders followed. Fields round Syracuse must not be burned, ostensibly to propitiate the grain spirits, but also to earn peasant gratitude. Soon the conference was over, leaving Timo alone with Theodotos to deal with Sicilian emissaries, inspect assault-machines, scaling-ladders, engineers, hoplite reserves, before dispatching them forward.

Syracuse, however, was secondary. The real challenges would begin after her capture. Much depended on the leader's wits in that cosmopolitan, unsteady city. Meanwhile, he maintained routine, officiating at ceremonies, receiving delegates, dictating reports and replies.

He particularly enjoyed regular sessions when soldiers, water-carriers, muleteers, even Sicilians, cooks and slaves could approach him, with pleas, suggestions, complaints even against the Equals. Here he was at ease, pleased with his new verbal agility. To each man his disposition which, if the gods willed, could form talent. For himself, gods were to be met not in journeys inwards but in venturing outwards. Better men achieve both. Meanwhile, he was at everyone's disposal.

Once, seated under a pine, he had been accosted by a Cretan pedlar, a trespasser undeterred by hostile faces. He had been denied free food, been insulted by officers, even by scullions, wronged in the sight of earth and sky, seen and unseen.

'You, General, are worst of all.' His voice altered course like a drunkard's flute. 'Your villainy is atrocious. You steal eggs from widows to pay these ragamuffins, the world rings with your boasts. Your hands have long been drenched with blood, your very breath is stolen from Hades.' Short and fat, he was dancing with indignation. Timo's quiet inspection, others' ribaldry, some threats made him caper the more, until, overcome by breathlessness, he had to cease.

Timo had been ostentatiously patient, occasionally nodding, as if at an old friend. Voices called on him to have the gasping intruder whipped. He held up one hand, to Theodotos, in charge of military discipline, so that soldiers leaped forward, always glad to witness a thrashing, particularly one so markedly deserved.

Expressionless, still seated, Timo signed to Theodotos to bring forward two small bags of coin that had arrived an hour ago from Catana. Incredulous silence followed, through which his voice was very clear as he handed the Cretan one bag. 'Had you, most respected sir, told me anything I did not already know, you could have earned yourself both bags. As it is, I regret . . .'

Even the Cretan joined in the laughter. Our Timo.

Though conscious of his age, he delighted in joining youngsters in their dawn games and dances on Four Winds Hill, from where the sea, still dark green, seemed hung from high, white ridges of cloud; dances spontaneous yet perhaps older than winds; dew glistened on thyme and grass, the bee rose, the bird darted; the lithe, tanned bodies exhilarated him as he moved amongst them to catch a ball, clumsily, arrive last in a race, sing, slightly out of measure, or stop a fight between two incensed youths, rebuking them as if in joke.

'You can both buffet more fiercely than I can, but I know exactly when to strike and where to strike, which you do not. So, embrace and forget.'

Suddenly tearful, they did so.

4

Timo learned from Xenophon, placing the most heavily armed in the vanguard, thus setting a manageable pace. Black Cloud would greet him at Syracuse; meanwhile he trudged with the hoplites, leading, along the narrow, dusty track under baking cliffs. His grey hair and fading skin might have been foreboding but for his knowledge of the men's identities and natures. He had already recognised a Kallias, handsome, winning, untrustworthy, and knew where to station him in battle. Encouraging, confiding, telling stories, apparently tireless, he could enjoy the immemorial jokes. The more ancient, the more loudly applauded.

'Who decides when sober, obeys when drunk?'

'A Persian.'

A chance to retell yet again the story of Xerxes having the sea thrashed, for unruliness.

Despot Dionysius, the Canary, was a favourite butt.

'More appetite than teeth, our Dinny.'

'Sparrow-hearted, newt-loined, he should lengthen his stride.'

'Stretch his cock, rather.'

Hicetas, all knew, was dabbler in tortures, blood brother to Carthaginian crucifiers. One youth, jostling for Timo's attention, boasted a brass locket containing, hush, the dust of Heracles' Leaf, remedy for all mortal wounds. He, like the rest, incessantly praised his own deeds, particularly those to come. Timo encouraged him. Swagger, like song, helped morale. He kept them moving. They were exhausted at dusk, bivouacking by an almost dry brook, reaching for coarse, fermented barley, groaning for women. Timo mischievously told them of Artemesia, who had commanded a Persian ship at Salamis. The groans loudened.

'Why did I leave her? . . . Fat in the right places. Straight path to the lower depths!'

'Or a loving-cup lover-boy.'

The moon rose over a headland. Some older men prayed. The archers to Apollo, swordsmen to Ares. Incantations sounded further off, to cudgel the Fates, Night's daughters. Then further

stories and jokes: to rescue King Admetus from death, jolly Heracles had tempted those three haggard old girls, the Fates, into
drunkenness.

Most slept well, Timo in their midst, Theodotos beside him,
sleepless and watchful. Timo himself dreamed. Hermes, lover of
night deeds, sent a vision of a tree encircled by birds. Awakening,
he told this to his companions, explaining it as an excellent omen,
and adding, untruthfully, that the birds had pecked the tree into
collapse.

Next day they were early swinging towards Syracuse under a
sky bruised by clouds drifting from Etna in pursuit. Speed was
essential. Heat was parching the plain, scorching corn and barley.
The light was hard, each stone, leaf, crack glaringly explicit.
Dowsers were sent out. A thrill through the fingertips, the convul-
sions of a coin tied to a cord, could find water. Theodotos enjoyed
such forays. He would abruptly halt, stand motionless, lower his
head, then stamp; diggers would hurry forward, unfailingly
successful, the water brackish, stained, but, Theodotos added,
usually wet.

Exchanging lewd jokes, riding out alone, foraging, spying, fondling the animals, leaving many remarks unfinished, he remained
inscrutable. Younger officers feared him, sensing unnatural loneliness, profound as a moonless night, an existence of chase, mountain ambush, killings at fords, clansman's hatred. He was powerful
by example, more powerful still by withholding; he seemed everywhere, riding, riding, his lean, invulnerable presence disturbing,
yet also a guarantee.

Small crowds from the hills were now less suspicious, offering
volunteers, mules, loaves, warning that Carthaginians had landed
with elephants, their tusks bound with sickles; had poisoned
wells; that Suffete Mago was embracing Hicetas. Some of this
might be true. Plague had been released by a local god, and
irresponsible, too easily bribed, the troops were more interested in
a wagonload of village whores, themselves mercenaries, following
their bets.

The great Hanno had not been great enough to entrap another
Corinthian supply ship, now beached a few miles ahead. A trustworthy spy reported that a band of Mago's Libyans had been
repulsed north of Syracuse. Corinthian fireships had actually scattered Carthaginians outside the Great Harbour. Within the New

Towns, Hicetas held two of the four Sections, the others being already invaded by Eucleides and Telemachus, no pimply braggards and with less rancour and envy than could be expected, capturing the narrow, twisting streets with small squads linked by runners. The Citadel, closed and soundless, was still avoided by all contenders.

Timo was now a day's march from Apelles' force, within sight of the Citadel. For noonday rest he occupied a low, wooded hill, protected from Aphreliotes, the East Wind, by a walled, abandoned village. Here they would remain until midnight. He supped with Theodotos by a fire of dry broom and arbutus. Far away, light glittered on metal, perhaps that of Sicilian scavengers. The sun was sinking to a benign sea, nightingales trilled from lemon trees, men wandered at will through the village making small, inconsequential thefts. A distant island, like a tortoise, Theodotos said, was already fading in dusk. Jasmine and wild hyacinth flared briefly above marsh, then were extinguished.

Theodotos contemplated the wood, he jerked a thumb at the Citadel, faint above the massed shadows. 'Ripe fruit, Timo. Good for your teeth. More important, good for mine.' Then he wandered off, steathily, into the darkening trees, perhaps to assist the nightingales, perhaps not.

The night march was uneventful. Reaching the Corinthian lines, meticulously fortified, they were greeted by Apelles, dour, but almost managing a smile. All was prepared. Leontines, hungry, thirsty, were mutinous against well-fed Carthaginians, calling themselves advisers but behaving like slave overseers. Apelles had installed a small mint on the Achradina, key to both harbours, and had with false coins bribed an entire Section to surrender.

Mago was commanding forces within Syracuse, but cautiously, and precariously, from offshore, for Hanno still occupied the Great Harbour. Over-confident, he had divided his forces, sending one group to coerce Mamercus. Noting this, Apelles ordered his camp to send up wild laughter, which bemused the remaining Carthaginians into conviction that they were already routed by Neon, a young officer, promoted by Telemachus. Soon Corinthian laughter did not need to be ordered. Theodotos returned, smiling, but saying nothing.

Timo could see lurid flames and gushing smoke blowing up to

the Citadel, smudging the lower reaches. Scared of encirclement, Leontine outposts had fled deeper into the Old City, fatally squeezing into a narrow perimeter.

Street fighting, Apelles said, continued. At this, Theodotos, without a word, summoned his aides and rode off, to enjoy the turmoil. Wolf-man, strangler.

Timo would not be following him. Let the young men win their laurels. Later, he would have to take up his shield and hold fast to it. He was learning from Hermes, from Ismene, from chance and endeavour, to become I. *I*, rounded and entire, like the soul. Meanwhile, he summoned the main assault force, Apelles standing dutifully behind him, fully armoured, masked, corsleted, anonymous save for his plume.

'Here are my orders. Crown yourselves, all of you, with the brightest garlands. Let Zeus himself see you. Carry the scarlet banners of victory. Now, listen further, and, if there are spies amongst you, let them take note. It seems to me. . . .' His absolute certainty drugged them. Yes, at Rhegium he had outfoxed the Leontines; yes, the sea had calmed for him; at Taormina, omens rivalled each other to aclaim him. Now they heard him, laughed and stamped, then turned, roused further by the clash and swirl within burning Syracuse.

A boy rushed into Timo's tent. He was surrounded by secretaries, officials, quartermasters from Andromachus. Excited, the boy forgot formal salutations.

'Sir. A man from the City. He insists on seeing you. Clad like a rough sailor, but speaks your own Greek. He's got rings. Marvellous rings.'

Already the fugitive, flabby and smiling, was kneeling before Timo, who knew him from his coins. Youngish, fairish, nothing very much. The Beloved of Artemis, Dionysius II, Despot of Syracuse.

Dionysius was rising, slightly complacent. 'We dodged through their men, your men. Every street awash with blood. No wonder Hicetas hasn't joined in! At the causeway I pretended to sell fish. No bad performance, as my bag was empty.'

Uninvited, he waved a secretary from a stool, his hand flashed with jewels, and seated himself. Unwashed, his garb ill-smelling, his face unpainted, his thin hair awry, he was composed, then wheedling. Timo, watching him, still standing, had not spoken. The soft voice resumed:

'Lord Timo, my sun has set. I had my chance, never very much of one. My head was too great for my shoulders. I was raised to be a titled nonentity. All's gone. My sister, my wife and children got themselves raped, killed, flung into the sea at Locri.'

Behind forced tears he was proud of this too. Timo held up one hand, markedly bare.

'You'll be allowed passage to Corinth. The Archons will decide your future, if you have one.'

'Thank you, Timo. You've got a soul. If Hicetas had hold of me, he'd sell me to Carthage, where I'd end up on a cross. Not much future in that. Meanwhile, the Citadel will open to you. No one will resist. You'll find weapons for two thousand, well oiled and sharp, and will know where to use them.'

He was wholly at ease though he had deserted his men, thrown away his shield. No ruler, he had acted the part of one very badly, knowing some of his lines but uncertain when to say them or to whom, uncertain too where to place his feet.

He could be pitied. Behind the smart words and indeterminate eyes fear lurked like a trapped sparrow. Timo signed for others to leave them, and the two sat together through the long, troubled afternoon, as Syracuse seethed into collapse under the grim, sunlit Citadel, its marble lit by tawny flames beneath and the thick red sun above.

Timo's luck prevailed. Without warning, from the empty sky, a wind rushed shorewards, the sea rose, even in the Great Harbour, crowding Hanno's warships too closely, so that some were smashed and tumbled, others hustled to the Lesser Harbour where the Corinthians waited. Most Carthaginians were Mago's landsmen, depleted already, now bewildered and angered. Mago himself was not with them but, leaving them to Hanno, had sailed to meet Hicetas. They saw harbour walls crowded with scarlet banners, hundreds of armed, beflowered men shouting that Timo was Heaven-sent and invincible, wind and tide obeyed him, Hermes was with him. They yelled that Mago had quarrelled with Hanno, denouncing him as a traitor, that a Corinthian fleet was raiding Carthage, that Hicetas was imploring peace and holding Mago hostage. The Hellenic style.

Aloft on his flagship, the great Hanno hesitated. Used to wide seas, he had to grapple with fierce wind without room to manoeuvre; his swaying, disordered vessels were now top-heavy and under-armed. Too many archers and slingmen had been sent forward to Catana or into the City. When the wind slackened, barely a quarter of the Punic ships were seaworthy, and Hanno ordered retreat, itself a gamble through fireship and arrow.

In Syracuse, Telemachus had rushed the causeway, Eucleides joining him after prolonged slaughter in street and avenue, and together they scaled the Citadel, the enemy already piling arms in surrender.

At sunset, Dionysius was escorted to the Great Harbour, dispensing eloquent thanks, profuse quotations, now joined by Apelles and, with strips of bronze across their foreheads, a company of Equals. Timo then received seven Syracusan nobles, preceded by heralds with consecrated rods. He listened impassively. Leontine regulars and Carthaginian mercenaries were still being rounded up, rather brutally, by Deinarchus, glad of his chance. Both harbours were secured. Names sparkled. Neon, triumphant at the Victory Gate, Isias, captor of Apollo's temple; Demaretus; the two young victors lording it in the Citadel; Theodotos, who had seemed everywhere simultaneously, now in the lead, now joining common soldiers in a scramble for blood and mindlessness, now taunting a demoralised foe, now refusing quarter. He could be lying, drunk and exhausted, in delirious dreams of uproar and onslaught, a satyr after rape.

'We swear by Earth and Water, Timo, that our city is yours for ever. Syracuse, lighthouse above the dark sea, is a robe for your strength, a spear, a healer's rod. As a horse senses fear in its master, the Magistrates and people. . . .'

They, in opulence and finery, who must have backed Dion and Demos, Dionysius and Hicetas, in successive opportunities for privilege, were weaving a bright gauze of rhetoric in which words lost all meaning save a plea for survival.

On Timo's orders, the Corinthians entered Syracuse by night, so that their numbers would appear greater. Some entered it twice. Link-slaves flanked them, with flaring brands. Conch-shells screamed, the populace, famine-struck and plundered, nevertheless cheered the high, dim riders, strewed hyacinths before them, stretched imploring hands, cried *Euoi, Euoi*, each mindful of that whispered prophecy, 'the Arrival', culled from none knew where. A voice from the sky, a murmur from the sea, a whisper from the giant heart of the earth.

All pushed and fought to see the Liberator. Mistaken for Timo, Apelles received uproarious acclaim. Voices jabbered incontinently.

'His shadow, his *very* shadow, binds our wounds and griefs.'

'His smiles are the alms of the world.'

'He is taller than Thebes.'

Out of the firelit procession a figure lurched on to a smashed column, gashed, unsteady, crimson in flickering lights, goblet in one hand, bloody spear in another. Ares? No, Theodotos. The populace hushed in sudden awe. Then, he growled one word: 'Hicetas!'

It released a torrent. Hicetas had eyes like rats, his beard was a goat's tail, his pizzle dried lemon-rind, his tongue the blight of Sicily. In Old Times a bardic curse had swept off the head of a Doric king. Tonight we are all bards.

5

Perhaps, or perhaps not, fulfilling the Arrival, Timo was being discussed throughout Sicily, was known to all Hellenic states and colonies: praises arrived from every quarter: words like scents, like bundles of pretty, silken strings entwined in the bunched hair of Persian nobles: congratulations were delivered from 'Agamemnon': pledges flourished like Syrian roses, however spiky beneath glowing petals: proposals lulled like poppy-seed . . . a loan, an alliance, a defensive league against Macedon. Hellenes, Theodotos grunted, at their worst. Gifts dangled, over-lauded, but ready to be withdrawn at a grimace from fortune.

More solid were reinforcements from Corinth, the droves of Leontine fugitives beseeching protection from frozen-arsed Hicetas and implacable Carthage.

Whatever his seating arrangements, Hicetas had retreated west, to the Carthaginian colonists, seeking high walls and broad moats. Apelles, correctly, warned that he had further tricks in hand.

All now realised that, protected by the unseen, the Liberator despised bodyguards. Installed in Syracuse, he announced his intention to make public sacrifices, not forgetting that worthy but obscure god Andranus. This was not mere display. Inwardly he was wondering whether the campaign had not been ominous in its every ease. Beware. The universe hated the triumph of mortals. *Nothing fails more swiftly than success.* Nothing in excess, Lord Apollo taught.

> Yesterday, so mighty a Lord
> Now a sight to break all hearts.

Timophanes, Dionysius knew that demons, like gods, can be jealous or bored, destroying with a wink, a spiteful jest. *Born, Suffered, Died,* Theodotos had said.

Timo thought sadly of Ismene. She would have heard of the capture of Syracuse. To praise was not in her nature. Her smile was inward. She would prefer to love him as an exile than sit beside him in triumph.

Great crowds, Demos of Syracuse watched as, at the altar of Zeus, Timo officiated in white, simple robe. The white bull, horns painted red, neck wreathed with lilies, the flutes, the barley grains and myrrh, the libations, the blood, the fumes so delicious to Heaven. With all intent on the upraised blade, the music rising to a wail, two men edged from the mass towards Timo's back. An arm lifted, a glitter, a hiss. 'This for your brother. . . .' But already the knife had clattered harmlessly to the stone, its wielder himself stabbed by an unknown who at once fled, pursued by the nearest. His confederate rushed to the altar, clutching it as if drowning, moaning for clemency.

Timo resumed his office, the man was dragged away with the corpse, the bull fell, the crowd sang and stamped. Later, Timo's saviour was caught, on a rocky promontory abutting the Citadel. Surrounded by the ardent, the curious, the grateful, he said only that he was justly avenged. Escorted to Timo, he quietly explained that the dead man had been a hired killer, murderer of his father, and notoriously in the pay of Hicetas.

Timo embraced him. Later, he and Apelles discussed Fate, which unifies apparent contrasts and coincidences, making such a man bide his time until the precise instant when his anger is demanded.

People were dancing. Zeus himself had held a shield over the

Liberator. Gongs and tambourines, swaggering rhythms, in a city festooned with the effigies and emblems of Mother Corinth. Parks and esplanades were dense with happiness. Elesian winds from the north tempered the painful sunlight. Banners rippled, huge plywood paintings of ships sinking, armies fleeing were paraded, though many, caustic taverners observed, had already done service for Dion, even for Dionysius II. Phalli jutting from statues, and the herms outside porches were splashed with wine and left garlanded. Another bull was offered, to the Lord and Protector of Sicily. Who is he? Ah, yes. Poseidon. This time, however, because of the shortages, the beast was artificial.

No rain had fallen for weeks, children had died, and only the priests had averted wholesale famine, itself magnified by Leontine ravagings. During the Victory Games, the boxing and races, vaultings and dances, the hobby-horse wildness, the huge wagers, the moon madness in which a respectable magistrate tried to drink the sea and a woman interrupted a foot race to recite Euripides, Lord Timo was urged to take the Bow of Theseus and, from the heights of the Citadel, shoot an arrow over the sea into the cloudless blue. The Equals, gaily draped, actually did likewise. The arrows sped upwards, lines glittered, falling in wide, distant curves, Syracuse applauded, half mocking, then stilled, as by what Theodotos called a fluke of sunlight, Timo's pale raiment was slowly suffused with gold, so that many believed that, tall and shining above them, as if hewn from granite, backed by overpowering Citadel and depthless sky, he was Theseus himself.

That night the arrows returned; rain, plenteous and bountiful, restored the land. In the highest skies, music clashed and counter-clashed, harmonies sustaining the clear, bright air of Hellas.

Timo was quickly wearied by the praise songs which daily assured him that he had saved Syracuse single-handed, gleamed with astral light, had been complimented by Zeus. Choral odes acclaimed him as son of the Muses. 'Nine mothers simultaneously,' Theodotos laughed. 'Few will envy you.'

On behalf of the people, Theodotos had presented him with a fleece, deep purple, gold-fringed, able to control weather. Scarcely necessary, he muttered, avoiding meeting Timo's eye, to so effective a rain-maker!

Refusing Dionysius' resplendent quarters in the Citadel, Timo contented himself with two rooms on Achradina, within sight of the harbours. He always enjoyed masts, reminders of the world's utmost limits. Apelles lived in the Citadel barracks, Theodotos in some tavern backstairs, with a dog, a raven and a tamed white snake filched from a temple, the god pretending not to notice. In Council, urged towards the winged silver throne once used by Gelon, Heiron, the great Dionysius, by Dion, Timo casually ordered it to be melted down for Treasury funds. Burned homes must be restored, streets cleared of rubble, the harbours dredged of wreckage, New Hades emptied. Almost emptied, Theodotos amended.

Offerings continued, from throughout Sicily and beyond. A thyrsus, allegedly from the god Dionysos, more probably from a corporation anxious to grab street-corner sites damaged by fighting: a statue of 'the new Immortal', Timo himself: books for the State Library, itself left intact. Dionysius could at least be thanked for that, though he was already forgotten, the merest wisp of being, the flown canary.

He was known to have safely reached Corinth. The fashionable, lovers of any novelty, had hastened to entertain him, applauding his verses, repeating his malicious anecdotes, though at Timo's name he lowered his head. Apparently he contemplated setting up stall as philosopher of what he termed the second rank. Like an impious Sophist, an Athenian Sceptic, he would set the past to rights. Children would learn neat felicities: there had been no Wooden Horse, only a graphic synonym for Argive cavalry; Heracles' Labours were but public works performed at considerable expense; the Phoenix, so handy for poets, merely part of an Egyptian calendar.

Timo smiled. He had not disliked Dionysius, who accepted defeat with the same shrug as he would victory. He himself enjoyed wooden horses and labours: life should periodically enchant, before being reduced to a skeleton. The nymph strips by the stream, sticks and stones hearken to the sweetest of lyres. Tomorrow he would wash in Arethusa and perhaps be rewarded by a vision.

Oligarchs were reassembling, carefully presenting themselves, animals seeking shade, in shabby robes, as if driven to direst penury. Remembering the family dislike of Factions, he was not

deceived, but he needed them, as they needed him, to restore all
that Dionysius had airily neglected. The most fruitful of lands had
been plundered for years: half-starved cattle roamed streets over-
grown with thistle and grass, hungry deer, even boars, menaced
the suburbs, with many people too famished to resist.

Taxes must be remodelled, the Treasury filled, alliances negotiated. Mamercus of Catana must be watched. Always about to
visit Syracuse, to advise, to assist, he had not yet come. Andromachus was dead, allegedly poisoned. The powerful town, Akragas,
soggy with corruption, had sent tribute, but with clauses so slippery that Theodotos, who enjoyed such deals, offered to negotiate
them himself. Those swindling purveyors, he grinned as if before
belching, were noxious as a dead horse liver which, at five paces,
can suffocate three men and seven boys. In headlong skirmishes,
Eucleides, Deinarchus, at last receiving his due, and Telemachus
were evicting robber kinglets, mercenary gangs, nests of pirates.
Sicily, so crossed with feuding strongholds and tribal thiefdoms,
might one day merge Ionian brillance with Doric solidity, but
would scarcely do so tomorrow. As for Syracuse, Apelles called her
a Hellenic prow thrusting towards Carthage.

When not bargaining with merchants, wrangling with contractors,
losing his temper with alien merchants, losing it again with temple
commissioners, Timo enjoyed discussion. The purpose, the justifi-
cation, of life. Tidal ebb and flow, limitless, before the death froth.
After so many years he could now re-engage with it, testing others,
exploring himself. His rooms were soon familiar to many, often
chosen not for charm or amiability but for intellectual mobility, wit,
for experience, for cunning, all that enlarges. Most nights some
dozen would recline over common rations of bread and figs, olives
and wine, arguing about the nature of gods, the latest interpreta-
tion of Olympus, the laws of necessity, the balance between logic
and chance; about Mysteries and mystery, retribution, the price of
whores in Taormina, the strange relation between deformity and
good fortune, the opportunities of retrieving Ionian liberties; the
sanctity of harvest, golden pledge between gods and men.

Here, lined, pouched, Apelles lost some dourness. He drank
much, he even smiled.

'Despots breed like chickens. All turn with the wind, but, deep

down, are in love with the Great King. Philip would risk his own
throat for a diadem, and give many others the certainty of losing
theirs. When the cash runs out, they turn on the weakest states
and call it the breath of the gods. The bane of Hellas. Despots
would pull out every tooth in Syracuse to sell to the ivory combines
for a few more days in power, an extra column for their monu-
ment. When the bills come in, they decamp.'

As always, Theodotos' chortle was mirthless as oak-bark, but
fighting had enlivened him. He sat as if after a banquet, not
gulping but sipping.

'They can be a refuge against worse. Mob rule. King Demos.
Look at Athenian crowds! They sell all for a change, even for
disaster. Particularly for disaster.'

He did not appear perturbed, nodding as if at a joke not in itself
outstanding but hallowed by repetition.

A very young officer, Telemachus' lover, sat like a dog begging
attention. His small voice was nervous. 'At home in Corinth did
not Cypselus rule thirty years, unquestioned, like Zeus himself?
And the city prospered!'

Timo always encouraged younger men and pressed his shoulder. He was about to speak, then recalled Timophanes' admiration for Peisistratus, Despot of Athens, champion of serfs and
peasants against robber landlords, builder of roads, temples, fountains, endower of festivals, manufactures, blessed by the wounded. Yet he had snatched power by deceit, betrayal, savagery. A
lesson, but what did it teach?

To avoid answering, remembering too how Timophanes had
resented discussion, how Father had craved it, he smiled at the
youngster. 'I'm glad you remember Cypselus. One of the Seven
Sages. So long ago. The gods were with them, he with them.
Everyone was young. But never forget the outcome. He died. Well
enough. But most great men leave feeble offspring to restore
balance. Unwisely, he left rule to his own son. Periander. Periander began well. Reduced taxes, kept the peace. But then . . . forty
years of crazed bloodshed. And the great Dionysius held on to his
own power too long and lost most of it. And that wretched son . . .
but again, Syracuse rejected him not for his despotism but for his
incompetence.'

He sensed that these faces, respectful, concerned, were less at
ease than they appeared. Inwardly, they were appealing for a

declaration of policy. He had scarcely one to make, he was still groping for answers. He must try another performance, imitate Hermes. No longer wholly 'Our Timo', but using power to make it unnecessary, to rule in order to cease from rule. He listened to his own voice as if he were one of them. 'We don't control tides. We can only adapt ourselves, like helmsmen. Reject one despot, one faction, support another. But only for a period. The best strive to undermine their own authority. They obey Zeus, who equalises all. It demands much, usually too much. Only in Hellas can such a condition be thought of, even uttered aloud. It is a fragment of the Hellenic Idea, not all of which I can explain. I haven't the words.'

He was friendly, apologetic, slightly pedagogic, the oldest amongst them. Perhaps Apelles was nearest in understanding. Theodotos had no interest. Of the rest, some might already have received offers from Persia, or be considering ample opportunities in Ionia.

Timo was slow-speaking, even hesitant, seeing disappointment or perplexity settle over them. 'One man can sometimes see further, act more swiftly, than a Council, with its divisions and debates. There was Polycrates of Samos. He gave orders, juggled with the desires of Demos, the land flourished. Poets, musicians, painters . . . they flocked to him. At his will, a great mountain was cracked, to supply his people with water. He alone could have done it, and because he was alone it was done without question. Yet he lost all and, falling, dragged his people down to ruin. A crafty word from Persia accepted too hastily, and he died screaming on a cross.' He was speaking too fast, too loudly. He said as if in a small afterthought: 'Emergencies need the strong hand. But they get prolonged. Sometimes,' he laughed slightly, reassuringly, feeling the evening drifting away, like a sloop when mischievous urchins slice the ropes, 'a good ruler's lusts . . . even his games. . . .'

He had lost himself: a novice under test, or nervous beneath Timophanes' scorn. The pleasant supper had changed course, entering chilly air. The silence was awkward. He had spoken too much, revealed too little; he had confused. To restore the simplicity of wine, amiable exchanges, unexpected revelations small but useful, he tried a joke. None seemed to hear it, in a tension unintended, scarcely accidental.

He braced himself for what did not come. Apelles pondered,

fingered his heavy, squarish head, twisted his scant hair, as if
unaware of doing so, but said nothing. Equals, civil dignitaries,
alien guests, waited. Finally Theodotos flickered a smile, held up a
jug as if to an invisible presence.

'Tell us, my friend, tell us at once without boasts and tall stories
about certain wanderings, various adventures, where we can find
such men? Or is he amongst us? This all or nothing "Arrival".
Should we hail him, respectfully of course, as Dionysos? If so, bad
manners insist on saying that the wine he's provided is thinner
than might be expected, and there's not overmuch of it.'

Mightily relieved, Timo led the laughter and called for more
jars.

Alone, he could rehearse only all that he had forgotten to say. His
mistrust of the loudest voice, deepest purse, swollen populations,
his belief, learned in blood, that a ruler should confide but not
pander. Self-mastery. The overweening pride of Achilles destroyed more than it gained. When he himself enjoyed praise, it
restored a small pride upset long ago. No more. He remembered
Ismene's ironic smile.

Here, in Syracuse, he feared not Persia, Carthage and Macedon,
but Demos overthrowing government by shallow rhymes, mischievous slogans, caprice. An actor in a mournful tragedy had
gravely intoned:

> 'We Hellenes face the Magistrates.
> The Gods themselves are at our feet.'

And the entire concourse at once stampeded, deeming that Magistrates had granted permission to loot. Loot for three days.

Demos had applauded Timophanes' killing, then expelled the
killer. Demos exiled Aristides of Athens, wearied by hearing him
called the Just. Demos craved not better government but new
jokes. Peace, won by bloody struggle, drives youth to seek danger;
reason, carefully taught, can induce madness. Women too enjoy a
killing, indeed crave it, not always secretly. Thracians elected as
general a dead man, a Phrygian painter who, working on a mural
of Eurydice and the serpent, had died of snake-bite, a story
Theodotos rated as ludicrous as the death of Ajax.

Questions, demands, temptations. Someone, Solon perhaps, had said that the most difficult of all labours is to perform a gracious deed without demanding credit for it. He at last smiled. He found no such difficulty, save enacting the gracious deed. To deny one's Name is to besmirch posterity.

At this the smile collapsed. Aigle and her infant daughter would soon be arriving from Corinth. He must enlarge his quarters; marriage, like comedy, needs space. Owing them comforts, he knew, however, that he would be of no great comfort.

Already he was returning to old habits. Seldom able to sleep long, he wandered alone and unrecognised through Syracuse. Winding pavements were streaky with moonlight. Murmurs came from houses on steep streets. Street of Archia and Melissas, Circus of the Sons of Sisyphus, Market of Actaeon. Here he could feel supreme in freedom, in Ismene delight. That line of steps, that fountain, a wall needing repair, a trough mysteriously avoided, called to him more urgently than the grandiose, the absolute order and perfect symmetries demanded by new philosophers. He wondered at tiny discoveries: a flame jutting from a disused alley, three men staring motionless at a pebble. Outside a darkened tavern he was invited to wager on the duration of Lord Timo's rule. Ninety days, he replied, and I'll be back to gather my winnings. On the dawn shore he watched for masts against the horizon and, turning, saw high walls behind which were lives, plots, passions he would never know. The tang of the wind braced him for the waiting day.

He heard random whispers of 'the Arrival'. Once, a shape, abnormally tall, cloaked, spoke from shadows, the voice broad, slurred, perhaps from remoter islands:

'Son of Timodemos, you were born Orestes, you will be Odysseus, the Fiery, the Imperfect. You will end darkly, in the hands of Athene.'

6

Syracuse rejoiced, steeped in blue aura. Praise-bards compared Sicily to Delos at the birth of the Divine Pair, sweet as the nightingales of Colonos. Universal optimism forced abortionists to lower their charges. The Arrival occurred daily, miracles on demand. Routine sacrifices, to Zeus Xenios, Lord of Human Bonds, to Zeus Polieus, Father of Cities, usually ill-attended, were now crowded, excuses for drunkenness and lust worthy of Milesians. Processions were incessant, for the godlike Liberator, for Dionysos of the red-tipped pine-cone, the green tendril, the luxuriant grape. His emblems were everywhere; dice and balls, golden apples, mirrors, raucous bull-roarers twirled by boys with carmine lips, draped in fawn-skins, artificial snakes lacing their arms to the din of pipe and tambourine. Timo had 'arrived', Dionysos had 'arrived', Timo and Dionysos were one, invulnerable, invincible, immortal. A temple was being built to Timo, at Rhegium. A gigantic wooden lion, gilded and flaring, led a procession for Artemis. Mothers were telling their children that the new god in their midst had, long, long ago, earlier than Troy, been ordered by Poseidon to sacrifice his beloved brother. He had wept seven days, seven nights, and obeyed.

With quays astir again, sailors abandoned themselves to the Aphrodisia, hurling flowers at women, chasing them to arch and arbour, dragging them, willingly enough, from porches. Artisan clubs held night-long street banquets. Stories swelled like melons. Those scarlet victory banners had fooled the Suffete in all his grandeur, he and Hanno had struck each other, he had sailed to Libya, sick all the way, leaving Hicetas crazed with terror. Listen for more. The day before the capitulation, an amusing contest had occurred.

Fields around Syracuse were fed with fresh water. There, during the blinding, stifling afternoons, when the throat dried and the eye smarted, Leontines and Corinthians alike, against orders, slept or fished for eels. A good supper was itself a battle won.

That afternoon the Leontines heard their enemies noisily praising water for breeding eels, they congratulated the sea for being water and housing fish. And ah, the joys of repose, by rich mud in choicest meadows, well-trimmed, provident hills! Forget officers' stuck-up-noses, Sicily was large enough for all, blessed by the goddesses.

The Leontines, fuddled by heat, listened incautiously. They propped ears to a stalwart Corinthian. 'You fellows are Hellenes like us, teachers of Asia, conquerors of Troy. Yet you wish to surrender your lives, your livelihoods, to a nest of African snakes, to Carthage, who wants to stuff the world into her stinking wallet. A wallet, mind, stolen from others.'

Waving amiable farewell, he was replaced by a neat-bearded, dignified man, evidently of importance. The Leontines were now standing, weapons forgone. They forgot the baked earth and scorched air, the white and yellow sky trapping them all. His words were beautifully shaped, his tones made melody, lulling, yet edged with inescapable meaning.

'You fine fellows should give thought to the liberties of Hellas, our common Mother. You cannot really and *verily* believe that Carthage, *Carthage*, encourages warfare merely to entertain lazy women and a pack of slave-owners. Intelligent men like you! Of course not, assuredly not. By no means. Yet here you are, about to venture all for their tame eunuch, Hicetas. If he were a proper king, a Theseus or Diomedes, he would not be sniffing and snoring in luxury, leaving you the wounds and death-thrust, the black path to Hades. He would be in the forefront, against us, the sons of Corinth. Can you doubt it? Do you wish to perish, for such as he, as Mago, as Hanno? Or display the largeness of a free soul that each of you once cherished yet have forgotten?'

The Leontines gazed at one another, then at a crowd of Corinthians adroitly drawing up nets thick with silvery eels. Their own nets were slack and empty. Almost before the speech was finished, they were running forward, unarmed, to join the feast and volunteer for the invader.

The first horse fairs were erupting, jesting, deceiving, murderous. Skinflint bargaining, exorbitant promises. A new coin was rushed through the mint, stamped with winged Nike, Lady of Victory, crowning a chariot hero. Customs posts were manned again, cranes already swinging too many luxury imports; gold filigree, jade, the pearlike dildos used in women's private gatherings, and the depilatory ointments that men demanded they use. Peacocks for Hera, Bactrian baubles, oiled cedar planks, white barley loaves were reappearing, also the Sons of Aesculapius, a

A Choice of Murder

sacred caste from Cnidus which preserved medical secrets, with a paraphernalia of snakes, herbs, liquids, guaranteed to kill the living and raise the dead, sufferers jibed, though at a price that none had ever been able to afford. Murex vendors basked in the profits that follow shortages. Despite the bustle, however, people in all Sections were slow in seeking work. They cadged wine, spat beans against witches, enjoyed rumours.

'Have you heard? . . . Out there, under the soil, gold, silver, for us! As much as we can carry!'

The latest poet shouted for an audience. He had completed a heroic tragedy in three hours. 'There, on the towering heights, sleeps my destiny. . . .' He ceased, glaring at the mirth, unaware that he was pointing at a horse-trough. Musicians strummed good-natured catches, while effigies of Hicetas, Hanno, the Suffete, crammed with live rats, were burned under the Citadel, shrieking and hissing. The spectre of Carthage drifted away, grey in dark, golden dusk.

Apelles was training recruits. Theodotos, of sullen mien and angry purpose, had departed with Neon to receive the surrender of Messina, perhaps, people said, pouring a river down Etna on his way.

Timo had left Syracuse. He was tired. Domestic bliss was a coma, in Council he found himself at best attentive to the tracings on a shield, which led him away to a story. The ram or goddess on a ship's prow thrusting through early haze, a god confronting him in a dream, restored childhood: the quick smile of Kallias, a discus hurled towards the sun, hopes rising like an islet in the Bay of Thyra, only to sink again.

PART FIVE

Carthage

1

Who, save philosophers, can forget Carthage, black planet of
Africa, baleful southern light yellow but gritty enough to blind?
Images of Carthage choke and menace. The great metropolis
sacred to Tanit, sea goddess consort of Baal-Hamman, the Punic
Zeus. The tiered Phoenician capital laden with towers and cupolas,
temples, banks, arsenals, slave-hells, flaunts gardens magnificent
and soundless, dungeons yet more soundless. Throughout the
Middle Sea all races speak of coiled stairways and enfoliated
balustrades, resplendent domes, marbled lions and baboons,
lascivious demons and goddesses entwined, spawned from a reeling chaos, walls slitted and manned, rearing giddily above cypress
and palm, oleander and tamarisk. From here sail the war-fleets, the
ornate galleys of Spanish, Sardinian, Balearic and Sicilian gover-
nors, of statesmen, the long files of commercial and military trans-
ports, or with black sails, those of defeated generals returning for
crucifixion, war captives for mine, plantations, the oar.

Hellenic states are changeable as wind, but loveless Carthage
had, long before, bribed the wind, and her Empire was monotonous, like the eyes of the Fates. She was set on but one course,
mercantile expansion to counter ruthless Hellenic commerce, was
founded on monopolies, governed by a master race closed and
haughty, each head an emporium, proud even of its lice.

Continuously, the small are engorged by the large as monopo-

133

lists seek new markets, struggle to retain old. Carthage is developing Spanish silver, Sardinian ore, exploiting far-western copper, has marked for expropriation the key harbours of Syracuse. In Carthage, tall sacrificial topheths steam with fresh blood. Foreigners lower their voices when speaking of her, where, lest you forget, apes, jewelled, brocaded, can be mistaken for lords, and where elephants, thick grey clouds, are indeed lords. City of incinerations in molochs, ovens in which Cronos, father of Zeus, savours the first-born of fruits, beasts and, allegedly, mortals – those freezing screams, that incomphrehension, that obedience. A holy duty to be granted by Hellas, if the gods will it, is to withstand the Sacred Republic.

Carthage. The philosophers shrug her away as a city without principle, a mere sensation of brutal African hugeness, the virtue of magnitude, Semitic intensity. Armed elephants, giant black torturers, colonies wider than Illyria, sensational heights and nightmarish depths, impregnable palaces, conscript armies vaster than Egypt, ceremonial splendours, immovable glooms. Carthaginian deities are frowning, heavy, implacable. Khamoni, Mastman, Gurzil, Amman, Melkarth, Eshmun, Rabbet . . . barbarian coughs, savage imprecations, exhalations of curdled sky and diseased stars. Stiff, tight hierarchies. The casual, libellous chatter suffered in Hellas is repressed here with halter, cross, fire.

The Great King himself winces at mention of Carthage, reeking, snake-obsessed iniquity, and had once condescended to vomit, at which the court bowed, the chamberlains prostrated themselves and righteous gods approved.

Violence, incense-ridden and secretive, pervaded the Sacred Republic, vaunted ally of Etruscans and Berbers, controller of desert caravanserais. Look closer at Carthage, aloft on tribute, levies, protection fees, dues, insatiable, spending but to obtain more. Serene and inviolate? Probably not. Monopolists are friendless: scores of client states fear but do not love her, and independent cities strain to break her price-rings and prohibited areas. To the polyglot Sacred Republic, subjects, feudatories, allies, associates are alike parasites, natural helots, and ever in debt. Her senators, gods parcelling out the universe, dispatch delegations, secret missions, across Africa and Asia, they supplement alliances, debate mortgages, recruit auxiliaries from distant places by questionable means. They hear appeals and countenance festivals, and they turn their dark, unblinking eyes towards Syracuse.

Syracuse herself was debating Carthage. Council and Equals, though not unanimous, generally supported Timo and Apelles; that Carthage had weaknesses, perhaps fatal. Both liked to remember that Gelon and the Sicilian Hellenes had thrashed Carthage at Himera, establishing Syracuse as a Middle Sea power. As in her defeats of Persia, small Hellas demonstrated that giant conscript armies could be broken by dedicated and trained dwarfs. Quoting his father, Timo would compare Carthage to an overspecialised Spartan athlete. Wealth was all: her politics lacked theory, religion taught only obedience and sacrifice, people were mere digits. She could not envisage alternatives. Plague, earthquake, the unforeseen bewildered her, as proof that Fate cannot be bribed. Apelles would add that her military tactics were inherited from different circumstances: elephant onslaught, slave muscle, mercenary faith were fickle. One defeat, and her empire would rebel, clamouring for a moratorium on debts. She was incapable of nobility. To a Carthaginian, Theodotos said, Priam kneeling before Achilles was merely an easy target. Sensible enough, he had to add.

In his displeasing way, he substantiated Carthaginian vulnerability. In Timo's absence, partly strategic, Theodotos, uninvited, replaced him, angering not the Equals but the restored oligarchic nobles. They watched him, their eyes raking him for signs of fallacy or disloyalty, though vainly. At dainty suppers and opulent hunts they complained of the upstart with ragged dialect and jeering tongue, but, backed by the army, he seemed out of reach.

His features, ravaged as if by frost-bite, crinkled unpleasantly as he hinted at secret reports, unofficial couriers, even of his own uncanny adventures in Carthage, disguised as an animal, doubtless a weasel, scarcely a turtle. What need of disguise, peace-loving gentry wondered, though behind his back. Sometimes the educated man quoting Herodotus, sometimes the rustic boor, wild man of the woods, he was untrustworthy, leering and calculating. But his popularity continued: he was no jobbing profiteer; his tastes, though not pretty, were simple, understood by common folk, he disliked ostentation, was difficult to contradict.

The oligarchs listened apprehensively, the Equals, flush from unmistakable triumphs, less so.

'Carthage is rank with hidden fears. Like a cave stinking with blood, should I call it gore? Always haunted by something fearful, in Tyrian waters or those beehive tombs in Mycenae, where the ghosts make horrid faces at you. One of them tried to steal my neck – or was it my brother's?'

As though announcing a special treat, Theodotos gazed at his expensively robed and decorated opponents. 'They're importing outsize Libyans of exceptional ferocity. No addicts of laughter-loving Aphrodite and Zeus, protector of Peace. They love one thing only. Yes, you've guessed it. Women! And only one bit of them. You may know that they've learned from Egypt that a crocodile's cock – a leathery affair, you know that too, better than I do – if roasted, then smeared with honey, can give you eleven spurts a night. If any gentleman doubts it, I'll lend him mine – the crocodile's of course – acquired at mighty cost, and expensive to hire. Now, while some of you were gabbling about Himera and Marathon, I was buying up leather from some rascal Celts. Their fields dribble honey, even more than Hymettus. So, I've already been trying out that leather, suitably fashioned, not on you lot, but, through my usual agents, on our friends in the west, the Carthaginian settlers and their Libyan protectors. Leather goods are now dumped on their boundaries, inscribed as gifts from Africa. Disappointments may be unseemly. Each gift is streaked with honey. Poisoned, of course.'

He grinned with deceptive amiability, the Equals chuckled, the fastidious oligarchs smiled nervously but swiftly calculated prices on the leather-market.

A year after the liberation, though lines were inexact, two factions had evolved on the Council. The Peace Party, mostly oligarchic and commercial, cautious, afraid of provoking Carthage; and the War Party, headed, rather carelessly, by Theodotos, anxious less to start a campaign than, by shows of force, to warn the Sacred Republic against renewed invasion. Also, to warn Macedonian Philip. Denounced in Athens for seeking overlordship of Hellas, Philip was ever strengthening his phalanx, for defence, for assault, encouraged by Hellenic disunity.

For no known reason, the Peace Party was now styled the Followers of Noon – more vulgarly, the Sleepers. Their spokesmen argued that the Corinthian army was an excuse for military blockheads from overseas to retain power, for officials to redouble taxes, allow alien contractors and depraved speculators to rootle in the public purse. Lord Timo had accomplished wonders, who could deny it, but wonders are seldom repeated. Timo is elsewhere, why risk further? Hide your head and you won't be noticed. Speak fair words, and Carthaginian spies, in taverns, on quays, will report them back, soothing the fierce Africans. Apelles, incessantly demanding ships, arms, is a firebrand. Diplomacy is a matter of lawyers' courtesies, scented compliments, emptying a few wallets, entangling stupid barbarians with ambiguous clauses and equivocal options. Let all wait until Timo returns – genius settles all. Meanwhile, the streets can be induced periodically to revile sour tax-master Apelles, ruffianly Deinarchus and the rest. The gods enjoin us to be content with our winnings. Civilised men are content to amble.

The dispute quickened. Humidity made tempers fractious. To the War Party, Syracuse had won nothing, merely appealed to Corinth. Those most enriched by the flight of Dionysius were intriguing against those who had accomplished it. Appeasement appeases none, soft words inflame savagery. Carthaginian skies are fanged.

The populace, satiated with victory, inclined towards the Sleepers. All wanted glory, of course, but without having to pay for it. Any mention of 'the Arrival' now roused embarrassment or irritation. One man was badly stoned for doing so. Dram-shop, rabblemouth rumours were muttering that the capture of Syracuse had been no liberation but a plot engineered by Mother Corinth to reclaim authority.

Almost everything waited on Timo's return. But who was he? God, statesman, politician, Corinthian governor? An empire-builder like Dionysius I, a schoolmaster with a stick, like Dion? An adventurer? Or an accident, a Name magnified by absence? Or a half-bald grey-beard with stiffening limbs and shuffling manner who had fluked a triumph, then saddled himself with responsibilities that he shrank from sustaining.

Many had assumed that, with the fall of the Citadel, he would return to Corinth, Lady of the Isthmus, his Name secured, a beacon unquenchable. Yet . . . yet . . . he might be another tiresome hero steering for a collision, perhaps fatal, not only with Carthage but with Macedon. South against North. Civilisation against barbarism. Apollo against Ares. A prospect to make the intelligent and prosperous shudder, as at the unthinkable. At slaves demanding civic rights, a voice from the dead, the earth opening a path to musty, overcrowded Hades.

2

Woods were still thick, darkly glistening in thin, clear dawn, dense and tired in aching noon, but always taut with mystery, with presences within wood and water, furtive worship in deepest and nameless recesses where no writ pursued, where Syracuse was dim. Rivers dropped clear from mountains where small, walled communities lodged on precipitous stone platforms above ravines, still retaining some horror of the aged and unwanted hurled to death, a falling as in dreams issued like death sentences. Closed towns were hidden within vast steep shadows, level with eagle and morning sun, the sea periodically reappearing, flecked with gulls, a reminder of other voices, further distances.

Everywhere, even in the sorriest hamlet, anarchic feudings persisted, the deepest veins of Hellas. None knew better than he the pressure of reciprocal obligations, the dues of gratitude and vengeance, modes beyond laws and a Programme. A farmer would risk his family to grab a field, not from need but to spite a friendly neighbour.

For many weeks, Timo, with barest of escorts, had, in his old manner, trudged field and upland, emptying his head of debate and plan and quarrel. People usually recognised him, he knew not how, bringing him petty lawsuits, grievances, fears, begging him to receive some rustic Homer held by his folk as rival of Apollo, lord of beginning and end, whose soundless rays yet sound sweeter than nightingales, more poignant than swallows. The vine-dresser and woodman, the sailor and carpenter demanded voice, and he listened, patient and smiling, trusting his eyes as much as his ears.

In a lonely pass above the sea he might be ambushed, not by robber or mercenary but a craving for Ismene, coolly amused, welcoming, yet with her own joy of solitude. He thought too of that earlier Ismene, with a sister who had striven against those like himself, lawgivers who, on behalf of the people, can nevertheless outrage Heaven.

Each day opened rewards and discoveries. Barely visible in a narrow rug-hung forest cave waited a stone goddess, cracked, mossed, one arm broken, her face a blank slab, yet with stern power that forced a prayer from him, though one inarticulate and formless. Without majesty or beauty she appeared, not carved but hewn intact from one primeval boulder, and speaking from darkness to echoing chasms of spirit. Before that crude figure, within that silence, his fame was negligible, his Eleusinian initiation a charade. At her feet a fresh bloodstain began a story. Authority should not forget her.

Deep in the island, he enjoyed moments brief but full: Syracuse evaporated in the call of a nightjar, moonbeams on esparto grass, sunlight tipping the myrtle, the glow of cherry blossom, lemon, almond. Boyhood songs revived, he fumbled with old lexicon teachings. Cranes sacred to the moon, dolphins bearing off souls, chaste Artemis leading a wild pack through the night. Zeus of the Bright Sky was simultaneously lord of shadow, brother to the keeper of the Grim House. Tall, shining Olympus was simultaneously the blackest of depths.

At ancient crossroads and market squares friendly people gathered about him, not for a miracle but for a story, the traveller's bounty which became pictures grandly distorted by wine fumes and camp-smoke and the tall, grey authority of the stranger descended amongst them.

'Cambyses, Great King of Persia, Lord of the World, whose ardour with women once set alight a whole town, offended Apis, bull-god of Egypt, by stabbing his statue in the left breast. And he himself perished from an identical wound. And Pollexyanos of Delos dreamed, as we all do, but of a straight line cut on a rock. Listen, imagine, see. A priestess warned him against whatever flies. So ever after he watched for the eagle, the vulture, even the harpy, but, during a raid, was killed by a slinger's stone. Amongst three hundred companions, he alone died.'

In those last weeks in Syracuse he had suffered exhaustion, pain in head and eyes, the constant hammering of dispute, the crushing mass of detail. Now he was happy, binding simple folk to him with tales, and feeling quietly honoured. At midday when the earth swooned, in a barn where the owl called and the moth flew, he felt identities more revealing than Eleusis, cleaner than Delphi, part of a further island unperturbed by mainland conspiracies, the cultured weariness of Ionia, the philosophers pacing or sipping within cool, secluded colonnades, the hugeness of Asia and Africa. Like a fig on a south wall, a random exchange would gleam, bear fruit, endure. Like prayer, a story, urged outwards, transformed you within. Here, virtue need not be enforced by high words and sharp swords. From fireside talk, tavern maunderings, drunken stammers, came, disjointed, vague, yet persistent as a tune, tales not his own, memories of long-ago Crete, of peaceful citizens beautiful in form, attire, in games and arts, each woman an Ismene, with Zeus obeying his gentle mother, Gaia the Earth. Yet all had vanished. Earthquake? Pirates? Monstrous bulls sent by jealous gods?

Unannounced, Timo returned to Aigle in the dull house in momentous Syracuse. Theodotos greeted him curtly, as though he had never been away; Apelles, gaunter, depleted, bowed, with undisguised relief. 'Dare say you're still needed.' Theodotos' smile seemed to doubt it. 'Here, and in Corinth, such places . . . they want things to get better and better. But they won't, they can't, and' – his chuckle was like a rasping quern – 'they shouldn't!'

Somehow aware of his return even before he completed it, the Sections erupted, immense crowds were chanting his name, excited by the unspoken, rich in unmade promise. A few confessed remorse for backsliding towards Dionysius: his amusing verses, the huge profits extracted from his festivals, his jewelled, sensational banquets.

From the start, Timo trod dangerously through the network of lies; lies in Council and at altars, from behind walls, behind hands, hissing like fiery wasps, crouching like frogs, lies afloat, crawling, watching. Also reports, not always lies, of the long aftermath of victory: throat-slittings, tigerish castrations, disembowellings; the terrible red desert of losers.

Already knowing his decision, he heard the War Party, ostensibly urging only defence preparations; the Peace Party reiterating that enemies were inventions of interests. From both, wily praises trickled towards 'Our Saviour . . . the Incomparable . . . the Hero . . .' with cautious suspicion and malice.

Both Factions had reasonable policies, held for reasons usually despicable. The Sleepers, mostly landowners, were scared of risk; the War Party was led by shipbuilders, armourers, grain contractors, horse-dealers. He heard all, still said nothing, though convinced that, whatever prevailed in Syracuse, Carthage would attack. The constant suction, the obsession with Empire. Her credit depended on reputation for invincibility. She was supported not by loyalty but by terror and debt. Her gods attracted no stories, ribald and affectionate; teaching nothing, demanding blood, they received no love. He would not yet wager on the outcome, though this time he must lead for battle. Thus a new thrill, hooligan but complex, out of the past, as if of sacrificing naked Ismene to Moira's black, mouthless goddess. Momentarily he stood paralysed, then slowly resumed movement, shaking, like a half-drowned body before a fire.

Unauthorised he began training, labouriously, patiently, a small, mobile, light-armed cavalry squad, the Centaurs, to fight always within earshot of himself, wherever he might stray, and rush upon whatever he ordered.

Not all of the original Equals would now support him. Many had joined the oligarchs in buying up property on which to flourish at leisure. Returned exiles, too, regaining their homes, wished only for quiet. Their maneouvres convinced him that feebleness is worse than despotism, that many voices impair decision.

Carthaginian ships, pretending piracy, attacked commerce, but the Republic still withheld direct aggression. Persia blandly watched, though, when a loose island federation, misjudging Syracusan politics, raided north Sicily, Apelles considered it a Persian cat's-paw. When the Great King gave his slow, mannered orders, there followed silence, the silence of stealth, subterfuge, secret payments. A few cities surrendered, rather too quickly, bribed perhaps by the War Party, who needed a few reverses to bolster their arguments. Mamercus still wavered, fearful of openly defying Carthage, unwilling wholly to disbelieve in Syracuse. Disease, however, swiftly repulsed the invaders, survivors were dispatched to the quarries, sunless mazes from which none returned.

Macedon still advanced, east, south, mastiff-jawed Philip proclaiming his Hellenism. Reviled by Athenian demagogues as
barbarous imperialist, he replied in poor Greek that he was no
cannibal, then captured another city, on the fringes of Attica.

In Council, arguments swayed, nowhere, nowhere. Bigger men,
less paunchy, more candid, were now taking up stations. Apelles,
dedicated to stern *ananke*, Necessity, was at last speaking, less to
the factionalists than to the silent, intent figure between them, hair
grey scrub, eyes shrouded, the man of beliefs but no ideas. Apelles
was incapable of flattery, rhetoric, legalistic invective, flourish.
Firm and confident, he lectured them. Reluctantly, despite heat
and languor, they had to attend. Second-hand Nestors, would-be
profiteers, warriors who craved victory without fighting, shying at
the single word: *Carthage*. Many of his words were slurred, ill-
spoken or archaic, though no man smiled, starkly aware of im-
pending crisis. Heat and languor drained away.

'Examine wars. A city barricades a trade path or port, another
tries to crack it. Coalitions form, dissolve, re-form. Bubbles! Soft-
spoken truces, undated treaties. Carthage respects none of them.
Treaties are there to be broken. To lull, to deceive. She crushes the
sea-world and calls it the will of gods. Inordinate hunger. You can't
conciliate an angry viper, a wounded lion. Gifts will be snatched
with only contempt. Pity is unknown there.'

He paused, awaiting dissent, someone to excuse Carthage or
protest that she was too mighty to risk offending, but none responded. Theodotos was absent, Timo's features seemed unlit, his
mind far away.

'You ignore your own maps. The Pillars of Hercules, our western
lands, eastern Spain, are rich with men's needs. A triangle – fruit,
grain, metal, wine, timber. A single campaign can seize it all. Can
master Middle Sea lands, isolate Syracuse, strangle the mainland.
I'm not reminding you of *aidos*, shame. I am speaking of maps.
And . . .' – the steady, indeed monotonous voice, loudened unpleasantly – 'the crosses and smoking ovens of Carthage.'

Timo saw how Apelles enjoyed ships, was always glad to descend
from the Citadel to inspect a newly repaired hull, help tar a deck or
fit a new keel, shortening odds against the Sacred Republic. Once a
laurelled charioteer, he spoke of Hellas as racing against Carthage

and Persia. Syracuse, on the inside track, was slightly ahead of Macedon, the rest having fallen far behind. Bald, thickset, testy, he was thorough, indispensable, at ease only after the day's work when, with the younger men, he would let himself talk, impatient at all interruption, even from Timo, who would laugh as he remembered eager but callow Neon, the youngest of all, at an evening gathering when Apelles was speaking.

'I was bargaining outside a goatfold somewhere up-country, over a jar, a slave was for sale too, and some blunt-nosed Northerner, his pelt hung with heavy purses, getting impatient, took the jar, threw it against the wall, then, without a word, emptied a purse into the dust, buying both jar and slave. Then . . .'

Neon, cocky, cheerful, broke in: 'It must have been a very cheap jar.'

Apelles glared from beneath bushy tufts: 'No. It was a very expensive jar. I began . . .'

Neon was undeterred. 'Then it must have been a very beautiful slave.'

Apelles' brows almost joined. 'No. It was a very ugly slave.'

Meanwhile, Timo collected reports, weighed opinions, covertly manipulated the Factions. The Sleepers were taunted as cowards and extortionists. They replied with explosive appeals to liberty, goodwill, freedom. Many, too many, were susceptible to the careless smile, easy promise, grafter's proposal, reminders of past glory. Men who could die of ghosts, Theodotos said. The polished decades of excitement given by Dionysius I, Syracuse triumphant with scant talk of liberty and no practice of it. He had summoned assemblies, praised them eloquently, agreed to all demands however contradictory, then went his way, disregarding them, leaving the City happy in freedom to decide nothing, be responsible for nothing, only to enjoy the spoils of incessant conquest. All Hellas had bowed to Dionysius, Carthage had been rebuffed. Police agents, spies, certain disappearances, occasional spectacular executions could be overlooked in what had been a genuine 'Arrival' until, in the last years of decay, fatigue, even disaster, the mockers, the conspirators, the demagogues and factionalists crept from the shadows, and street gangs ruled.

Timo seldom argued about liberty and freedom. In Corinth these had been demanded more for the individual than the City, but here they must be allowed only after reconstruction. Freedom must be release from threat of Carthage and another Great War. The perpetual restlessness of the city-states, itself freedom, was perilous, so that ambitions for overlordship sounded more plausible, more possible. Such unity might be solution, or might reduce Hellas to an ant-heap, like Asia and Africa.

Unobtrusively he enlarged the Council with certain priests, magnates, retired Magistrates, even a passing philosopher, all looking to himself, independent of the War and Peace factions. The philosopher, native of Miletus, had injured himself on a boulder, though confessing his inability to prove the reality of obstruction and disposed to doubt his own existence. Just the man, Theodotos agreed, to be unleashed on the Sleepers. Though preferring the useful artisan, craftsman, farmer, and without wealth himself, Timo had no strenuous objection to the rich, save to those whose selfishness was overdone, and overdone too often.

Much was uneasy, currents astir under smooth surfaces. 'The Arrival' might yet be that of a Philip or Hanno. Small skirmishes were frequent with the Carthaginian colonists in western Sicily, though the Sleepers, headed by a rich salt purveyor, Aristodemos, insisted that these were provoked by the War Party, who consistently exaggerated external danger to maintain their position and increase taxation.

In Council, Timo still seated not in the Chair, which was always left empty, but amongst the others, in his rare interventions, was tentative and inquiring: 'My good friends, the question now is, not how we can keep the peace with Carthage, but whether she seeks peace with us. Is it not so?'

Apparently not. Aristodemos, claiming popular support, was at once suggesting trade treaties, sworn alliances, anything but resistance. Zeus loved the peaceful, harmony was essential to existence, only peace would keep prices stable and commerce secure. Losses to Carthaginian marauders were negligible. The Republic, the *Sacred* Republic, had indeed issued a solemn ordination against piracy, nay, an *indictment*.

Behind Timo, Theodotos muttered: 'That fellow! Uninterested in truth, careful not to be caught lying. Needs a gash on his hunkers.' He eyed noisy Aristodemos with hunter's stillness, a sudden glint on his thin, bitten face as though roused by the unmentioned and perhaps unmentionable. He fingered his beard as if testing a dagger.

Aristodemos, urging conciliation, won the loudest acclamation. Carthage would be informed. All gazed at Timo. Would he overrule this, had he the constitutional right, had he the power? Then many remembered the Centaurs, blinked uneasily and agreed, as Timo remained indifferent, to consider further. Aristodemos, aggrieved, said nothing.

Theodotos himself, always wanting to break from walls and doors, was quickly bored by discussion, preferred 'government by thunderclap', held that rulers of whatever persuasion at best created muddle, winning fame by efforts to control it, usually failing. Ambush, revolt, battle allowed no time for sea lawyers and rhetors, eyes bright for easy pickings and shadowy deals.

Occasionally perceiving Theodotos staring at a bird, tree, rock, Aristodemos would state that he was a wizard who would injure Syracuse, perhaps fatally, having very obviously bewitched the worthy but simple Liberator, now approaching dotage.

Hicetas was not forgotten. Though weakened, he remained a Carthaginian puppet. Then even Aristodemos was hushed by messengers from the further coast. Mago, grand Suffete, was said to have killed himself, to escape impeachment for miscarriage at Syracuse. His corpse was rumoured to be publicly impaled, an offering to wrathful gods. The Senate had certainly assembled its largest fleet ever, for the final conquest of Sicily.

Early summer. Risking opposition in Council, from the streets, even from Corinth, Timo dispatched troops to occupy untrustworthy cities, and, with professions of affection and praise, to overawe Catana and the now unmistakably shifty Mamercus. The short campaign, under Telemachus, was successful, and, by a bare majority, a war loan was established, subscribed reluctantly on Timo's personal guarantee, and rapidly spent.

He did not neglect the drama, unexpected confrontations, which sustain people like bread and wine. Captured by Telemachus for sheltering a Carthaginian crew, Leptines of Apollonia, notoriously cruel, pelted by his own subjects, was hustled before the Council. Scarred in defeat, haughty, he stood in chains, addressing his accusers as though declaiming to a vulgar mob.

'Overcome by no man, betrayed by fortune, I shall die with my Name untarnished, knowing that my welcome among the Shades is assured. Posterity will acclaim my deeds, Zeus himself. . . .'

As if awaking, Timo, standing at the back, raised his hand. Timo *Somatrophyolax*, and, at his quiet rejoinder. Theodotos nodded approval, like a master whose pupil is fulfilling promise.

'Your words, Leptines, are cool as swans, yet graceless, clumsy and inappropriate, and your tone is unacceptable. You forget, in your recital, and your surely inappropriate reminder of Zeus, a certain hallowed line – that Zeus with all his heart hates the bray of swaggerers. As for your talk of death, you forget that Syracuse is not a butcher's yard, it is certainly not Apollonia where you've ruled like a mad or scalded cat. By all means, if you think it worth your while to continue an existence so sorry – you might agree, less than a scallop shell – you can certainly do so. Zeus will scent no rival, Heaven will remain unperturbed. Depart, therefore, not to the Shades, already overburdened with scoundrels, nor of course to Olympus, but to Corinth, where you may meet another illustrious personage occupying a place to which he is unaccustomed. The austerities of exile you should welcome, for they may teach you manners, prohibit your vileness, lend you a respect amongst civilised men hitherto lacking. You will, no doubt, wish to express your gratitude to us?

Leptines did not. His mouth opened, and remained so. He was led away as though swamped with poppy juice, a few councillors giving jeering bows, mock-deferential smiles. The agony of others strengthens the soul and gratifies the jealous dead.

That week, Theodotos, lover of risk, approached Timo by night. Aigle was asleep. Grimly determined, he uttered six names, rich oligarchs, leaders of the Sleepers. Aristodemos the foremost. He was convinced that all had been seduced by Carthage.

'You have proof?'

'Certainly not.'

'What can they gain? If we lose, Carthage won't reward them. None of them are moonstruck . . .'

'They hate you, vultures on the peck. Hatred can be moon madness. Probably they want Carthage half-victorious, Syracuse half-defeated, with themselves as happy go-betweens, pleasing to all. Diplomats! Foppish pigs. A fireship perhaps has its own pleasures. Pleasures itself like a schoolboy. But no one can love Carthage . . . save a gorgon . . .!' He winked, as if cherishing secrets best not disclosed, his voice, like his expression, now perfunctory.

'Early people were half-animal, could exchange thoughts without speaking. There weren't words to speak. They may have sung. I have some of this . . . I've seen these fellows' plans and hopes . . . written on the air, though clamped inside them.'

'That's your evidence?'

'What better? Trust me, Timo. Accuse them, and you'll get a lawsuit inexhaustible as Zeus' ramrod. They'd squeeze out every particle of law known and unknown. Demand a verdict and they'll bribe any jury out of its senses. Meanwhile . . .' – he opened his arms, then clapped hands together, twisting them as though strangling a goose – 'meanwhile . . . Carthage sails. Mind,' again that unpleasant grin, 'to be really safe, we should kill everybody.'

Timo deliberated. Not for long. Theodotos' spirit, all gristle and bone, mastered him; he already knew that he would not sorrow, that he loved Theodotos, whose very sting was a sharing, his bite a blood brotherhood.

'Say nothing. Let them . . . what you decide. . . .' He would offer no sacrifice, beseech no pardon. The greater good did not please but ordained. Enough. If he perished under the elephants or the knives of factionalists, he might become one with Timophanes.

The disappearance of the six, explained as desertion to Carthage, to Persia, caused uproar, accusation, dismay, considerable fear. For the first time Timo faced hostility: shouts of 'Killer . . . Despot . . . Fishgut. . . .'

He greeted this unalarmed, unsurprised. The wheel turned incessantly, Syracuse had ever dangled between extremes, loving the sensational while denouncing it. Soon he must let her know that, say, a snake had crossed his path, from the right, thus mightily propitious. Through the senseless one restored good sense.

No snake, however, was required. Within days all knew that Carthage had responded to Telemachus' goadings. Her fleet was advancing on Sicily: eighty thousand men, elephants, four-horse chariots, commanded by Hamilcar and Hasdrubal, renowned, unconquered, primed to link up with Hicetas' battalions. The mercenaries, Libyan, Numidian, Egyptian, Berber, were supported by the Republic's most dedicated regiment, the free-born aristocratic Sacred Band.

In Syracuse, mobs yelled for immediate advance, instant battle,

gods flashing crowns on request. Victory must have already occurred, the Council mendaciously delaying celebrations.

When Hamilcar landed at Lilybaeum, the mood swerved, then
fell away. Carthaginian strength was fantastic: elephants blocking
the sky, javelins a mile long, chariots pulled by hydras. Murders
were forgiven or praised, fishgut forgotten: a fearsome stillness
ensued until, from flocks in shivering panic, a measured stamp
began, a single momentous thud from dust and gloom, and the
cavernous heart of the city:

'Timo . . . Timo . . . Timo. . . .'

3

The Equals rejoined, rivalries and jealousies forgone. Embraces,
pledges, toasts, tears. One obstacle alone between them and stupid, crumbling Carthage. Demaretus, Eucleides, Telemachus,
Deinarchus, with the rising young Neon and Isias, strode to the
house in Achradina.

Timo was reclining at ease, in an old gown, a roll of Hesiod on
his knee. He appeared surprised but formally hospitable. Despite
the early hour, windows were shuttered, candles shining from
small terracotta jars. He had begun to avoid bright lights. Behind
him, at a table, scarcely glancing up in greeting, were Apelles and
Theodotos.

The visitors' faces, ambitious, excitable, beardless or lightly
shaved, encircled him. The dim, inconstant light worried them.
Deinarchus, always anxious to lead the pack, hastened to speak.

'Timo, let us consider. . . .'

Apelles and Theodotos, out of range of any inclination to consider, shuffled quartermasters' reports, mint declarations, sought
letters from Mamercus.

'Sir, don't do it. You have risked enough. Why risk more? It's
appointed for the young to fight and die. The people need you here.'

Ah! He saw the smiles come first on faces wide-eyed and strenuous, which then composed themselves. The handsome youths, the calculating Deinarchus, respected him, but for his crimes distant and recent. They saw him defying the gods, the laws, slaying whomever he wished. Now they sought their own turn. Briefly inattentive, he saw Kallias crouching over him, eager for his naked thighs. His sudden wince would be mistaken for rudeness.

He still seemed more intent upon Hesiod – *Often an entire city has suffered because of an evil man* – deep in himself. Then, rough, dismissive, he looked up at Deinarchus who, the oldest, unpleasant, reliable, part hero, part intriguer, was the most uncertain of his standing, pleading for supreme command, though from Timo's tone he must know that this was hopeless. Admitting it, he continued, his square, short-bearded face deferential but still authoritative, claiming his due.

'The City's overcrowded. Hordes of idlers. We can raise forty thousand, by force if there's trouble. I could have the sergeants and recruiting banners sent out at once.'

The others supported him, if unwillingly. In the artificial light, the small drab room, they were clumsy, too numerous, their grace and vigour useless, while, as though unaware of them, Theodotos and Apelles organised the future.

Timo's sigh was courteously regretful. He laid aside the Hesiod. He was fatherly, approachable but assured of obedience from those whose force was already spent. 'Not so, Deinarchus. We'll need five thousand. Theodotos will know whom to choose. Volunteers. We're not Carthage, conscripting a herd of brainless animals craving to turn traitor. They'll probably choose to fight with the sun in their eyes, to brag they've mastered the sun.'

Already he was thinking ahead. Defeat of Carthage would tilt the entire maritime balance, cut the monopolies, perhaps check Macedon. He was already signalling dismissal, touching every hand, as though each young officer were his chosen.

'We'll sacrifice to Demeter and that daughter of hers. We'll curse Hamilcar, add another curse for Hasdrubal, no less. We'll wait three days to discover whether Mamercus overcomes his fright and sends us the men and supplies he's promised. Promised,' Timo said, clasping the last hand, 'but not, I remember, on oath.'

Noosed by Timo's Name, merciless reputation for inordinate fortune, for guile, for story-telling, swearing loyalty to himself alone, sixty Thessalian horsemen landed from Rhegium, seeking no wages, scenting spoils, as news of the Carthaginian invasion sped across the Hellas.

Timo himself welcomed them, a resplendent helmet concealing his ageing head and weakened eyes. He had perfected his style. A judicious untruth, the over-familiar smile, the feigned recognition. Their randiness, excelled only by Pan, was a hazard, yet in crisis they could transform battle, not invariably for the better. 'You honour me', his voice was nicely judged between professional confidence and professional acumen, 'more than the gods.'

Hermes, forgive me.

Caustic and exacting, in borrowed regalia, now the barbarous champion, cast-off Jason, Theodotos also greeted them, with foul jokes that won instant respect. 'A virgin met a ram and a bear . . .', returning to Apelles with information racy, sardonic and unnecessary. 'Before battle, Apelles, they gorge on mushrooms, scarlet-capped like a Hittite giggle-stick, spotted white. Gives them frenzy. Wild courage, wild fear.'

'Men to be watched,' Apelles considered, then drily, 'by you, Theodotos.'

The Thessalians themselves gathered about Theodotos, feeling kinship, though avoiding his eye, reputed to turn yellow under the moon. They heard that he prowled the night, complaining of irredeemable hunger, and was greedy for the action ahead. Rich bodies, rich meat. Prudently, they called him 'the Blessed'. With him, they would snatch rewards.

The three days passed without signal from Mamercus. His perfidity was publicly cursed, as pollution, and Apelles, in a rare outburst, vowed that his name would be obliterated though never forgotten. On rumours that a few Syracusans had deserted, colluding with Sicilians, vengeful and sullen, Timo proclaimed the execution of a traitor with the sword that had slain Dion. The City rejoiced, not wholly knowing why.

The Carthaginians, with Hicetas' 'followers', who ventured where he himself did not lead, were already moving. Scouts reported them heading, in compact formations, for Estello. Simultaneously, Carthage offered a barrel of gold for Timo's head. On hearing this, Timo promised to supply the barrel, and throughout next day walked the City unattended and without armour, a red ribbon round his neck, to much laughter and goodwill.

The month of Tharlegion ended. Timo called for the five thousand volunteers, announcing that the Carthaginians were gathering at the Crimesus, challenging him not to battle but to punishment.

This news dispersed the elation. Through long, hot, dusty hours Apelles and his staff waited outside the walls. By dusk, however, only three thousand had responded and he methodically reduced these by some eight hundred. Excuses were more numerous. People were praying, were at essential work; swallows fleeing from a jagged column of wind. Syracuse was crown of Hellas, the gods would provide.

Timo was despondent, but Theodotos only smiled, hastening to address the volunteers. They considered his grin malicious, his promises insulting but his demeanour reassuring.

'In the battle, which none of you can escape, only heroes will gain burial-rites. The rest we'll leave for kites and wolves. Their spirits will be homeless, my word on it. Make certain of your own. You can trust Timo, you trust my brother Apelles. You can even', his grin was even nastier, 'trust me!'

Surrounded by the Centaurs, themselves noisy and confident, counting up dead Carthaginians and fugitive Leontines, Timo led out the Syracusian army. He had had to accept some mercenary hoplites but trusted only the volunteers, few but hand-picked. The mercenaries, however, hearing that they were not to defend the City but directly assail the huge Carthaginians, shouted that Timo was demented, condemning his force to death by killers whose ruthlessness dismayed the gods themselves. They then departed in a body, leaving the remainder downcast.

They were marching towards the Crimesus and surely disaster. Timo felt their mood on his back and finally clambered on Black Cloud so that they could see him better. A gesture was expected. Peitho, goddess of persuasion, help me.

Reaching a bare, brown hillock he ordered a halt. Pressing Black Cloud up to the summit he looked down at the men straggling beneath him. Upright against the sky, he stationed himself with the sea breeze behind him so that all could hear. The Centaurs ranged him. The senior officers, Apelles, Theodotos, Demaretus and the rest stood at the bank, alongside the cavalry, all hearing him.

'Zeus is with us, Hades awaits his due. He has called to us but his words were cracked, they fell apart with a clatter that scared our Lady Persephone and will certainly get the better of Hamilcar, Hasdrubal and that dainty Lady Hicetas. Remember, Syracuse overwhelmed Carthage at Himera and broke Athens in the Great War, avenging her genocide at innocent Melos, deemed disgraceful even in Macedon. Meanwhile, in token, we have received a rich gift, though not from Hades. Now, I challenge each one of you to name it.'

Cheered, they tossed off guesses, officers readily joining in. A truce? Plague in the west? Relief army from Corinth, from Catana? Earthquake in Carthage?

Timo shook his head. Only the Thessalians stared silent and impatient, not understanding, anxious to reach the Crimesus and stain it scarlet.

Unexpectedly, Timo allowed himself what he had so seldom, the enduring, sometimes unendurable habit of Theodotos: a laugh. Dry and emphatic, an axe splitting tough wood; startling.

'No, my valiant friends. None of these, but much better. You already know but, in your eagerness for victory, swarming to be first, to be Best of All, you've already forgotten. So I remind you, and each of you will grow taller. Be careful not to damage the clouds! We may need them!'

Horseman in the sky, undisputed, both in a dream and out of it, he paused, inviting further visions from the expectant mass. A banquet on Olympus, a march to the world's end, lives merging into an irresistible, inexhaustible phallus thrusting beyond mortal life.

His words fell distinct as coins down still, late afternoon air. The drooping sun strewed him with gold. Black Cloud himself was motionless, as if listening.

'Mamercus, royal Mamercus, brave Mamercus, Mamercus with the soul of a louse and the heart of a sparrow, promised us help. Like a Celt pledging to repay a loan – but in the next world. He has broken his word. Those worthless mercenaries have crept away, abashed by the company of real warriors, the splendour of Syracuse and Corinth. The bad apples have shrivelled. Stop your tears, you won't have to cover your backs. You, who took Syracuse, who exploded the grasshopper Leontines with no more than a belch, to put it politely as a gentleman should to gentlemen, who blew away the Canary. So. . . .' Timo, beneath his feathered casque, was grinning like a tavern-keeper, knowing his men, knowing life. 'We've the best of it. We are spared poisonous breath, boasts born in a latrine, jokes that blight every loaf in camp, faces that curdle the excellent wine which Apelles has procured for us. Because . . . – he gazed down, mild, apologetic as if repeating a verse already heard too often – 'they, and facing-both-ways Mamercus, will not be joining us. Thus victory is certain. We shall see Carthage on the run, Hicetas lowering what's left of his head!'

Cheers began, laughter was immoderate, but, with artful timing, he raised a hand for quiet. 'You can rejoice further. I too am a betting man. I've wagered your pay with Theodotos, the old ruffian, that we'll thrash Carthage in a day. So he'll be paying you double!'

He allowed the applause full storm: the stamps, the clash of weapons, the friendly jibes at Theodotos, who bared his teeth, spat, then gave a sudden jump, both arms stretched as if to tussle with the sun.

Despite heat, the march to the Crimesus must be swift. The small army accepted it, alight with prospects. On wooded heights, from furtive valleys, Sicilians would be watching, hoping against odds that all conquerors would devour each other. The priest of some river god approached Theodotos, demanding a forest in return for the goodwill of a sacred well, which would then refrain from being poisoned. 'Bramble-arsed offspring of a goat.' Theodotos smiled courteously, though his dark eyes glittered on the worn, yellowy skin.

Priests have double tongues: in Greek accents they would be learning Carthaginian runes and hymns, flavoured with praises sufficient to spray a suffete's midden or gild a paradise.

Etna was hidden. Clouds were high, summer hard on fields, lying deep on hillsides. Occasionally the marchers heard, or seemed to hear, a dulled medley of sound drifting towards them from beyond hills, against which they muttered charms, repeated certain numbers. One number assured complete protection, but in a dispute about its identity, one fellow lost an eye.

The sun was harsh, the gnats vicious, and three thirsty days left most dispirited, worried by the aura of Semitic Carthage; the elephants, the innumerable warriors, the ferocity. Rumours of evil furnaces and prolonged, unnatural torture. Small birds had vanished, those of prey hovered hopefully. Moods wobbled like mercury, emotions were pared: stark as rock, snake, knife or as Timo's nodding plume ahead.

They had enfiled through valleys, bypassed small, closed towns surrounding the dry plain of Crimesus. The enemy had reached powerful Entella and was occupying the river lands.

A halt was signalled. Experienced Equals mounted a blue heathered rise, hoping to see the Carthaginian dispositions and there, across the mile or so of flattish scrub and stone, easily reached in a sustained charge, was the shining, rippling line of water and, close behind it, very clear, the dense wedges of armoured men, the flapping standards, grotesque hues, the shuffling, ornate elephants. Theodotos identified the huge, elephant-hide shields of the Sacred Band, pledged to defend the Republic to the last man. These were some two thousand. From spies, Apelles learned that Hamilcar led the cumbersome chariots glinting on the left, Hasdrubal the centre, mostly foot-soldiers. On the right, cavalry, a motley crowd, Apelles judged.

He turned to Timo; the weathered face with the young, sharp eyes, was composed, as always. 'A divided command. Always risky though we've done it ourselves. But with such numbers. . . .' He shrugged, stared out again. 'One lot will break bounds to outmatch the other. In Carthage a general gets gigantic rewards . . . but, if he loses, he'd better die in the field. Now, if I'm right, if one of them crosses the river on his own. . . .' He was suddenly luminous, very content.

Deinarchus stepped to his side. 'But they've chosen a marvellous defence . . .'

'They won't keep it,' Theodotos the Blessed said in his grumbling way. 'An army like that, slaves and hirelings and jobless from a hundred cities . . . they can't defend. They can only attack. Understanding nothing at all. Accursed.'

Timo scarcely listened. He was no strategic planner and, in battle, the best plans dissolve. Fighting to rescue Timophanes, amid the din and anguish, he had been aware only of half-heard, contradictory orders and improvised blundering. His role was not that of Apelles, Deinarchus, Demeratus. He had courage, not showy but useful. He had obstinacy. Chiefly, he possessed a Name.

While the Equals discussed, he contemplated not the enemy but his own force. Indeed, it was small, even puny; morose, complaining, mercurial, but, while he lived, it would not retreat. Apelles had not descended, but was giving orders to keep the men busy: point arrows with obsidian, oil shields to make them slippery in the hand-to-hand, sharpen blades, groom the horses.

Timo wondered whether to address them. They usually expected it. He hesitated, awaiting words, awaiting Hermes. Not only Sicily but all Hellas might depend on this battle: Macedon, victorious over small cities and scheming cliques, remained a pimple beside this momentous exchange. But to speak thus, at this crisis, was lawyers' stuff, sonorous, echoing, but unreal, like that invented for Pericles.

Leaving the Equals to their plans, he moved along the ridge, averted from the plain, gazing at thin grass, bee-swarming heather, paths traced on sloping turf and stony, irregular terracing. On a dark-green mound a heron stood, uninterested in the commotion below. A movement from the further side of his own hill attracted him. A peaceful convoy of mules, bearing parsley, drooping like filmy wings over the beasts' flanks. Soon, the troops too saw it, pausing, gazing, all briskness evaporating in mournful shock. The omen atrocious, for parsley is used for tomb wreaths. Blood pulled down their hearts.

But the god spoke. Timo felt words rush into him. He summoned dark-haired Demeratus, was brusquely incisive, back in command. 'Get a bag of drachmas, pour out half and give it to the muleteer. Buy all his stuff. Every shred, every sprig. You'll be a grocer for all time. High praise! I want it distributed. Bring me enough to make myself a coronal, then I'll give them some sort of explaining and attend to marching orders.'

Shortly the army was surprised to see its general donning a clumsy green circlet, then inviting them to do likewise. This was the session before battle, for seasonal exhortations – the birthright of Hellas, the liberties of hearth and motherland, a mention of wives and lustral libations.

But he was informal, off-duty, one of themselves, wandering

between ranks, addressing each sun-smitten, tousled head as it flickered before him, instantly replaced. All were festooned with parsley: round the neck, across the forehead, behind the ears, on wrist and arm. His failure, or the parsley's failure, would leave them torn, pierced, nailed. Meanwhile they glowed, pushing to hear him, handling their parsley as they might amulets.

'We're going to win fame as parsley kings. Why? Listen. It's true that here in Sicily parsley is for the dead. But which dead? Not us! You'll be presenting it in person to the sons and slaves of Carthage. Many of you are Corinthians, with long valour and short memory. Don't any of you remember that on our Isthmus victors are crowned with the sacred herb of Aphrodite? And what is that?'

Pause, then, in hoarse, gritty unison: *'Parsley.'*

'Verily! Indeed! An excellent cure, moreover, for sick fish. Could any fish be more sick than those barbarian conscripts over the river pushed into line to face us, and wishing they weren't.'

He was sauntering, pausing to examine a shield, a cooking-pot, inquire of one man's name, another's dwelling. From further away, the Equals, the new, aspiring leaders, quick-tempered and ruthless, watched him: grudging, jealous, with misgivings, with relief. No real warrior, like Philip, like Hasdrubal and Hamilcar, he might yet, in this fiery contest, prove a great captain. No orator, he could yet transform a mob to an audience. 'Don't let the elephants scare you. Theodotos will tell you they're more dangerous to their own side than to ours. Likely to panic. Stupid beasts, left over from Chaos. A god blundered, then lost interest. Or got interrupted, probably saw a nymph and put the tail in the wrong place. . . . Anyway, I'll tell you a story. Yesterday, or last week . . . some-time . . . I saw in the sky – what do you think? Elephants? Of course not. An eagle flying, clutching a snake! I don't need to tell you who is the eagle, who the nasty snake!'

A hoary story, endlessly repeated from armies long dead, and they loved it, demanding more. Our Timo, godson of Hermes the joker, and throwing them jokes like spells.

'And whom are we deigning to conquer? Cowardly Hicetas, who sees an enemy only from his back – indeed, from his backside! Hook-nosed Hasdrubal who spent all night looking for a coin, which was in his hand the whole time! Hamilcar, who fell down a well seeking his own star! His father was a belch, his mother a fart, and between them they produced a loser. Remember poor old

Mago. Hamilcar's wife was fertilised by a cross-wind from Libya, so she got two snouts! As for his grandfather. . . .' He spread his hands.

Shouts: 'Tell us the grandfather, Timo!'

His protesting sigh was theatrical, evoking raucous encouragement. 'When young, ugly as a gorgon's liver, he loved a fly-by-night whore. Wanted to ram her, but alas, no go at all. She kept her rear-end covered, but teased him with it relentlessly, and charged him just for that. Then began overcharging him for merely imagining her slack and cockle. All he got was dreams about her, up-ended, naked as a fish. And, true bastard of Carthage, he loved collecting money, hated spending it. So think of him, poor old granddad dreaming of spouting into her like a geyser. Like that nameless fellow who burned down Artemis' temple, to be remembered for ever.

'But like all of us, he couldn't keep his tongue from clacking. At this, the precious whore got angry. Dreams of me, does he! Not a stitch on. Plugging me with his dirty thing, or trying to! Messy little squid! And for nothing? Certainly not. You pay me, my fine stallion, she ordered, for without me where would your silly dream be? Nowhere. You've dirtied me in your own bed, so pay up!

'At this, even he protested, swearing by all the unpronounceable gods of Carthage, dangling not a dirty . . . thing, but an empty purse. Wailing, threatening, she pulled him to the judges. Carthage is that sort of place. The judges conferred like drunken owls, then ordered him to produce a certain sum. Granddad did so, not very cheerfully. He'd stolen it from his sister. He laid it before the owls and the whore, you can imagine, reached out to grab it, stuff it where it belonged. But the judges stopped her. Not so fast, my pretty! they said. They *pronounced* that, as the case depended on a dream, she was entitled only to the money's shadow, which she could take away at once, if she could. She lamented like a Kotyan fishwife when her putrid cuckold turns up unexpectedly.

'Then the judges added that granddad was due for payment from her, a fine, for having trespassed on his sleep! So he got back his money and got a fine too. So it all ended well enough, save for his having whelped a son who produced this abominable Hamilcar, who'll be remembered not for his ancestry but for his flight from tomorrow's little skirmish.'

The cheers must have reached the Carthaginians and roused the sensitive elephants. The Hellenes no longer saw a face worn and ridged under the silvery mat of hair, a burdened frame and withdrawn spirit, but a young champion out of spring rain, a graceful lord of renewal, a Parsley King.

4

Few slept, though the huge moonlight blocked any likelihood of night attack. On higher slopes, pickets watched for movement from the river. Heather, rock, water glimmered in level consistency.

The bright moon of Artemis. Each general was with his own men, vague heaps huddled among foothills, horses shuffling in a disused quarry.

Only Apelles sat alone. Beneath the pallid sky tinged with dark blue and green, lit further by Carthaginian fires, were soundless messages for himself alone. Moonflakes, shadows, stars had tongues. Shapes behind shape. In such long moments gods stirred, ghosts filtered from tree, boulder, tarn, an abyss spread from solid ground; Spartans would summon star-gazers to advise the fate of a new-born baby; there opened the ivory gate of deception, the horn gate of true prophecy.

Apelles was considering less the battle than the need to maintain Timo's Name. Out of this, many thoughts oppressed him. He sorted them, contemplated them, waited for them to clarify, cold and chilling as Artemis herself riding in the night, solitary, absorbed.

Death hung, cancelling time. Soothsayers had told Achilles that, by sparing Hector, he could appease powerful gods, divert Fate, prolong his life, though feuds of blood and honour forbade such temptations. Life is obligation, pacts must be observed, friendship's dues completed, Patroclus, the incomparable, be avenged. *But*

Achilles wept, dreaming of the beloved comrade.

Carthage and her hordes dwindled, despite the line of camp-fires. Apelles had long known that the Bronze Kings of Hittites had fatally trusted mercenaries, whose souls were as large only as their pay. Not defeat but victory would now be the danger. Gods are jealous, triumph demands a sacrifice. Timo's Promethean adventures imperilled him, risking the counter-blow, slow but determined as rot. Yet he must survive. His work was unfinished.

The moon glared from the ashen sky, shrinking star and fire. Artemis, uncanny as twins, Virgin of the Silver Bow, a frozen weight on the heart. Apelles, Lord General of Syracuse, knew that she was aiming directly at him.

Peril must be borne for Timo, his Fate safeguarded. All knew that the sun must not stray from his appointed track but, should he do so, threefold Fate will pursue even him. Timo might be fated to die at Crimesus, but it is the onus of manhood to act as if no Fate existed, to challenge destiny: otherwise an Achilles would be but a toy of slime and chaos. Apelles sat like a stone. Who was this man to whom he was pledged?

Throughout Hellas, Timo the story-teller had become a story. In infancy he had worsted Sophists, had pulled a lance from a sacred tree, been embraced by Aphrodite, overcome the monstrous at crossroads. A rock had addressed him, he understood birds, learning from a hawk that he would achieve a wonder and sacrifice himself to himself.

The real Timo? He displayed affection like a strategist, but could he ever have loved? Certainly he avoided passion, an affliction sent to unman and ruin the inordinate, so that self-love was the rudder essential to reach fair havens, to maintain order. Beloved as a teller of tales, he apparently set no store by them. Usually he said little, while provoking speech from others. He would examine a statue, listen to singer or rhetor, but expressionless. His head might be a single room or a fortress divided by bolted doors, behind which sat the adventurer, the husband, the father, the lawgiver. His jocularity might be genuine, but only with inferiors. Sadness nourished his authority, a sigh lurked within his laugh, his eyes could catch fire but remained uneasy. Probably his spirit was sustained by curiosity. He loved questions: a slave's name, why a rich man spent his wealth on oriental flowers, why one expert sea captain so seldom attracted a reliable crew; whether luck had meaning, even purpose; whether luck existed.

Theodotos, brutal, intemperate, might know Timo, but none knew Theodotos, who spoke only to lock up his thoughts.

Mortal life proceeds through defeat and recovery, restoration of balance. Timo's ancient crime was working itself out, like poison from the flesh, in his unceasing labours. The will of Zeus. The Idea of Hellas.

Apelles, suddenly fatigued, fancied he could hear distant singing. Carthaginians? But the voices were eerily high, not animal but scarcely human. The Hellenic general, renowned for taciturnity, discipline, caution, shivered in the warm night, for he knew that the sirens, beautiful but treacherous, sang their sweetest songs to the dying.

Dawn mist curled over the Crimesus, sheeting the plain. On the hill, Timo waited, already unmistakable in scarlet corslet, golden bracelets, his crested headpiece a flash of white and scarlet. Demarchus, Telemachus, Demeratus were with him, about to rejoin their troops.

As if before Troy, the dim air was filled with gods. Eyes in the sky watched river and plain. Obeisance had been paid to the sunrise, itself invisible. Timo had poured libations to Timodemos and Timophanes, prayed to Hermes, Giver of the Favourable Instant, had considered proclaiming a vision of Victory on a cloud pointing seawards towards Carthage, but such tricks had staled. Someone might fluke a glimpse of a devout toad or the Archer God who loved Corinth. The Blessed, wolf-man, had already excited his Thessalian desperadoes by parading a wooden gorgon, to shock ill-fortune. Showing fangs, he announced that Carthage always sweetened his gums.

Timo closed his eyes, opened them. All remained grey. Through dimness, irregular blocks of men were now stirring, horses being led forward, fires extinguished, the little army moving to orders from Apelles. Deinarchus on the right, with cavalry, Demeratus and Eucleides on the left. Theodotos and his erratics conforming to no plan, ready to gallop into any gaps offered. Plans, commands, all restraints are hateful to Thessalians. Apelles himself would remain near Timo, leading the hoplite centre, an arc of spearmen, archers, slingers, seven deep, though, whatever the orders, his mounted Centaurs under young Isias would be following close.

Flutes sounded, thin, sharp, despite the muffled air. Later they will resume, for music helps heal wounds, sometimes recalls the dead. As if responding, the sun was edging through the lower mists, disclosing the Carthaginian masses, the chariots, armoured wagons, the cloudy but powerful elephants, while on the higher slopes the scantiness of the Syracusan army was still obscured. The Thessalians, already mounted, clustered on flat ground, were chafing, barely stilled by Theodotos.

The air was spiked. Timo fancied a quiver beyond the river, from the rampart of shields, wheels, beasts. Bracken and pine glowed on hills, then dazzled. Would the Carthaginians, over-confident, venture everything and dare a crossing? Warming, the last haze rose from the plain and dispersed, light flashing along the Crimesus, no broader than the renowned Scamander, snatching at fierce details in the African host. Silver coins planted on a charioteer's head, gold filigree blazing on an elephant. Even at this distance veterans identified colours, weapons, garish standards, of Iberians, Libyans, a scattering of Celts and Etruscans, a Numidian regiment, Berber auxiliaries and, surrounded by giant, black slingers, a group of women, metal-plated, bare-headed, probably Sarmatians from the Euxine. Near these, very appropriately, the Hellenes joked, was a company of Leontines, at sight of whom rose a sardonic cheer.

On poles, above convex shields and triangular iron helms, glinted carved lions, horse-heads and, on scarlet spears, several human heads and grinning masks. The glory of Carthage. The quiver quickened. 'I see them dance,' Timo spoke loud enough for his words to reach the serried ranks behind him, 'but I don't hear their music.'

He signed. From leftwards, trumpets pealed and a Thessalian, his spirit capering, overflowing, scarlet-tipped javelin upheld, was already crashing forward out of damp undergrowth, through sunlight, his fellows in crazed pursuit. Theodotos amongst them. Arrows whistled, curved, fell, a rider lurched, a horse collapsed, but the charge sped on, nearing the water, reaching it, the leader whooping some forgotten rhyme, then drawing rein, hurled his spear over the river into the packed metallic squares, tensed, waiting, flanked by Nubian conscripts gripping black whips.

The entire Carthaginian army was now exposed, a mile of

infantry mixed with cavalry and chariots, each end weighted by elephants, painted, feathered, bejewelled, tusks glittering with blades strapped tight. The exact centre, savagely, obscenely taunted by the Thessalians who, riding undeterred by arrow and dart, sprayed it with javelins, was held by the Sacred Band, a rampart of shields and spears, tight, motionless, packed with as much honour as Carthage could ever muster.

Could the Carthaginians but keep to their side of the river, not wide but strong and deep, they could be impregnable. Timo and Apelles urgently searched for a break in the ranks, while the Syracusans, still held back, cheered as Theodotos galloped back unscathed, his troop madly singing, more arrows dropping behind them as they lifted weapons at the uproarous greetings, swords clashing on shields. Almost at once they were regrouping, primed for further extravagance, Theodotos himself flush with hunter's lust.

Apelles called. From the far bank an unmistakable tremor, then movement. True. Undeniable. As if recklessly unaware of the Syracusans shuffling under the hill, either the two Carthaginian war-lords, more rivals than colleagues, had ordered a crossing or were unable to restrain it. Then a cry from Deinarchus. He too had noticed.

The Syracusans stood poised, exultant and quailing simultaneously, gut-loose. All seemed enlarged and fateful. Tall chariots and horses four abreast were slowly pushing over a ford, a few wagons fortified with brazen shields and crammed with swordsmen following, men and animals finely controlled. Behind, waiting their turn, stately as a ritual procession, banners limp, golden standards aching with mottled light, their devices lumpish as congealed oil, stood the Sacred Band itself, shields fiery circles, then, meticulous, perfected, stepping down as one into the river, and, as if on parade, reaching the further side, chariots deploying around them.

Throughout his every nerve, Timo felt men shake, toughen, then shed consciousness of all save the approaching shock of arms. Could he but hold them a few instants more, he could snare the witless Africans. The ford seemed narrow, too narrow for an army so swollen with gesticulating, perhaps hysterical conscripts, ill-armed reserves, with slaves and baggage. Less than half the Sacred Band had crossed but already, lashed forward by the dread ox-hide whips, mercenaries were descending, floundering, inextricably tumbling amongst their superiors. Apelles, almost within reach, would be noting the slack discipline, the wilful risks. Order was disintegrating. Horses stumbled, a wagon was stuck, and now, in deeper waters, the elephants had started, powerful, but perilously slow, impeding the mass behind. Once over, the monsters stood puzzled, ill-tempered from mounting, uncontrolled din, goaded with difficulty to the outer horns of the Carthaginian crescent. This, Timo thought, must necessitate further muddle.

Horses fear elephants. The Chariots, stationed too near them, would have to slant centrewards, exposing their sides, a gift to Deinarchus, Telemachus, Eucleides, let alone the Thessalians who, yes, unleashed perhaps by Theodotos, more probably by spontaneous will, the leap of the blood, were renewing their assault, bearing down on the still frail Carthaginian right, while the chariots, somewhat indeterminate, were attempting to manoeuvre in front of the immaculate Sacred Band. At its rear, confusion seemed swirling, perhaps another wagon had faltered, the banks becoming muddied and slippery. The horses of chariots and cavalry were uneasy, tossing heads at the clumsy bodies and screaming commands. At last. Timo, Timo *Somatrophylax*, jabbed up his spear, Apelles nodded.

Trumpets again, hoarse and chattering. The regular cavalry at once started, following up the dust of the Thessalians, in strict order, gathering pace. Sunlight raged among the distracted chariots, at last managing to swing towards the foe, in a single block, advancing in molten heat against the Thessalian irregulars and, if dodging them, ready to meet the Syracusans with spear and arrow. Behind, led by Timo, in parallel formations, the hoplites advanced at jogtrot. Spears, bows, slings.

A voice darted from Isias, covering the rearguard with the Centaurs. 'Trust us, Timo. Don't bother to look behind you. . . . Don't risk your head by turning it.'

Metal clanged, horses reared from dust-clouds which distorted all – elephants lost outline, were a jumbled mess of skin and metal, rearing waves, wheels were jagged, one, from an overturned chariot, still rolling, faces all eye and tooth. Duels pounded, chariots drove through, were repulsed or careered unmanned into oblivion. Already at grips with the Sacred Band, tall, bearded but faceless beneath low-brimmed casques, perhaps closing on

Hamilcar himself, Timo could only strive forwards: his body lunged, aimed, rammed home with toxic exhilaration, stooped and twisted of itself, for him to follow. In fits of exhaustion he had abruptly to stand helpless, a spent swimmer, cramped, almost blind, drenched, yet defended from out of the air by axe, stone, dart, shield. Brays, yells, curses, wordless howls covered him, a medley of pain and joy; red froth, dirt, the thuds, the tearings. Restored, at one with the tumult, he had random lucidity, hearing a familiar voice, sensing from stupendous crashes a Thessalian crushing of chariots, recognising that Apelles, like a Homeric prince, still lived, shouting, encouraging. Out of the fray, Telemachus' raw, gashed face, more dim chariots, a shuddering, transfixed horse, Isias swooping like a trim bird of prey, then gone.

Continuously reinforced, the Carthaginian wings seemed to be converging, to envelope and overwhelm. Tusk and trunk, vast in the infernal dream, loomed, swayed, receded or toppled, terrified and mad, once overthrowing an opulent, black-bearded officer on to a crowd of spears. The Sacred Band, diminished, bloodied, fought on, silently, in a circle of mashed flesh, a severed hand gripping a trident, trampled shields, artificial beards falling on to a ripped belly, a dead, open mouth. The elephants were now invisible, horses on both sides faltered, overcome by the reek of blood, the sickly light, the heat, the dark equality. Lives gushed, pouring away into the earth. Boulders smashed Hellene and Carthaginian alike, splintering, mangling, while Timo, with Centaurs now dismounted, strove for mastery. Orders were impossible save those of insensate Ares howling for massacre. Instinct governed the undulating flood, the shapes, distorted, desperate in murk, sinking back again.

Continually the Syracusans divided, struggled to half turn, wheel back in brief, frantic pushes. Two elephants stumbled on the loose, blinded, blood-spattered outlines of Chaos, trumpeting, stamping out the wounded, staggering without direction, until swallowed in the red dusk. In one clearing, despite the missiles, demented horses, ravaging blades, several Syracusans stood as if immune, passionately quarrelling, finally assaulting each other until abruptly dispersed by a Numidian onslaught, naked, blood-eyed, stabbing all before them until falling themselves, attacked from the side. Weapons sparked and struck as if of their own, detached in the stinking pall from bodies discoloured, gasping, thrusting, dripping from crunch and collision, sickening in brutish impact. A monstrous spawn from Tartarean couplings, a maze shot by lightning. An inhuman call. A sight of Theodotos, helmet lost, breast armour missing, but still mounted, deftly killing, short spear hideously wet, face and body shining above swarthy bodies split, wavering, falling into death, or torture from hoof and foot.

Timo's strength was diminishing, prolonged only by brief re-treats covered by Centaurs, themselves still largely intact. He knew little save chance: chance to strike, chance to evade. Twice Isias had replaced his weapon. The Sacred Band, depleted, high above mounds of their dead, fought on, undeterred, trained, methodical, their shields thick ovals of blood, flesh, hair. But again pausing, barely upright, Timo saw, or thought he saw through the con-fusion, storm-clouds, low, purple blemishes closing over unnatu-ral lights of battle, and yes, wind gusting, driving rain towards the river. He contrived to shout encouragement, his voice enormous, followed at once by the wind roaring, beating, the air filling with hard edges as hail slithered over skin and metal. Feet slipped further on human mud. Breathlessness, hectic clamour, madness, an unending groan.

Barely coherent, at last reckless, Timo grabbed a bewildered, riderless horse, risking all against the terrible shields and blades, the square black beards. He was up, again shouting, making ground. A streaming eye swelled as if to block him, incredible din was solid within the gale. Scarlet surf, another cascade of hail. Screams like giant marrow splitting, sough of Titans, all vampires, famished for blood, clawing. Underworld shapes, foul scents.

But Isias was near, the Centaurs plunging, scarcely aware of broken chariots, oozing corpses, the hurricane above. The Sacred Band flinched, its line bulged, sagged, uncertain in failing light, flayed by frontal hail, yet recovering, obdurate, wounded but still powerful.

Further off, Apelles had fought his share, once rescued by a manic Thessalian charge. Overall control was long lost, the battle was shapeless, he struggled as if alone, sensing that the barbarian mercenaries were faltering, though attempts to flee were throttled by overseers turned executioners. He had successfully manned resistance to Libyan onrush, led a foray against Berber spearmen, but throughout strove to keep sight of Timo. He now recognised through the gloom, quite close, Timo's crest rising, falling, imperilled, amid a hash of steam, blood, hail, clumsy dance of arms, the quick, blurred flashes, densities of filth. Butcher's cauldron of pain. He felt Timo drawn by an inexorable magnetic pull into a patch of Etna horror, seething, deathly, in this mouldering light in which all bodies merged, jerking horribly in the gloom, and as if growing useless wings as storm broke the sun. Within this, from poised, black skin latticed with blood, an axe was raised at Timo's back.

Apelles knew his moment, saw his chance, rushed on the Numidian's flank before he could strike, open Charon's dark river. Timo was still fighting unaware, Isias reeling from an unseen blow. The struggle heaved through vast avenues of sound. Wind still swept hail on to Carthaginians, but mercenaries were in panic revolt, terrorised less by the combat, the whips, than by lurid twilight, the black and red slime, apparently depthless, and the unseen. Lightning ripped the clouds, revealing an elephant on its knees, its death agony honking, honking like a primeval mating of earth and sky while the fury still blew, as though lashed by outraged gods.

The Sacred Band stood, thrust back, undeterred by rain, by deserting auxiliaries, but with strength slowly flagging. Elsewhere on the spectral, disordered field mercenaries were beseeching quarter, crouching helpless, fleeing to the river, even their masters now hesitant, straining to see, even to stand. Armour itself now fatal, draggling; once fallen, none could retrieve himself from the swamp. A snap, a whistle, a neigh as if from the earth, a naked breast sprouting feathers.

Drenched, riven, almost abandoned, weapons now ponderous, almost immovable, the black-beards were retreating before the lighter, more nimble Hellenes, now shrieking victory. Behind them, the Crimesus was overflowing, first in rivulets, now in misshapen torrent whipped by the storm, while from hills more water eddied and foamed, entangling the floundering remains of battle, though, in and out of shadow, in ferocious insets, persisted the hand-to-hand, the tooth-to-tooth. Outlaw figures, flurried surges and falls. On higher ground, fugitives were being speared, screeching in a dozen languages. Thessalians, vague, gigantic and irresistible, rode the earth at will.

The sun reappeared, scalding, entire, showing the Carthaginian wings shattered. Chariots and horses, elephants, artillery machines, corpses made a sacked town, convulsed by the dying.

Three blinded horses, lopsided and precarious, still dragged a
chariot over the dead and wounded. The last of the Sacred Band
were swept aside by Theodotos, even in death their mouths set,
their eyes ungiving. Rain slackened, dried; yellow lit a vile, tortured world with labyrinthine ferocity.

Surviving Equals could discern a meagre pattern. Elephants had
charged their officers. Deinarchus had triumphed without knowing it. Demeratus had heaved a decisive counter-blow, fancying
himself retreating. Theodotos had charged far beyond the battle,
returned, heard a flying report that Timo had fallen, and in animal
fury, doubtless growing claws and poison-sacs, regrouped his
followers for the last swoop.

The sky healed. Through air still streaky, flute and pipe dropped
low, mournful notes. Under the unblinking sun, which like a
wounded bird was suffusing the west with unsullied radiance,
splinters of orange, blue, green and yellow, flies had spread a
black, glistening counterpane over the acreage of human trash . . .
lopped thighs, a heap of knuckles, grinning throats. Kites squatted
on tallowy flesh swollen like wine-skins and, through bluish-white
death fumes, scarecrow Sicilian women were creeping forward,
exhalation from ravine and scarp, marsh and cave, or the dank
earth itself, to strip and knife the dead and wounded. Whores of
warfare, on ground blotched with red slurry.

Fugitives were rounded up for slave-market and quarry, ceasing
to curse Hamilcar and Hasdrubal, who would have reached the
coast, but mute, resigned, numbed by the invisible aura of Timo.
Spoils were being piled: decorated bucklers, elaborately chased
swords and shields fallen from the generals' retinue, the flaunting
standards, bundled equipage, chariots, in high, irregular cairns,
memorials to the battle of Crimesus.

In their leader's tent the Equals were swilling, boasting, swapping their tales. Eucleides had sliced a black Titan, Neon overthrown
a naked youth on a leopard. Deinarchus' exuberant stratagems had
cost Carthage ten thousand.

Further off, amid stench and offal, Apelles lay dying, crumpled,
tiny scum round his stiff, grimed lips; at one with the gaunt music,
the rank, bloated, fly-smitten bodies, the packed, discarded
weaponry, the curdled air. The Numidian axe had cleft his shoulder

where strapping had broken, as he accepted the death meant for another. Watched from afar, two men knelt beside him, Theodotos and Timo. He was speechless, his eyelids twitched, his breath faded. Rites had started, the chants, the prayers, the lamb burned for Artemis Agrotera. Tomorrow he would be burned with the others, on pyres already being stacked by the river. Clean flame would outbid the worm, races and dances speed the soul, hymns be intoned to Calliope, Muse of Heroic Song.

PART SIX

Government

1

The Persians had arrived, somewhat overdue, to present the Great King's congratulations on the overthrow of Carthaginian Sicily. An interview with Timo was to be kept as private as possible in the city of spies and scatter-tongues, where secrets were often lavish chances to speculate, invent, embroider. The envoys had already been publicly received by the Council, men simultaneously smiling and impassive, lips and eyelids carmined, beards curled and jewelled, some with beryls in their ears. The populace grinned at their mauve, pointed caps or turbans fixed with emerald brooches, the sumptuous cushions carried behind them by glittering slaves – doubtless eunuchs, people said contemptuously.

Timo, in conference in a secluded room in the Citadel, was enjoying the talk. There were chairs for all save himself. They had seated themselves without realising this so that, left standing, he had already gained a small advantage as if not sharing but granting, like the Great King himself.

Listening with a courtesy that the army had not seen, he studied them. Faces adorned with clever eyes, thin lips; subtly powdered and tinted, a daub here, a line there, ingeniously adding a further expression to those concealed beneath. Their perfumes shrugged away the coarse smells rising from street and market, harbour and fish-mart. Their voices, clear but weak, seemed to chime faintly, with a Greek purer than that of quick-speaking Corinthians. Now

slightly deaf, Timo welcomed this. He was enjoying the conference, despite the fatigue in his legs. Such Persian lords were
always illustrious, silken men of knowledge, even wisdom, or
apparent wisdom, with graciousness, with wit, and an occasional
hint of the comic, of which they were unaware.

They had been complimenting everything: the splendour and
power of the Citadel and New Hades, the fame of Syracuse, the
awesome Crimesus 'negotiation', the wine and satyr-shaped cakes
before them, which they praised elaborately, dangled, contemplated with wonder, without actually consuming. Still the talk
purred and wandered, serious converse in which he could join,
more directly, more crudely if you like, about the origin of gods
and the nature of the sun, the new Hellenic lyric, developments
in dance, in philosophy. *What is man?* Pindar of Thebes had
written. *What is he not? He is the dream of a shadow.* The ambassadors
plied words like scalpels, like tweezers, like unguents. The divine
does not create, it experiments, like the godly Timo himself. His
adventures were contrary to all logic, but logic is but the last resort
of the civilised. Euripides had written that wisdom is not wisdom.
How could a Philip, a Hamilcar understand that? Comprehension
was reserved for the guardian of beautiful, sea-girt Syracuse.

Discussion shifted to whether magic powers could be inherited.
A thickset, bearded envoy volunteered, rather casually, that his
own mother had possessed such powers, though, dying, had
transmitted them not to her daughter, and not, as was frequent, to
a ring . . . he looked complacently at three of his own – black,
olive, emerald – but to his own favourite scimitar. Now endowed
with the knack of invisibility, it made him irresistible in battle,
should he ever deign to use it, which hitherto, of course, he had
not. Whether it was now present, hanging from his belt, or even
from his hand, he did not disclose.

'We bring sovereign gifts to illustrious Timo and time-loved
Syracuse on her island of islands.'

Bulky, shimmering, in phosphorescent white and green, the
Persian unrolled the ritual phrases, sanctified laudations. Timo
gazed down with requisite care. A well-tried appearance of informed deliberation remembered from Timodemos, adept in
Council, at home in assemblies. Behind him a table gleamed with
golden dishes, silver chalices, with onyx and turquoise, with ex-
quisite buskins and resplendent mantles, with sceptres, ceremonial

swords, belts crusted with opals, points of light twinkling within blacks and browns. Arrested waves of crafted opulence.

Timo's show of hands was deprecatory. 'Honoured lords, it is not for me, not for Syracuse, to accept gifts from your master whose shadow falls over all the world, but for me to send such gifts to him as do not detract from his greatness.' He was confidential, almost affectionate, a spare, grey man in quiet robes greeting those stationed beneath him in insatiable power. Unfamiliar with such austerity, which made them flamboyant and excessive, the envoys coughed, blinked, gave soothing inclinations, inexpressive nods, then, as if at an unobtrusive sign, returned his smile, though wary of its implications. Yet his manner, diffident, grateful, seemed as sincere as a Greek could ever be.

Timo, despite his hearing difficulties, judged his moment. 'My own poor gifts are already corded and sealed, for your long-ships. On behalf of Syracuse I beg forbearance for their paltriness. But our hearts are willing, our hopes eager.'

Another Persian spoke. 'Our Lord will accept your gifts, not indeed for their value, for he is royal Persia and Media, the Sun Incarnate, World Father, but for the willingness and eagerness which you so eloquently present. Likewise, he, he himself, deigns to suggest that you, Lord Timo, cross the seas so that you can embrace as brothers, consult, deliver and receive advice in veritable harmony and return so much strengthened, protected by the divine which illuminates all. The Great King, as all know, makes no journeys, otherwise he would of course seek the hospitality of Syracuse. In his unmoving posture he is superior even to the sun.'

Timo's face was worn, very lined, frayed beneath tired eyes, yet his carriage was undeniably that of the victor of Crimesus, humbler of Carthage. His reply, unexpected, did not bely this. He was stern, more shrewd than he looked, and slightly malicious. Unarmed, he was his own weapon.

'Nevertheless, my friends, I may venture, my dear friends . . . the sun has observed a Great King bestirring himself towards Greece, who proved a less than agreeable host.'

His smile erased offensiveness, his hand was appeasing, so that the reference to Xerxes, with his twofold defeat by Hellas, elicited only a wily shrug, even a glimmer of amusement, instantly withdrawn.

'Indeed, Illustrious, nothing remains still. Your sword has broken Carthaginian monopolies, African barbarity, dazzled even calm, wide-eyed Egypt, long so indebted to Persia. And', the tone was unchanged, 'what delicious wine you proffer, what cakes . . . the bees of Hymettus, no doubt . . . the artistry so long acclaimed. . . .'

Wine and cakes remained untouched despite their allure. Holding fast against weariness, Timo never forgot that beneath the glories of the Persian monarchy, the smoothness of satrap and eunuch, were botched, twisted figures impaled for dissent, or suspicion of treasonable thoughts. He braced himself for further proposals.

'As we see it, Illustrious, your own greatness is by no means concluded. Far from it. The city-state, the signal achievement of Hellas, of course, praised throughout the earth, cherished by gods . . . has yet, you may agree, you may concur, reached, nay passed, its noon. Another understands this, while probably understanding nothing else. The Macedonian. Doughty fighter, of course, champion brawler in a bad year. Nevertheless. . . .'

Another voice continued, casually, as though in contrived afterthought: 'He too calls himself a liberator, yet with eyes not upon liberties but on supremacy. Over Athens, over Ionia . . . perhaps more. Further east, further west. This is unnecessary, unseemly, even, so to speak, dangerous. It need not occur. An alliance between Sicily, Persia and Egypt would abash Macedon, contain Carthage, leaving Syracuse overlord of Greater Greece. No offence to Heracles, naturally.'

All, Timo himself, laughed tolerantly, though the main allusion was serious. The High King of Macedon, while owing his throne to popular vote, claimed descent not only from Achilles but from Heracles, and was still encroaching south, annexing cities, rescuing Delphi from a Phocian rabble, who, probably with his connivance, had plundered the temple and been rewarded by earthquake; then with ostentatious modesty presiding at the Pythian Games, with fair words, tempting promises, yet simultaneously threatening Athens whose love he craved. Athens herself was denouncing him, seeking belated league with her rivals, Thebes and Corinth. Conditions for another Great War, which Persians knew would obliterate Hellas. The Macedonian phalanx might prove unbeatable, and prove itself a despotism over a burned-out land.

Philip, Timo was thinking, professed Hellenism, but did he know the warning of Herodotus of Halicarnassus, that divine law shatters overweening greatness? Campaneus of Thebes had been slain by Zeus for striving to clamber into Heaven.

These Persians knew, the Athenian demagogues knew, what Sicily neither knew nor cared, that unity under Macedon would secure Hellenic liberty, while destroying the liberties of Hellas, the Idea, thus Hellas herself. The docility of vastness.

Doubtless reported to Persia, Philip had hastened to seek understanding, even alliance, less with Syracuse than with 'Greatly esteemed Timo – saviour of peoples'. In his quiet way – he too had some vision of a once and future Hellas – Timo remained courteous but guarded. He must delay his course, parry as long as possible. Equals, Council, Demos, months after Crimesus, were still inflamed, headstrong, with hankerings, increasingly uttered aloud, for the lost empire of Dionysius I, he who had gibed that terror makes the best government. Evidently, in the Great King's tortuous scheme of power balance and shifting alliances, such an empire could be restored, underpinned by Persian funds. Here was a dream of a Hellenic peace, the Hellenic genius tied to a single will, with Persia turning east, wounded Carthage isolated. And Macedon?

'We shall talk further.' Timo politely hospitable, stood with the mien not of Liberator, Rain-maker, Conqueror, Parsley King, but of a trustworthy, unspectacular magistrate, due for retirement, slightly disappointed but without complaints.

He still dwelt in Achradina, dutifully talking to Aigle, fondling the children with whom some deafness was not displeasing, in what Timophanes had called the Hen-coop, the women's quarters. He had sent an invitation to Ismene, but she was dead, had been found hanged, seemingly murdered. Speaking of her to none, he mourned her in solitude, recalling their kingfisher partnership, aware that she could not be replaced. He had known little of her; now he knew less. A light flickering in mist, held for an instant, then extinguished for ever.

Henceforward he flagged more than he admitted. Headaches would leave him prostrate and trembling, short, pointed stabs ending as abruptly as they began. Nameless colours flooded his vision, but he avoided doctors. Later, the Sons of Aesculapius on their island with their vaunted cures might be an excuse for travel. Journeys always helped disperse the muddle of existence. Far from cities, in light abnormally clear, he would see a bird alight on a twig – Dionysius II inheriting a flimsy throne: a peasant girl smiling – a summer wave.

He was relishing younger men less: Isias, Neon, Telemachus – their harsh ambition, their need to flaunt, grated. Their elders were no better: the greed and rancour of faction. In the manner of victories, the defeat of Carthage had settled little. Victory – rats, horribly swollen, gorging by the Crimesus, where, against his will, a temple was being erected to his Name. The cities still nonchalantly quarrelled, grew fat, lost all, began again, foundering on immoderate dreams, betraying Proportion, the Idea. Athens massacres the population of Melos, retribution inevitably follows. The gods thrive not on sacrificial fumes but mortal follies, which they nevertheless punish.

Disowning the renewed, inevitable chatter of 'the Arrival', 'the New Aeon', 'the Renewal of Time', Timo had returned to acclamations from Syracuse, from Corinth, from all Hellas and beyond. He was Heracles returned, a purged Theseus, he was Prometheus the Foresighted. Seamen in the Piraeus, villagers under Olympus, women secluded in Ionian courtyards, Macedonian hunters smiled at his battle quip that Carthage danced without music.

He was offered sacks of coinage, a grain monopoly, but accepted only a wreath, which he laid by Apelles' statue, and he gave the sacks to the army, the poor, and prisoners released from New Hades. He did accept a small farm near the city, its steading somewhat dilapidated, but with several fields, an orchard, a stream. There, in old age, he would prepare for the Ferryman amongst cattle and bees. This was not distant. Forebodings were plain. An insect crawled, he stamped, it remained unharmed; he stamped again, it was only a shadow vibrating in sunlight.

He had already suggested his resignation from politics. He no longer felt Chosen. Turbulent young bullies reverenced him for defying laws of god and man and butchering his brother. He embroidered what he most feared. His genius, he knew, was negligible, his courage mostly doggedness, his aura fraudulent, a reflection of luck. Let Deinarchus and his set court the impossible.

Syracuse would have none of it. In every street, people repeated the saying, *A crowd of rulers is bad, let there be one.* Already they craved the all-wise gardener, planting, uprooting, burning at will. In Council and Assembly even the most ardent factionalist, the wealthiest oligarch, the most ravenous monopolist spoke sententiously of the Odysseus amongst them. One Odysseus at the table is needful; five hundred in the market-place is not.

He grumbled, he objected, but accepted, knowing that others' heads were so lowered over the trough that they no longer saw Persia, Carthage, Macedon, even Thebes, Sparta, Athens, even Corinth. He was more alone than in the years of exile. Apelles had gone, and not only he. Handsome, ambitious Demeratus had left, to join Philip and win greater renown than cleansing Sicily and chasing off Hicetas. No real loss, his talk was monotonous as surf. Little echoed. Eucleides too had gone, stabbed in a quarrel. Moreover, almost immediately after Crimesus, Theodotos had stalked in, rudely ignoring Aigle.

'I'm leaving you, Timo.' He seemed vicious, then the chipped, soiled features relented. 'No, not you. We'll always be the wolf and the fox, in the forest together. Within call. But . . .' – the darkly veined hands rummaged in the beard now reverted to the straggling and dry – 'walls, streets, too many throats. I'm stifled. Riff-raff places. And you've done it all. You don't need me.'

Chilled, Timo knew that he did. Carthage never forgave, Mamercus and Hicetas still scuttled for power. Some crisis with Philip must surely ensue. Carthage remained powerful at sea. Corinth was hesitating, doubtless over options presented by Macedon, while taking credit for the liberation of Sicily.

Scrawny, unkempt Theodotos retained a laugh like a wound complaining. 'We Greeks!' He scowled, his face seemed itching, he stilled it awkwardly. 'Sometimes you pick up a stick and the stick moves. I wish your sovereignty well, of course. On my knees', he added, though remaining on his feet, his grin lopsided, grudgingly pleasant.

They embraced, he tramped away. Timo sought the shore. The gull, the fresh sea, the space. Fate was absolute in Theodotos. A blackness swarmed in his blood, charred residue of the defeated and banished, huddled in unmapped valleys and woods, refuge of bear, wolf, viper, forcing him to seek shadows, mirthless jokes, perversity. Once, drunk, he had been tempted to join feeble Dionysius II. His was a restless intimacy. He might be more Titan than man, with a black taint, always striving to escape the flesh, then dragged back to the brutish.

Not one of those eager to assault the sun and call it Arrival, New Age, Theodotos lacked interest in the future.

Timo was dejected. Hereafter, he and Theodotos would pass each other only in dreams, soundless, gliding, deaf, almost sight-less.

His own life, however, showed that most men contained swamp and desert, the poisoned shrub, the tusk and the forked tongue. Xenophon told of an Armenian king appointing a wise philosopher to educate his beloved son. Later, he accused him of corrupting the boy. The philosopher, wholly guiltless, before execution, took his weeping pupil aside. 'Do not be angry with your father. He does this not from evil but from ignorance.' Years afterwards, the king confessed that he had killed out of jealousy alone.

Meanwhile, he still must work. Obligation ruled. Victory was the chance to destroy bad corn, cut off the rotten. Reconstruction was urgent. A Constitution. Colonial policy, foreign policy. An expedition against Mamercus. The oath-breaker, desperate, the axe at his neck had joined the Grasshopper, fugitive Hicetas. They had negotiated with bruised and wrathful Carthage and already, dodging the Syracusan defences, Giso the Ever-Victorious, squat, ruthless, had landed a small force in the west. No Crimesus threatened, but Etna erupted, dismaying the populace, which at once called for Timo.

Supported by the Council, most being anxious to harry their game and win the prizes on their own, he demurred. Deinarchus and the younger men could settle the absurd Hicetas, the perjured Mamercus; an Ever-Victorious was by divine will fated to disaster. Meanwhile, he himself was needed, not to charge west and rout the discredited, the doomed, but to assist reconstruction at home.

People were dissatisfied but acquiescent, the troops, in pig anger, called for Timo but were overruled. An oak promptly foretold the destruction of Hicetas, an oracle announced that Mamercus' women would gain more renown than himself.

News came that, skirmishing near Konhas, Mamercus had cap-tured one of Timo's favourite young captains, threatening cru-cifixion unless he were granted a favourable truce. The Council hesitated, the streets were wrathful, Timo advised immediate ad-vance, and Deinarchus with cavalry, Telemachus with hoplites,

moved west. He had no misgivings of the outcome, no hesitation
because of the possible death of the hostage. To yield to Mamercus
for the sake of one boy would be absurd, though only news of the
youth's escape stilled his tears. Giso's mutinous conscripts would
gain little from Sicily. Reconstruction was more absorbing than
Giso, and more menacing, despite wearisome arguments, inter-
minable meetings. Creditors, often first to leave an ill-managed
city, were now back, demanding compensation, revenge, prizes
for exploits they would have achieved had they been present. The
poor regarded the State as a depthless pool of awards. Sophists
arrived, and, before departing, lectured on the community of mankind, in which the rights of all were defended by wisdom alone.
Just so. Theodotos would have enjoyed listening, though not for
long.

He, Timo, retained personal style. The Council had rounded up
scores of those mercenary deserters and besought a reluctant Timo
to judge them. They were dragged into Dionysius' theatre, mocked
by crowds armed with stones. Timo, for once at the old Despot's
throne, dismissed an attempt to plead. He spoke very clearly,
deliberately, without passion.

'You are here to listen. Be still, while I praise your ingenuity,
extol your honesty, your respect for oaths to those who trusted
your valour. Others may recite an ambrosial ode to your deeds, to
the example you gave Hellas in days of trial. May Zeus, guardian
of oaths, protect you. May you bask in Lord Apollo's bright day.
May you live for ever.'

The crowds grinned contentedly, polishing sharp edges. The
victims, famished, almost naked, gazed tragically at the white-
garbed, unadorned, slightly stooping figure of the fearsome Timo,
so merciless, so many-tongued. As though recollecting a detail, he
added: 'Your due reward will not be ungenerous. We are not
Asiatics, Africans, we are not even Celts. Let it not be reported
that, in the gaze of fortune, Syracuse disregards those who merit
her attention. So get you all gone, with your so very precious lives,
rejoicing in your spirit in the respect of your fellows . . . gone from
Syracuse before sunset, to boast your skills before all men.'

In a long, critical moment the swarming terraces waited, silent,
numbed, uncertain, the sharp stones quivering. Yet the man at the
podium, solitary, protected only by his Name, withstood the
chance of revolt by a small, rather shy smile. Frustrated, outraged

or puzzled, Syracuse impulsively cheered, forgoing vengeance, the delights of blood, though not hoots and curses as the deserters were hustled away.

Fate can be defied, but not with inevitable success. Soon, all Sicily heard that they had been massacred at Rhegium. 'I myself was at fault' – Timo showed no marked concern – 'in offering to use such men. Their deaths remove stains. Not', he allowed himself the rare laugh, 'bloodstains, of course!' Dionysius I, after a lifetime manipulating Syracuse, must have learned that government should be an art, is never a science, but is actually a roughneck game, watched by those liable to boredom, prone to hysteria.

Politics had swiftly resumed. Syracuse merely waited on Timo's will, but, like Dion before him, Timo had invited political experts from Corinth to frame a constitution. Its ultimate value he doubted. Constitutions are no more than those who work them, are precautions against the exceptional, the heroes, monsters and comedians who burst the bonds. Meanwhile he sat with a moderate oligarchy, the priest of Zeus the nominal Chief Magistrate – very nominal, Theodotos had said.

He kept a reserved demeanour, few words, a capacity to surprise. Open deceptions at Delphi, more subtle ones at Eleusis, conferences, diplomacies, agreements alike showed that if politics is sport, government is theatre, Zeus himself a versatile actor, now a swan, now an eagle, now a golden shower.

In his house, in memory of Theodotos, he had built an altar not to the goddesses of Fate but to Chance, the uncontrollable that controls, whom the Blessed dismissed as Muddle. Theodotos was sceptical of Fate. 'An invention of priests, Timo. Like the calendar. A plaything, yet a device to turn us common folk inwards. Usually inside out!'

Theodotos was amused yet respectful of slippery Alcibiades, flawed gambler, charming renegade, mocker of gods, mocker of men, contemptuous of those who weigh out life like grocers. Over too much wine, Theodotos had grunted that Alcibiades and himself, not Timo, not Hamilcar, not the Great King, were 'the Arrival', men of the future.

Not art or science but sport made Timo wrest a vineyard from a bumptious aristocrat who had refused duty at Crimesus, worsting him in court, though his own case was dubious. He had not desired the vineyard, only to see the affront on the high-boned face, spoilt, petulant, hear the onlookers' ribaldry, and imagine the jest of Hermes, master of knavery. The populace recognised the knavery, and a popular song soon buzzed like a bluebottle: 'Timo, our honest cheat'.

Daily, rhetors, petitioners, Sophists, praise singers, merchants, contractors, slave-masters, proceeded to Achradina, beneath the lowering Citadel. He received them pleasantly, praised Aigle's housekeeping, spoke of retirement, but ended by referring them to the Council or mentioning that the army needed recruits. Lobbies besought him to ban effeminate boy dancers, sacrilegious ditties and rescind his recommendation to grant citizenship to propertied aliens and even Sicilians. Mainland cities implored protection against Macedon, Ionians his influence against Persia.

A ruler sits back, lifts a brow, ends a session, reveals all or nothing. Tricks of the trade. He knows what scrapes behind well-reasoned debate. The man urging a larger fleet has recently embezzled a wood. His neighbour, sunk beneath debt, makes a cogent plea for a job in the Treasury. Demos applauds, but government by streets keeps no street clean. One seeks no permission from the crowd, but appears to consult and inform the assemblies. In matters of religion, the manumission of a slave, the fate of a murderer, the popular vote have weight. Elsewhere, no. Crowds are already murmuring about 'Greater Sicily', with Mamercus and Hicetas still at large, Giso awaiting reinforcements. Few even in Council comprehend Theban negotiations with Macedon, movements in Ionia, Philip's new military tactics. Gold itself is too often reckoned not as fluctuating currency but a sublime yearning: drops of the sun, aura of gods, the deep blood of the earth. How we Hellenes love the undulations of words; ripples in a quiet pool.

One must endure impatience while councillors clamber for position, generals calculate spoils, Demos craves sensation. Too many rulers are in a hurry, too many officials in insufficient hurry. A new legal code allows rights to slaves, causing disquiet. Remnants of the old War Party back those calls for Greater Sicily, running after the latest teacher but remaining unteachable.

Distrustful of debates about legal government, Timo preferred the details of administration. Reproached for wasting himself on the trivial and beggarly, he admitted it, and continued. Too many slave-boys were being castrated for Persian markets, too many infant girls 'disposed of carefully'. He received deputations from guildsmen and supper clubs, accepted offerings of grain and cheese, dispatched offerings to ill-tempered Etna. Amused when a fishwife sent a slave to complain that in bed her man had stolen her coral anklet, pawning it, he decided to visit them; the delinquent might allow him a hunk of bread, a dose of sour wine, an invitation to mind his own business. His expectations were fulfilled. Seated under a walnut tree, outside a warehouse, on board a fishing-craft, he listened, ventured an opinion, told his stories. 'In Boeotia, in a forest more ancient than Cronos, there once lived. . . .' He accepted from a charcoal burner a hare – 'for your pot'. Hearing that quayside taverns were suffering bloodshed, he inspected them himself and discovered that all had red walls. Gently, he suggested they be repainted blue. The landlords grumbled, but violence dwindled.

Aristocrats thought him vulgar, demagogic, scheming; he acquiesced, undeterred. He was more interested in instruction from an Athenian philosopher who had known Alcibiades. 'You should', the sage told him, 'abandon the idle drift of politics. True history is that of the soul, which knows not Athens or Thebes, Persia or Carthage. It crosses all frontiers, embraces all men, knows not party or feud. The wise are at home in themselves. Socrates rated his own truth, dignity, even life, above even the common weal. He disdained to save himself by flight.' Admirable. Yet at the Crimesus, a Socrates, fighting bravely, might pause and, in finespun phrases, query the need for it, in all amiability letting companions perish; an Alcibiades change sides, pleading the urges of his soul. Such men were clever, doubtless they were forerunners, and they were dead. Others must live.

'Most persuasive, my dear sir. But now I must leave you, on behalf of a certain anklet. . . .'

With considerable ceremony, Timo summoned the Centaurs, embraced them as brothers, then, amid tears, disbanded them. Now he walked the streets unprotected, quietly drinking at a disorderly stall, accepting a platter of soiled figs. Well-wishers protested, for Syracuse remained Greek, thus quarrelsome. Within a few weeks of the Crimesus, he was attacked in an assembly. He had wasted lives for his own profit, he had usurped powers. He kept silent during the savage harangue, despite the attempts to shout down his accusers. Saving them from mob fury he eventually stilled the uproar, remarking conversationally that he was grateful to the gods for hearing his prayer, that free speech should be restored to Syracuse. He would now make use of it himself! Arraigned for illegality in the enlarging of slave rights, he agreed to appear before the judges. Acquitted, to lavish plaudits, he said, with well-staged apologetics, that he feared the secret of justice was favouritism.

That summer, with Deinarchus and the fleet young men absent on the way to glory, Games were afoot, celebrating not only victory but reconstruction. Statues of the discredited were smashed, for roads and walls, baths and temples. Timo had protested against the demolition of Dionysius I, Dion and others, then made play of surrendering to popular demand. Less ostentatiously, he enabled returning exiles to regain their homes, selling others at fair prices.

Provision was the daily refrain, amongst high born and slave alike. Provision for the wounded, the destitute, the wrongly imprisoned, so that many imagined that *provision* was a new god seeking a temple.

Sometimes despondent, harassed by eye-aches, burdened with Athenian reports of Macedonian intrigues, Timo had to submit to the sunlit temptations of the Persian peace. Persians, easy, pleasure-loving, could grow like peaches on a wall, pruned and ordered by hands not their own. The Great King offered his brother, Timo of Corinth, of Syracuse, of the Crimesus, a palace with white pinnacles piercing the sky, a retinue of nobles, an allowance scarcely calculable, a throne in the Grand Jewel of Persepolis, even a share in the compilation of annals. Ambassadors would arrive, with formal offers, and indeed had done so.

Reports from Deinarchus were not sparing of self-praise. Continually retreating, Mamercus and Hicetas had not yet risked battle. Timo was more concerned with an issue, for which *provision* must now be made and about which all Syracuse, swiftly forgetting Deinarchus' exploits, was clamouring. The Persian guests would be watching. The Citadel, arrogant, fierce, with which Dionysius I had replaced a small, elegant acropolis, though still dominating the city, had been severely damaged by the siege and was now used only by scribes, clerks, visiting notables. On so valuable a site all Factions were making claims. The military demanded it for a perpetual garrison, overawing dissent, aliens, the Sicilians. Carthage would take note, Macedon likewise. Their spokesman, Demetrius, a building contractor, guaranteed to restore it from the effeminate embellishments of that nerveless lap-dog, Dionysius II, at a cost by no means exorbitant. The priest of Zeus wished it to become a shrine to the three-in-one Genius of Syracuse: the Father, Fate and of course the Liberator. Several elderly aristocrats from out-lying estates urged its claims as a parthenon, statues of Heiron, Gelon, Timo promoting virtue through example. Proposals followed for a bank, a civic warehouse, an arms foundry, a palace for the Liberator.

To all this Timo listened, grudgingly admiring the ingenuity of corruption, occasionally smiling. Moderate corruption oiled the chariot, too much would corrode it. So, of course, might too much virtue. Seeing all, Timo knew when to close an eye: remembering much, he had learned how to forget.

On a hot, weary afternoon in Council, acrimony blazed, until exhausted, flushed, all turned to the mute legislator inconspicuous within a crowd of financiers. The silence drooped, then became emphatic.

Timo remained seated. The debate had bored him. To rely on a Citadel can ruin a city. Then he spoke. Later, throughout Hellas, fluent voices disputed his motives, piled up arguments, analysed, construed, sometimes coming to blows. All false coinage, for he had decided only on mischievous impulse with, behind it, the sense that, about to give an order, he was somehow obeying one. Sober reasons could be invented afterwards.

'I suggest', he spoke without concern, yet with an underlying incredulity of any likelihood of opposition, 'that the solution is plain. Even simple. Let us destroy the Citadel. Let in the light.'

The Persians had returned for their answer. Stately, glistening in brocaded shawls, trailing sleeves, their hats and turbans an ex-quisite line of fancy, design, hierarchy. To match such grandiosity, delicate, perfumed responses are necessary, familiar to any son of Timodemos, beloved by annalists, though on such occasions these are seldom actually present to record them.

'My lords of Persia, the Great King, Darius – I lower my voice – Son the Highest, the Ascent of Light, the Begetter of Truth, has honoured our small Syracuse with offers so dazzling that their fulfilment would halt the sun in his track and make all the world pause. I myself have barely strength to offer a reply. Others, the truly accomplished, the verily great, would crave to be where I stand, ennobled by the greetings from emissaries of a mortal god, whose radiant empery enchants all us suppliants who dare regard it, we pursuers of naught but a dream. Yet, in Hellas, we have risked a separate tradition. We have often presumed to think that government should be near enough to see and touch. Our skies are puny, I would not wish them greater. The gods have long upheld them. To you, they have awarded wider domains, more magnificent, more wondrous, which we admire but do not envy. We thrive on diversity, on what, in my muddled way, I can only call complex singularity. In your loftiness and exaltation, you may see no more than the squabbling of children, yet you may concede that a child's insight can sometimes be keen and his disposition generous. In his almighty wisdom, the Great King cherishes singleness, the ease of uniformity, the delights of the sun which shines upon all. And in truth, Persia is the sun, we Hellenes are the stars, many, changeable, visible only when he deigns to retire. However. . . .' He paused, invitingly, teasing, sombre, none could say; the Persian faces were immobile, but held as if at a drama.

'The Persian Empire is stable as the universe itself. It is the eternal rock of creation. In our own fragment of earth, rocky indeed but no rock, all is changing. The people have voice, often a discordant one, though music is sustained by discord. Moods prevail, frequently for the worst. Perhaps, very soon, Syracuse will open her eyes and see me clear, in my mistakes, misapprehensions, indeed misdeeds. Then in my mischance I may have to seek my home amongst you, at the feet of the Great King. I trust he in his magnanimity will receive me as I, in humility and smallness, have welcomed you, as my admired friends. You are generous to me – let me venture one word in return. Hellas remains divided, Persia can overlook Syracuse. Yet one man in Hellas should not be overlooked. To name him is unnecessary, perhaps offensive, and for him I hold no rancour, indeed some esteem. His eyes periodically turn east, and wherever he looks his army follows. Your master is immune from the tiger's bite, the slave's knife, the gods' jealousy, but even he can be irritated by the fly and the wasp. No more. I have already extended your patience. Darius' wisdom is infinite. I have but an old man's sagacity. His offer will be remembered throughout time itself. Syracuse, centuries ahead, will survive through its splendour, warmed by the imperial sun, fortified by greetings superhuman, pouring out gratitude fresh and pellucid as the waters of our own Arethusa.'

In short, a blatant refusal.

Their mightinessess of Persia bowed, they bowed low. Slaves were already amongst them, with wine-bowls, platters of fish-strips, salted rye bread, skewers of pork and fowl. Compliments were lavish but dainty, citations apt, goodwill flourishing like a peacock's tail, Timo, throughout grateful for attention, the veteran leaning on his spear.

2

'Let every free-born man attend, each with crowbar, hammer or mace, to strike his blow at the tomb of despotism. In return, treasures will enrich us all. Temples and halls, baths, markets, libraries and gardens. By this we show trust in our gods, disdain for our enemies, love of ourselves and our ever-flowing island.'

The heralds proclaimed the Festival of Liberation, slaves and poorer citizens acclaimed *Lord Provision*. Glad of the holiday, hordes rushed to hack down both the Citadel and New Hades, no longer recalling which Dionysius had erected them.

Observing the excitement, the heaving bodies, the crashing ramparts and pediments, the triumphant cries, the departing Persians, suitably redrafting events, foreseeing rash Timo's imminent downfall, must have noticed discontent from old soldiers; and even the least of governments need to find work for the jobless, who, as proper Greeks, leave sowing, street cleaning, building and repairing to slaves.

They could report more. Glaucous-eyed Giso, stubborn son of Carthage, gathering, even inspiriting the Leontines and Catanans, bullying their uneasy kings, had marched on Palermo, received

Punic reinforcements from beyond the Halycas. At Iceta, Giso encountered not Deinarchus' army but Phocian auxiliaries under Isias. He had over-rashly attacked, might just have succeeded, had Deinarchus moved to support him. Deinarchus, however, had resented the young man's share when spoils were divided after the Crimesus, and refused aid. Isias fled, after most of his men had perished.

The Council made the best of it, announcing a trifling reverse, owing to Apollo's grudge against Phocians for plundering Delphi. The citizens, still fresh from having dismantled the vainglorious Citadel and evil New Hades, knew better, blaming not Apollo but the Council for having entrusted the army to self-seeking generals and inept youths.

Timo himself was annoyed. Incoming news was no better. Giso had wheeled on Deinarchus and Telemachus in a battle, enforcing Syracusan retreat. Still over-confident, Deinarchus regrouped, counter-attacked, was repulsed. Driving all before him, Giso was manoeuvring to advance on Syracuse herself, mocking her outposts, encircling them, pushing on, distributing crude rhymes about those who destroy their citadels, vainly attempting to appease the mighty.

In the Carthaginian camp, Mamercus, his misgivings overcome, and always proud of his poetic skills, produced verses to encourage his followers and give them reason to boast. He much enjoyed such words as *epic*, *triumph*, *godlike*, was somewhat condescending to *Fate*, of whom he reckoned himself patron. His praise singers, handed his verses, regularly intoned them, to the displeasure of Giso, ascribing the Phocian rout to the greatest of all warriors, the sovereign prince of Catana.

> Those bucklers, gilded and purple,
> With amber and ivory inlaid,
> In battle quailed before my own shield,
> So small, so unadorned,
> For which I paid so little.

Hearing this, Giso, opulently arrayed with purple sash and gilded armour, remarked that His Highnesses' shield, picked up far behind the battle, was not only small and unadorned but unused.

King Hicetas giggled nervously, giggled again when Giso, never deferential, remarked that he hoped to greet him at the next battle.

In Syracuse, crowds surged from all Sections, cursing Deinarchus, reviling Isias, calling for Timo.

Without apparent enthusiasm, bereft of almost all old companions, he ordered his armour, murmured deferential words to Black Cloud, but felt old and discouraged. Again, despite noisy threats against Giso, jeers at the two kings, volunteers were less than a thousand, excuses were numerous and ingenious. One man had seen the ghost of Dionysius II, who was by no means dead. Another had planted a tree which must be guarded by himself alone, for it would bear jewels he would donate to the Treasury. Survivors from Crimesus had suffered wounds invisible but incurable.

Two days later he was jogging through late summer haze with men unknown to him. A sooty smudge from Etna was becalmed on windless blue. His silence disappointed those who had heard of his stories, jokes, encouragement. The hills were cauldron harsh.

Watched by suspicious peasants and slaves, passing burned fields, robbed hamlets, they reached high-walled Calauria, squalid above its swampy ditch, a hill-town near a crater inhabited only by demons. Timo was offered the sight of them but brusquely declined. He would soon, he added, be seeing Mamercus, one demon too many. On the flat fields beneath, in a tumid, oppressive atmosphere, Deinarchus had assembled the last of his forces, some two thousand, mostly infantry. Quite close, Giso would be planning, destroying, commandeering, conscripting, ignoring the two royal suppliants whose lands these were.

Timo at once realised that Deinarchus and Telemachus were affronted by his arrival. The older man was sullen and suspicious, the younger had lost ardour. With them, ignored, abashed, was Isias, astonished by defeat, rushing to an extreme of self-mistrust. All three were dismayed by the destruction of the Citadel, symbol of military authority. The welcome awarded Timo throughout the camp was unwelcome to them, suggesting an inquest on the campaign. Timo gave Isias a kind word, said less to his superiors, revealed nothing. He could see callow officers jostling each other, all wishing to lead, to catch the future, none wishing to follow. The two generals would lead a charge but skirted the imposition of order. Apelles would have cashiered the lot, Theodotos uncaged a charnel-house leer.

Cheered by the arrival of the Liberator himself, indifferent to the Citadel, the soldiery recovered animation, though for two days Timo lay unwell, eyes covered, receiving no one, hearing, or seeming to hear, whispers that he was overripe, a mildewed Nestor clinging to laurels proper to youth. He recovered in time to hear news, grudgingly delivered by mouse-eyed Deinarchus, that Hicetas, aggrieved by Giso's hauteur, had withdrawn his force, the largest, to a hill beyond the swift Darmurias river. A further message suggested that the Carthaginian himself had encouraged this move, unwilling to share victory with such as Hicetas. Also, that he had detached his army from Mamercus through suspicion of the number III.

Timo questioned local guides, then, with the only two trusted officers, inspected the troops. Deinarchus, grizzled, short-bearded, stumpy, professional horseman, greeted him as he would any veteran of mediocre experience, unreliable health and slight deafness, appearing amongst the valiant for reasons not yet explained.

'Sir?' His tone was insolent. The long, glistening ranks shifted uneasily. Parading in the noon heat, they suspected tension among the leaders. The late defeat rankled, a baleful and inescapable stare. Garbled rumours had made them suspect that Giso had sacked the Citadel and could now sweep the sea unopposed. Those who had fought at Crimesus loved Timo, those who had not, feared him. Telemachus was uncertain. Isias kept to his tent.

All waited. Timo was deceptively courteous. 'I see a fine array, I see famed leaders. Yourself, Deinarchus son of Cyprian, you, Telemachus. I shall hope to see Isias. I see some who helped me in my inexperience at Crimesus. My thanks to all. Now, Deinarchus, tell me who commands this vaunted company.'

He spoke so that all could hear. Quickened, sensing the momentous, all held their breath, fearing to miss a word. Beneath his cold frown and raised brows, Deinarchus was disconcerted, fearing a joke. Powerful warriors can be helpless against jokes, against song, against ridicule.

The wait was long, until the general found voice.

'Yours, Timo, is the greatest name in Sicily. Undisputed throughout Hellas. But for the ardours of battle, are you certain . . .'

'Certainty, Deinarchus, can itself be uncertain. Each one of you

has his choice of the fittest to lead. The Best of All. Yet the gods will
decide.'

'The gods?'

Deinarchus was deriding, Telemachus and his group wary, not
trusting their favour with Heaven. The men, beginning to break
rank and gather round Timo in the familiar way, scented the
beginnings of a story.

Folding his mantle into the shape of a rough dish, Timo gazed at
it approvingly. 'Good. Each of you, I suggest, now pull off his seal
ring and drop it in here.'

Perforce they complied, humouring the old fellow. His thanks
were a trifle too effusive. Then he covered the rings, and only the
young aides could have noticed that an extra one had been added.
He shuffled them like a Syrian roadside conjurer concerned to
make his small trick more elaborate. As always in such moments
he seemed younger, his smile had schoolboy artfulness. All was
suspended until he abruptly pulled out a ring, held it aloft. It
glittered, packed with promise. Large, flattened, it held an inscription of Nike, goddess of victory.

He affected surprise. Trapped in his will, Deinarchus and his
staff could only wait. 'Which of you distinguished campaigners
claims this ring?'

Silence. Glances crossed like darts but dropped helpless.

'You all know that the gods love the valour and spark of youth.
Yet they have compassion for the aged, the halt and the witless.
This young man' – he pointed to the aide beside him – 'will honour
himself by telling you to whom the chief danger is assigned, from
whom the principal sacrifice may be demanded.'

The youth's voice was unflinching, proud. 'Sirs, this ring is the
Liberator's own. With it I saw him mark the written surrender of
King Dionysius.'

Even the officers joined in the acclamations. Timo let Deinarchus
outline his plans, then approved most of them, though insisting
that Isias be given a chance to restore his Name. In need for this,
Isias would worst Ares himself.

Having risked division, the enemy could be overcome separ-
ately, only Giso possessing real strength. First, the Leontines,
scattered along the Damurias. Hicetas, referring to his ill-health,
had entrusted command to Euthymus, best known as a court poet
adept at composing flattering odes. Envying Mamercus' poetic

renown, at sight of the Syracusan advance, he rode forward, in coppery armour, upholding a curved Asiatic sabre, his smooth, plump head bare, and at once signalling pacific intention, he mocked the foe with imitations of Euripides. At a glance from Timo, Deinarchus ordered a halt and the Syracusans squatted to listen, indulgently, glad of respite after the usual hot, brisk march customary with Timo. A small, high cloud, a flock of birds, paused as if to listen.

The clear, somewhat epicine voice danced above them, the poet's horse lifting its head appraisingly.

Corinthian ladies, crawl from your beds . . . he continued, jeering, scurrilous, lewd, periodically applauded by some two thousand Leontines behind him, while the Syracusans, in equal number, patiently listened, slumped in trickling heat and flies, but ready to attack at the word from Timo.

Euthymus, gratified by his performance, embellished it further, in stock theatrical gesture pointing his sword at Timo.

> 'If you are a woman, which I doubt, you are ugly
> and scrawny,
> So, Medea mine, return in safety to your women.'

The Leontines were delighted, shouting 'Medea mine', while Euthymus gaily assured them that they need fear no women, no impotent old stallion, no untrained boys.

Timo waited, indifferent to this performance, perhaps using his deafness, though Deinarchus and Telemachus were raging, riled by *Corinthian ladies*. The Leontines were jubilant as Euthymus' exuberance welled over. 'Timo? Ah! Blind beggar with a plate, a cripple wanting to lead the dance, a walnut rattling in a dried pig's bladder.'

'Yes, indeed!' Timo murmured, more glad of his eyes than his ears. He had seen between hills red and blue striped tents where Hicetas would be crouching, fearful of outcome by water.

The Greeks too had seen them. Suddenly impatient with the foolish, vaunting poet, they scowled, muttering about Hicetas' foul armpits, gardens of worm-fed leaf-mould, his diseased cock, then looked to their blades, intent upon butchery. Hirelings of Carthage could expect no quarter: midden-flies were loathed even in Hades.

Alarmed, the men across the river rising without being ordered, Euthymus turned horse, turned tail, was absorbed into his still

applauding force, to spin a few more golden analogies in the few
minutes remaining.

The savage afternoon sun had slackened. Distant trees, hitherto
fiery and molten, now seemed wispy, arrested smoke. Hicetas'
tents dwindled. A tiny breeze quivered, the river gathered pace
but, undeterred, angered, the Hellenes, forgoing all order and
discipline, bounded forward, cavalry and foot alike, breasting the
water, clambering the bank, surging at the Leontines' carelessly
grouped centre as if at Hicetas himself. Flight was precipitate,
defence feeble, the assault roared and thrust, only Euthymus
attempting a confused rally, to be swept away in frantic retreat.

That night, while Timo feasted his officers inside Calouria, Isias,
dismounting from a headlong gallop, rushed in to announce his
capture of Euthymus and Hicetas.

While Deinarchus led the army towards Catana, Timo must deal
with the captives. He had few feelings and less to say. Feud and
vengeance were in the blood of Hellas, too powerful to be resisted,
even had he the desire. In much pain is much retribution. Though
concerned more with public justice than clan revenge, the Furies
were back, white-robed, with tragic beauty. They held no comfort
for Hicetas, a shabby nuisance, husk in the wind. Still remembered
was his drowning of Dion's children, to whom he had professed
friendship. A sacrilege. As for Euthymus, to spare him would
insult the *Corinthian ladies*, now bravely set to confront not only vile
Mamercus but Giso of Carthage.

He granted no interview. The corpses were burned without
rites, the ashes thrown into a slave latrine.

Before he could rejoin the army, he had further duty. The wives,
concubines and daughters of Hicetas, captured by Telemachus,
were dragged before the archons who obsequiously declared that
only illustrious Timo could decide their fate. Surrounded by a
citizenry, spiteful, malignant, rowdy, after years of Leontinian
exactions, Carthaginian encroachments, Timo, from a marble judi-
cial chair, strove for self-control. His head ached intolerably, he
disliked this small town and its brutish people. The very air, dry
and tawny, was wasted, a mere passage for dust and illness. The
Furies must have departed, contemptuous of matters so cheap.

Yells, spittle, a shower of pebbles and filth greeted the prisoners, a dozen women, in torn black gowns, alike worn to a common dejection and hopelessness, the children behind them parched, bewildered, scared, clutching their own fetters, dwarfs who had aged overnight as if from some rotting potion.

They were roughly lined before Timo and assailed with foul advice throughout the lustreless squares from the roofs and windows. Soldiers strove to maintain some residue of order, awaiting commands which did not come. Timo, enthroned, omnipotent, yet felt in a haze, through which shouts, gestures, figures moved shrouded and incomplete; a malodorous half-dream, a degraded mirage. Those before him, drooping in stained black, could no longer plead, ogle, protest. The oldest, Hicetas' mother, almost hairless, eyes sunk deep, almost invisible, in cracked, waxy flesh, had been particularly reviled and pelted, deemed to have incited her son against Dion's children, jealous of their youth.

Timo strove for consciousness, his head throbbing. He could see shapeless, stunted forms, prostrate or slanting and, save for a slow tremor, a whimper, as if carved. Stricken lips, tangled hair, gobbets of terror. The massed onlookers slowly went silent, hushed as if awaiting a lascivious satyr play.

Yet a word from Timo, light as a moth, could have swayed them, reprieved the prisoners. No word came. Behind his strained vision, his pains, was impatience, a pent-up need to escape this squalor, then a repulsive yet appetising memory of death: flesh parting, the jolt on the bone, a unique softness like warm juice on silk. At a small flicker of his hand, guards closed in triumphantly, stripping and mauling the victims, then, accompanied by a crowd now intoxicated and hilarious, dragging them to the town ditch. There, staked in the mud, they would lie slowly drowning while their judge still sat, virtually alone, but crowned with new epithets. Restorer of Justice, the Avenger. Our Scythian, the troopers chuckled.

The Scythian himself relished none of it. Feelings returned, nerves responded. He had again stood at a crossroads and now faced a new path. Always suspicious of success, he had made sacrifice, killed others, scorched his soul. He would not be permitted to forget. The lawgiver might have transgressed the law, might have fulfilled it. To deliberate further was useless, and, weary, resigned, he must resume his last campaign, his further killings. A

fated spirit. He might perish, honours upon him, favoured by
fortune, though Honour might scowl.

Catana was besieged. Deinarchus, who enjoyed battles but disliked sieges and strove to avoid them at whatever cost to strategy,
greeted Timo with some relief. Mamercus himself was within the
town, and both generals were resolved on his capture. Giso, encamped further off on the shore, was a mere barbarian trespasser,
but Mamercus, a Hellene, had broken faith. An oath, like atoms,
like comets, must keep station.

Himself no lover of sieges, Timo traversed the terrain. Landscapes have their own language: a broken wall was site of massacre, a lonely grove was reputedly the refuge of a proscribed
Sicilian god, from branches of a dried-up knoll hung bodies pecked
and torn.

Around Catana were stacked giant catapults and rocks, guarded
by bored troops heartened by the sight of Timo. His presence
would shorten the business, guarantee victory. Drawn by his
Name, a band had crossed from a Corinthian colony in Dalmatia,
ready to accompany him to wherever he ordered. From their leader
he heard that High King Philip had worsted a Theban confederacy,
at the Chaeronea, yet still wishing to ingratiate himself with weak
yet long-famed Athens, was threatening Corinth. Cackles about
the sham Hellene, would-be Agammemnon diminished.

The officers looked at Timo. He said nothing. His eyes still
ached, he thought not of busy Philip but of Timodemos' last
illness.

The siege had been desultory. The heat, snakes, afflicted all:
listlessness was dispelled only by Timo appearing at an unexpected moment, by the arrival of the Dalmatians and sallies from
the besieged, by fears that Mamercus would forgo dignity and
appeal to Giso for help. This indeed occurred. Halving the besieging force, Deinarchus happily marched seawards, making for the
Abdus, surprising the Carthaginian van. Giso despised details.
Punctual sentry-go, well-sited stockades, defensive lines did not
befit his style. During his over-prolonged afternoon sleep, from
which he could escape only to his harbour, Demarchus ordered the
attack. Neon and Isias led a zestful charge, the older man following
up. The Carthaginians were routed, though, with Deinarchus
allowing his men to plunder Giso's camp, they rallied sufficiently
to retreat in some strength, cursing sleepy Giso.

Timo oversaw the siege. The Dalmatians, excited by a new battering-ram and by the catapults, pleaded to storm the gate, after a barrage, scarcely awaiting assent. Timo knew men; better, he understood moods, the captivating or irresistible moment. It had come – let it slip and it might not return.

The gate was breached at first onslaught. A tower was fired, few would die for Mamercus. Knowing this, he fled, disguised as a porter. Timo ordered the prisoners to be dispatched to Giso, an unenviable journey with grim welcome.

Their arrival prompted Giso to disembark for Carthage. At his dictation, scribes wrote that he had departed with ceremony, requisite to the Sacred Republic, having settled the occasion. More literally, he had shirked mutiny, disease, Sicilian hatred, the miracles from Syracuse.

Mamercus found a ship, and sailed to Italy, where his few followers deserted. No ruler wished to breathe air polluted by the faithless and he was forced back to Sicily. Peasants, with a nose for profit, swiftly recognised him and he was soon in Syracuse, lying strapped to a sled, pulled at a horse's tail at the rear of the triumphal procession for the Peace Treaty with Carthage.

All had been threatened, all been overcome, Ceres and Persephone had returned, clustered with violets, harvest sheafs, garlands, the offerings of fifty cities. Greater Syracuse!

At the head, on foot between Deinarchus and Telemachus, surrounded by the other leaders, Timo trudged laboriously, often breathless, reliving much. The flowers falling, shouts scattering, songs starting, as they had for Poseidon, for Gelon and Heiron, Dionysius and Dion, for the storm god so helpful at the Crimesus, images trundled through Sicilian dreams, through demented, animal hordes now hailing him as a god. Could he really be so? Some transmutation of soul, some accession of light? Some rare view over the earth: Troy and Corinth, Chaos and Order, heaped for himself alone in a single glittering crystal flashing hues lost yet mysteriously familiar?

More likely, the gods could help him no further, had, at this thunderous day, this swarming concourse, already deserted him. Telemachus plucked his sleeve, pointed to a children's choir, a captured elephant, but he was remembering an illiterate stranger from Delos, who, reaching Syracuse, covered a pedagogue's eyes with a cloth, then induced him to read a line of Pindar's, written in the dust behind him: *What man, what hero, what god, shall we celebrate?*

Then, a turn of the way, and he might be consigned to join Mamercus. Earlier, a mob had stoned him for killing Dion's children, and when told that the murderer had been Hicetas, voices yelled that this mattered not at all, his name was Mamercus, quite sufficient. In a tiny prophetic insight, Timo saw the creature's end. The crucifix on the shore, the braying din, the naked king escaping the guards, rushing headlong towards a pillar to ram himself to death. Recaptured, wild children cackling and capering around him as if the ground were too hot, he was then hauled aloft, his screams unheard.

Timo willed himself to continue. In swelling, tidal release, thousands of faces smeared with peony juice, stained with vine leaves, blotched with wine, all urging him into immortality, he imagined Moira's startled eyes, Ismene's amused incredulity. A rumble of thunder, tribute from Zeus.

In mindless rote he saluted gilded masks of Dionysos, the dancers circling a sacred tree and clad as the Graces, holding wreaths of violet and plum, offspring of earth and sky. From the acropolis topped by the Citadel's jagged wreckage, more choirs chanted new odes to Peace, Liberty, though Hera would receive no white heifer, Zeus no black ox, only agonised Mamercus, flat against the sky.

Dust, fierce sunlight struck his tormented eyes, his slipshod limbs like chains. Little was coherent. He had ventured too far: in slaughtering those women he had surrendered to the black, subterranean Titans. This gaudy, rowdy Triumph was hollow, dangerous. All Sicily trailed behind him, but his back was undefended. Retribution was already invited. Up, up, to the temple beneath the Citadel's desolation. *Endure my heart*, Odysseus had muttered. *You have endured worse.*

Hermes could remind him, Ismene would have known, that whatever he had ventured, he had not travelled very far from that lonely cave on the Isthmus, the stories, the hideous joy in a killing. Cruel, vengeful, capricious, he might indeed be a god.

'Timo . . . Timo . . . Timo . . . *Euoi.*' Deinarchus was fading, all others drifting far behind him, leaving him to the world's plaudits. The name rebounded, leaped higher, atop of Syracuse, flower of cities, star of the seas, to be swept high over waters, over mountains, to land perhaps on a crucifix on which a body, exhausted, drained, savaged, lay in its last convulsion.

3

'My dear, I was giving ear, my favourite one, to the tragedian Damon, son of Konnos of Cos. Delightful sequence! He was talking, talking well, of Prometheus, referring to him as the compressed energy of the unyielding. Some of us, of course, prefer a butterfly lyric to a huge and obdurate pyramid. Then he likened Achilles' shield to the sensitivity and protective strength of his own imagination – nay, art. While he thus entranced us, I could not resist a vulgar intrusion, pointing to blood trickling from his boyfriend's room. "Ah!" quoth the illustrious son of Konnos. "That makes a very telling metaphor." Perhaps wisely, he withheld this from me. One learns. An Orphic adept, high and dry from too few beans and no meat, informs me that I was once a tortoise. I may one day become a leaf, a high wind showing me the wide, wide world.'

The speaker is scented, pinkish, in a yellow robe tinged with scarlet, woven in the latest Ionian mode. No longer young, he still wishes to pass as such. He is slender rather than scrawny, his face more crinkled by constant smiles than withered by age. His eyes remain light, his baldness is worn like fashionable headgear. His companion, actually young, is heavy, dull, hesitating between admiration and disquiet for the other's adventures and reputation.

They sit in a myrtle grove overlooking the Isthmus, watching the sunset, the bobbing masts, the returning fishermen. Between them a jug of second-quality wine, saucers of curved, phallic cakes, plums baked in pomegranate juice. Giggles fluttered around them, half concealed from 'neighbourhood girls' in transparent Coan silks, who would have to wait.

'Dionysius, the latest rhyme about the Macedonian . . . scarcely fare for your pupils . . .'

'They probably composed it.'

An apt obscenity can repel demons, dislodge the great. Philip, the crowned yokel, wild man fumbling for cultural manners, eloquence, the respect of academics; the Great King, painted acorn; a Scythian war-lord breaking his back attempting to suck his own

cock; all quailed before wit. Masquerade of futile power. Oddly
immune was that sack of virtue, Timo, praised for all-seeing, now
said to be going blind as a mole. If true, he can reflect on Democritus, blinding himself in order to see more clearly. He may have
found atoms revenging themselves for betraying their existence.

The talk continues. The skirts flash and glimmer between leaves.

'He lost his nose in that last skirmish with Philip. Finding it
amongst the thistles he prayed to Aesculapius to heal it. The god
complied, as gods often do, though in their own way, a trifle
oblique. The nose was replaced and stuck, but, too hastily . . .
upside-down, so his appearance was altered, not markedly for the
best. His sneezes caused confusion.'

Buffoon hero of a street song in which a despot opens his mouth
and a canary flies out, Dionysius had for a season been a welcome
exhibit in Corinth. He had style and, confusing him with his
father, market crowds swarmed to see him. Novelty, however,
quickly palls in Hellas. He was soon reduced to cheap taverns,
grateful for a place at a gentleman's table in return for anecdotes
and gossip which lacked staying power. Reduced to five slaves,
seven gowns, a few jars of cosmetics, he began correcting lady
songsters in their phrasing, social climbers in deportment, advis-
ing festival managers on plays, odes, processions.

He enjoyed such work. A god who creates by a mere flick of the
hand misses the delight of moulding, honing, rewriting a scene,
adding a lyric, training a particular smile, manipulating a verse:

> We run with the god of laughter –
> Labour is joy and weariness is sweet.

Midnight loneliness is cured by the rapture of sudden discovery:

> The celebrant runs entranced, whirling the torch
> That blazes red from the fennel-wand in his grasp.

He still enjoyed reminiscing about Plato, amiably refuting the great
thinker's disdain for popular art, his belief that the just live happily, the unjust wretchedly, that all men seek virtue, failing only
through ignorance, though a dinner at the College of Sophists, a

stroll through the fish-market could disprove that in a trice. Un-reason can promote order, wise laws induce chaos, to understand the good is not always to follow it; good, like evil, can be tedious, or lack cash value. Curiosity is more reliable. Another's body can excite, the Universal merely fatigue, a swallow's chirp outbid the Ideal. Plato was what he himself had feared, nothing but words. He was what power should not be: a teacher with a long whip, a baker kneading people to perfection, a farmer consigning bright weeds to the oven, an alchemist refining rich matter into thin soul.

Doubtless, of course, the properties of sand, vertebra of a fish, movements in the sun, will unravel the mysteries of Fate, free will, mortality, currently explained, very unconvincingly, by Athenian and Ionian Platonists, for considerable fees.

Dionysius paid nothing. He declined into obscure poverty, until unexpectedly rescued. An invitation had come from Philip of Macedon, attending Games nearby. Granted permission by Corinth, he was dished out before Philip like a chipped statue of third-rate quality. Hellenes love such demotions. Summoning him to his side, a burly, hairy creature, Philip had at once spoken of his writings, in serious mockery. His dialect was thick, not always comprehensible save by the rough accompanying gestures of fist and thumb. Also, he was drunk.

'I know your tragedies, Dionysius. I know your songs. They imitate your father's. He himself imitated Sophocles. I am sur-prised that rulers should have so allowed themselves the time.'

He had not been servile. 'Sir, one ruler can allow himself time during those hours when another sinks into his own cup.'

More of a gentleman than was realised, Philip stared, grunted, then laughed. 'We can all learn from you, Dionysius. A royal teacher who can teach royally.' Eventually indeed, through an anonymous grant from, he believed, Philip himself, always anxious to cultivate intellectuals, he opened a school for boys. Very successfully. Invitations returned, so did money. His favourites lingered after formal classes had been dismissed, their pedagogues clustering outside, grumbling, gossiping, libelling, ready to flap their cocks at the nearest pugilist or wheedling pedlar. Mother Corinth has the virtue of lacking decorum.

Dionysius has found he loves teaching, craving to make these trim, rapid-speaking lads see nuances shimmering within daily life. Most teachers have imaginations long covered with fur, rely on stale repetitions of Pindar and Theocritus, know little of value save tax evasion. He himself is paid well to teach Homer, but how much better Euripides! Sky and ocean, wit and satire are mightier than Achilles, gods are pupils of mortals, are but possibilities mined from within. Divisions of being. Could one but erase the ox-witted butchers, stupid beauties, empty if versatile deities ransacking maidenheads. *The mightiest were there, and with the mightiest they fought.* Worm-eaten rubbish! Heroes hunchbacked with lies too big for them, twisted nerve-ends of memory.

Homer reduced being to doing: a truer artist strives for lost moments, to arrest the fleeting, the barely seen, the misunderstood. The past, most of it invented, seldom stylishly, is unnecessary. The poet thrives not on analysis but half-knowledge, the intermingled, unfinished flakes of life. Athena's clear eyes demand total truth, that of a shipwright or bridge-builder accounting for the most minute detail. She is Lady of Success, at odds with wayward, unpredictable Dionysos, who builds no ships and whose bridges would swiftly collapse, but whose hints, gleams, sleights of fancy enrich existence and bemuse those thundering bores, Achilles and Heracles, and Philip of course. One lives by becoming, not by reciting Homer, or praising Sparta's unending 'wars of defence', her progress backwards. Plato himself had wanted Homer banned, for displaying gods in unseemly behaviour, showing warriors afraid. He preferred squares, triangles, circles, to Heracles tearing the air apart when monsters were absent, to Artemis with her cold charms, debatable goodwill, menacing solecism.

Father had the finest library in Hellas, rifled from conquest and extortion, could swap with Plato citations from the new physicists, Leukippos of Miletus, Democritus of Abtera, who reduced glittering, leopard-skinned Dionysos to five thousand atoms, eleven miscomprehensions and the meanderings of flux. But already the perfect symmetries of Platonism are leaving experiment and query to cranks, and the vulgar still hope for 'the Arrival', simultaneously wishing to be loved and to be sacrificed bloodily.

His boys are still free. At tales of death by fire, by poison, their chuckles win his small prizes. Plato too believed that, to discover talents, early schooling should be amusement. Yet the self-educated are most open to sparkle, to distant calls. 'I can see it for myself,' a boy had cried angrily, giddy with perception.

Much learning, Heraclitus knew, produces little understanding, though in a sentence Orpheus had exposed the secret of existence. *Zeus is man, Zeus is immortal woman*. Haloed in ignorance, yet knowing, the boys parade their charms. Bare legs under short chitons, urchin beauty. He enjoys promoting their jealousies, love matches; seeing the cheeks flush, fists clench, mouths tremble. They should never grow austere, disciplined, thinking, behaving, breeding according to civic plan, the rule of the imperfect by the perfect, reinforced by spies and soldiers. They should move not into some brutal symmetry but to offer myrrh to Erato, as desire wakens, to select the choicest aphrodisiac for their lord of wonders, Dionysiac redeemer.

Today, in Hellas, religion is relapsing into dreamy fables, philosophy into word-splitting pedantry, science into mysticism, anger into ill-will. In Corinth, new literates read only phallic drivel, write only complaints.

Lining up for his kiss, the boys patter away into twilight and he withdraws into a shuttered room. Slaves hover, dim outlines calculating his mood, ready to strip, or suffer his verses, or prepare a supper.

Life pleases Dionysius, though most dismiss him as a languid trifler. All Corinth had chuckled at his visit from the caustic philosopher, Diogenes of Sinope.

'How little, Dionysius, you deserve to live in this manner.'

'You are kind, sir, to commiserate with me in my misfortune.'

'Misfortune! Commiserate! What are you saying? You surely don't mistake contempt for sympathy! I'm merely aggrieved that one so enslaved to comfort, who observes an old age like your abominable father's, should survive on the gross rewards of despotism. Surfeited by the luxuries of this sluttish city.'

At his first banquet here, he had been greeted by a self-styled wit, who mockingly laid down his cloak as though for the ruler of Syracuse. He retained his bearing, bowing, stooping, returning the cloak, begging his tormentor to examine it in case some part of its intricate designs had already been stolen. Another Corinthian had accosted him. 'Dionysius, you knew the great Plato. Did your talks with him teach you nothing?'

Couldn't the horrid fellow use his eyes? To transform tragedy to comedy is not despicable.

I am an interesting fellow, yet a sequence of moods; now spokes without a centre, now a rim without spokes. I have my importance. Forgotten peoples minted words, contrivances for invisible futures. I help to preserve them, reissue them, train them for new vistas, dispatch them to dissolve boundaries. *Dusk, Bridge, Perhaps.* Words obvious; *Dance, Fire, Blood.* Words prophetic. *Tragedy. Black.* The epitaphs and prophecies of tribes. A barbarian onrush could scatter the lot, pervert them, obliterate the most vital. I teach boys to foster and cherish them. Words, as Pindar wrote, outlive deeds.

I never became a true poet, never achieved a unity, or made meaning fully consonant with sound, merely had aptitude for phrases which stand isolated like handsome sentries.

I lack charm and loveliness which excuse so much. Alcibiades, who loved Athens enough to betray her rather than have no part in her; ugly Socrates, teasing his judges for their own good, will be forgiven and remembered, even be awarded temples. I shall not. They might have appreciated me in Persia, the connoisseur's true haven. I have sailed into port, perhaps the wrong port.

Corinth is now crowded for the Hellenic Conference, so flamboyant, so futile, blaring exultation of a new Hellas, satirist's delight. Embassies, agents, knaves, fairground managers, greedy artists. Thebans, Athenians stuffed with Persian gold; Thracians, Illyrians, Ionians; ugly Macedonian charioteers misshapen as boxers. Sparta, grim, decayed, wounded, carrion city, has sent no one. Denounced by that agitated bucket Demosthenes of Athens, as would-be despot, the High King is expected and will bore all by discussing Hellenic culture in barbaric Greek. His brat Alexander, born of the snake queen, is attracting curious tales.

From Syracuse, Timo's plenipotentiaries have arrived, much flattered, assigned quarters, far grander than the Macedonians'.

Master of Hellas save for Timo, Lord of the Middle Sea, Philip has already sent word that he will receive me. 'You dare not refuse,' a boy told me, in love, in alarm. But I can. In his blunt way, Philip is still showing sympathy, intolerable, but, if he falls, if Fortune slings him down and all reject him, I, Dionysius, the despised fugitive, a painted old man, the Canary, will unbar my door and embrace him and his gold-maned, beautiful Alexander.

The boys gibe. 'Heard the latest. A man saw a bear imitating King Philip. But no. It was Philip himself.'

Adventurers are necessary. A Timo, a Philip, shatter pernicious notions of inexorable Fate. Religion asks all-important questions, gives less than important answers. Notions of soul obstruct curiosity, perhaps for ever. Plato holds the soul a circle, without end or beginning. Grandiloquent, fateful and perhaps fatal, anyway meaningless. In the surely inevitable collison between Timo and Philip, each great enough in his manner, might perhaps be that single song 'Arrival', a verbal bauble which might yet hold truth.

Both are loved by the unthinking. Philip is scheming to attack Persia. Timo has won mightier victories, has also killed surreptitiously. They have sinister glamour. Ageing men competing for the world's acclamation. Their rivalry, or their love, may destroy Hellas. Both elbowed their way into history with more effort than grace.

Bleary-eyed Timo treated me with kindness, without pomp or boast. Hicetas would have strangled me. Yet such as he are only the tints needed by a painter, a pose surviving but in effigy. Reputation is a gift of poets. Plato himself may be remembered only for my quatrain, jesting that he was born of a virgin. And I? The Canary? Certainly not. Failure? Of course. Yet I shall be remembered by those unborn, in lands undiscovered.

A gesture can be expected from Syracuse. Probably more. The city-state was obsolete. He, Dionysius, having escaped it, could be called victor.

4

From the Hellenic Conference the Macedonian king, whose forbearance to Athens was surely a bribe – for praise, for help against Persia – sent gifts to Syracuse and, to Corinth's greatest son, a private letter with ornate flourishes, complimenting him for the overthrow of Carthage, mastery of Sicily, thanking him for black-eyed Demeratus. In fewer words he implied that, as defence against Persia, he was willing to become Captain-General of Hellas, while beseeching great Timo's approval. Greater Syracuse,

Greater Macedon. To the man in Achradina whose eyes were dimming, the issues were nevertheless clear. Philip wanted over-lordship of Hellas and a Persian war. In Syracuse the old War Party would welcome this. Traditional liberties would be discarded. For-mal alliance with Macedon, success against Persia would bring Hellas, Ionia, Etruria, Spain into a vast, unnatural growth breeding unnatural agonies. The daydream enjoyed by few, none of them trustworthy. Old rivals trading as one, powerful as ancient Phoeni-cia; a common coinage, invincible army, almost a single god. Tempting but fraudulent, it ignored Nature.

Warnings abounded, stacked like Celtic skulls. Athens had col-lected treasure for a confederation against Persia, then embezzled it for her rebuilding. In Sparta, Macedonian gold was rotting her muscle-bound simplicities, already corrupted by immoderation during the Great War. Thebes and Corinth were not much better. None appreciated the necessity for limits.

Persia remained Persia, Carthage bemoaned her wounds, Egypt was following ferocious Nineveh and luxuriant Babylon into inert oblivion.

Though he could see less, he heard more. Behind the shouts for Greater Syracuse was the demand that he, undisputed hero, should vanquish Philip or collude with him in cut-throat glory. But a city's genius seldom depends on talk, most equivocal of gifts. Socrates, remember, held a discussion of logic, and by logic proved the number of teeth in a horse's head. He then irritably expelled an incautious, doubtless ill-favoured youth for suggesting a visit to the market to examine an actual head.

To win a debate seldom feeds the people, digs a canal, pacifies a rebel or convinces restless Syracuse that alliance with Philip would be to surrender the Idea to the weakness of brute size.

Factions were rowdier, more volunteers left, impatient to join adventurous Macedon, but, without formal constitutional powers, Timo still kept the balance. His Name restrained the loud-mouths, awed the seaboard lands, though he committed himself to no one. His reply to Philip outmatched him in eloquence, compliments, even grammar, but committed him to no more. He congratulated the High King for successfully storming a hilltop village. But, from the victor of the Crimesus, this could have sounded ironic, though to young, polished Alexander more than to his strenuous but obsessed father.

Philip wanted blood brotherhood, but so had Kallias. The season was too advanced for military action. Not until the spring could a Persian campaign be started. Now occupied with unrest in his highlands, Philip probably received this with some relief.

Placating, reassuring, encouraging, through his very silence, soothing by deafness sometimes exaggerated, almost sightless, Timo groped his way forward as though under water, none, despite his refusal to carry arms or be escorted, daring to obstruct or assist him. A half-smile, adroitly performed, a single, meaningless word cheerfully uttered, could induce Council, Assembly, Demos to assent to a proposal which, if explained, would appal them.

He was having to overcome problems of space, raw edges, dim substances, preparing for the last dark strata. That temple of his by the Crimesus had already provided cures for blindness, plague, old age, but was unlikely to do likewise for him. His priests might dress as goats, hide themselves in horse-masks, though they would do better to tell stories to children.

In what was probably a dream, Hermes had bidden farewell. 'You need us no more. We are but stages of spirit. Numbers!'

In that stony exile, numbers had indeed sustained him. He had once lodged with a tribe so scared of numbers that, to count aloud, particularly count the people, caused panic and accusations of conspiracy. A beloved youth, thus erring, had been forced to leap from a cliff. Even the Captain-General, on an unlucky date, might meet horror at crossroads. Philip would, despite his adopted Hellenism, always prefer command to debate. Some understanding might perhaps be reached with Alexander.

He was alone, thus, save for the dangerous impulses within, he was free. King Sisyphus, King Theseus, Heracles Best of All, knew those impulses. Zeus himself was not only the Centre but Lord of Crooked Counsels.

A rumour, later proved false, reached Syracuse that Philip had boasted that no other kings ruled in Hellas, so that none could dispute his supremacy. At this, the Council sent a message to Timo. Council and Assembly implored his attendance, a deputation of politicians and officers arrived to fetch him, removing all obstacles, gently nudging him on.

Within the violet and gold vault of the temple of Zeus, notables of

Sicily, Syracuse, Corinth and the Islands were assembled. Roseate shawls and tunics, yellow and white robes, jewelled ceremonial weapons. Covering the slopes of the acropolis, under the incomplete rebuildings, crowds, slaves and citizens mingling, stood expectant, identifying the big names. Deinarchus, Telemachus. . . . A star gleamed in each head. Now the severely robed delegation from Macedon, greeted with respect but not warmth, now the Athenians.

Inside amongst flowers, on an altar under the massive central arch, lay a crown of golden leaves clustered round an emerald wide as a thumb. Before the altar was a high, antique chair from Halicarnassus, carved with puma heads, covered with a lion's skin, slightly frayed and discoloured.

At Timo's entrance, the shout topped the murmurs from those seething outside. The high priest, stout, hairless, with faintly blotched cheeks and a manner fortified by wine, probably un-watered, stepped forward. The gold pin at his throat was suffi-ciently large to detract from a hauteur liable to be confused with high-mindedness.

Timo, in his usual plain white robe, stood between two sup-porters. From the priest he accepted a small blue krater of wine. Instead of laying it aside, according to custom, he drank copiously, arousing smiles as he affected to restrain a belch. Our Timo. Then he touched his lips, to dry them, or conceal fatigue, even a yawn. His humour was at odds with the priest's unctuousness.

'You, Timo, son of Timodemos, found Sicily a nest of bullies, despots, barbarians, a hateful morass of violence and oppression. You have cured all, taught us to behave better. Today, aliens are pleading for entry. Great towns are repopulated. Ceres recognises her own island, and you yourself as kin of Orion, before whom dance the sacred Pleiades.

'In former times, every ninth year, the Minos of Crete would stand before Zeus to accept his wisdom. You, Timo, need not wait so long. So now, on this very day, under the eyes of the gods of Hellas, we invite you, we beg you, to agree that Hellas seeks more than one king, and accept this, the crown of Syracuse. On your head, in your grasp, in your breath, hang the fortunes of civilisation.' With a slow, considered gesture, he pointed to the golden mass amongst the flowers, then made inclination towards the new king.

Unassisted, stooping, neither hesitant nor assertive though with a small suggestion of each, Timo emerged into strong light, blinked, stood still, then, forestalling the priest, stepped back, turning towards the crown and picking it up, examining it as though for faults, so that several old campaigners exchanged winks. When he nodded approval, many laughed, though they quickly ceased when, with a tiny shrug, he moved again and, very carefully, placed the crown not on his own head but on that of the lion, stuffed and a little askew, topping the State chair.

Timo's best remembered words had always been impromptu. He had inherited his father's facility, his judgement of words and occasions. Now, however, he took a scroll from his sleeve and slowly uncurled it, shaking his head as though discomforted by the length, before reading it aloud, with pauses deliberate and emphatic, speaking with a power that surprised those who had mistaken his irresolute sight for weakness.

'Masters and leaders of Sicily, sons of Hellas, we have done deeds together. My own are not greater than yours, though not always less. I have learned not to despise the despicable or underrate the small. The small have a true place. They should link hands as our fathers did against Xerxes. Hellas is small and divided or she is nothing, only a mere portion of the Great King's gilded beehive. Our cities face a common task: to maintain diversity without conflict, sharing without subordination. Our liberties are those of selfhood and, like each one of you, must respect limits. The Idea of Hellas, not the Kingdom of Hellas. I owe no disrespect to Macedon, but the conquest of Persia would destroy not her but ourselves. The Parthenon of Athens, dedicated to truth, beauty and valour, like her empire, was built on the profits of bad faith, theft, cruelty. In victory was defeat. Some of you crave Greater Sicily . . .' – he gestured towards the crown absurdly perched on the lion – 'a royal Syracuse, overlordship of Hellas, mastery of the world. I do not. That I should wear a crown would not strengthen Hellas. The strength of the King of Macedon owes nothing to his adornments. At best we should be a brake on the piling up of armies, embarkations to the unknown. I seek another strength, secure as an oath once was.'

On the strained faces devotion, professional courtesy, diplomatic concern were being replaced by perplexity, a flicker of grievance and doubt.

'You have honoured me by offering the crown of Dionysius. I do you the honour of refusing.' Clutching his paper he was reading from it, not monotonously but still with the measured, sententious emphasis of an actor. 'The rule of one man is an enormity, necessary only in crisis. Here there is no crisis, only opportunities for all. Rulers, cities have their time. Zeus succeeds Cronos. Change can be necessity, it can be sensation. You must choose. Novelty, like love, should perhaps be rare, deeply rooted, as Sparta once understood, though perhaps understanding little else.

'My own power was created by time and event. When they pass, so must I. A ruler must listen to the hum and the tick of the years. The Athenian philosopher tells us that the people fatten their champions into greatness. But another line should be remembered. *When the Despot first appears, he is a protector.* I am, you see, warning you against myself.'

Slowly, firmly, he turned his back on the crown, his shadow extinguishing it. 'To rely any further on me, my friends, would be to cripple yourselves. You who have withstood Carthage, restored her island to the goddess. A ruler must be able to forswear long-loved customs and traditions, discovering new styles for new problems. Government indeed is no science, it is not an appetite, tradition or plaything. I deemed it sport, but see now that it is an art, rigorous, painful, sometimes fatal. The ruler constantly seeks solutions, is often mistaken, perhaps always mistaken. His ear is more important than his mouth. When the problem is solved, never for all time, for time indeed is but a blink from the eyes of Zeus, the ruler must say his say, then go quietly away.'

The stillness was profound, communicating itself to the populace outside. All Syracuse waited, not quite believing, as if at the voice of Fate.

'We Hellenes are not puppets jerked by the master's hand. We have no master and should always resist one, though discontent and impatience grasp our souls and we desire all things at once. We shall risk defeat rather than pause for an instant. You would soon be denouncing as despotism what you have applauded as wisdom. This quicksilver disposition renders government more difficult, though it also quickens the spirit. Our freedom is not a birthright, it must be wrested, be maintained, be defended, though it can be cruel as Asia or Africa.'

Timo's face, now more obviously fretted with age, gazed at them with gentle defiance.

'I shall remind you of the words of Athene, written down by

Aeschylus, son of Euphorion, words which I myself, once condemned as a man of violence, have had to ponder. He shows the
vengeful Furies placated:

> 'But violence is unnecessary; use
> Persuasion to halt the outcome of witless threats
> Before it drops to earth, spreading plague and disaster.'

He smiled, he was now conversational, apparently adding certain
sentences to his prepared speech. His eyes were restless but
watchful, as if intent on a pool where fish are leaping.

'You may have heard stories of Babylonian mortals long ago,
driven out of a perfect garden at Eridu, where four rivers meet and
where death was unknown, for their imperfect behaviour. They
rebelled against perfection, preferring to wander, escape their
great god, Ea, for adventure and indeed death. Guiding their
flocks though marsh and desert, they had at last to use, and enjoy,
their brains. We remember Odysseus, in no haste to achieve his
long-desired home. Like Great Kings, the gods offer inertia, but an
Odysseus chooses diversities and risk. Perfect rule can thrive only
on drugged sleep. Idleness and dreams. We Hellenes are different.
We enjoy questions more than answers. We are not humble. We
demand challenge, dispute, revenge. And I shall tell you my
secret: I have never felt very strongly about any of them. A few
friends I have loved, loved more than all else. The rest was mostly
accident, bits of luck, useful mistakes.'

Boredom, disappointment, scheming were stilled by the quiet,
convinced voice, the friendly eyes which seemed to address each
separate listener. Braced for further admonition and exhortation
they were now surprised by his dexterous change of stance.

'I have been talking as your companion, whom you have
allowed a certain say in our affairs. You have shown me your
hearts, you have offered me your generosity. Let me end by telling
you a story, one close to my own heart. It was told me long ago by
our friend Theodotos and I have never forgotten it. You too will
remember his stories.'

He gave a playful sigh, a sort of relish for the unseemly. The
mirth was considerable, some of it lewd. That high, piercing Hellenic laugh aimed at all, and which can topple great ones. They did
indeed remember certain stories.

Timo was apologetic, gazing at his sleeve as if detecting a tear. 'You may not be so gratified by this story of mine. It contains no love for a swan, no flash of buttocks, no desire for one's own daughter. All the same, listen. Do please listen.'

His smile, beneath grey brows, dim eyes, pleaded, charmed, conquered. They all stood, ringing him, scarcely breathing. He had no need of the uplifted voice, the imperious gesture, the tricks of persuasion. All Hellas seemed behind them, hushed, looking up at him on a height now unearthly.

'There was once a youth, heir to the greatest king in all the world yet the vilest of men. Daily he pondered his father's ill-fame, his cruelties, his disregard of Zeus. A king who had long forgotten that if you betray, mock or deceive the gods, they will ambush you in ways unforeseen and astonishing. Then he died, smitten with a foul disease, though his body was less accursed than his Name. His son ascended, he towered over the earth, and, very young, very ardent, vowed to succour the poor, do justice to slaves, cleanse the temples, restore the dykes, root out criminal magic, soften the taxes, seek peace with neighbours. He also craved wisdom, so he summoned the wisest man then known. "Write me", he begged, "the story of mankind, from Prometheus to ourselves, so that I can learn and submit myself to the right." The sage departed and three years later he returned with twelve books. The tale of mankind. But meanwhile . . . and bear with me, my lords of Syracuse, masters of Sicily, fathers of many children, my story may be badly told but it does not lack meaning, and indeed does not lack a conclusion. . . .'

'Meanwhile, I say, the young ruler had discovered that kingship is more than quiet reaping, sowing and the occasional cock-crow. He had faced rebellion, invasion, plague, murrain. Justice was many-faced, truth was complex. Taxes were still needed, so were armies. So he requested his teacher to shorten the great work. Three years later . . . I see I do not astonish you . . . the sage returned with nine volumes. But the king, no longer quite so young, was too harassed to read so lengthy a narrative, and again the writer must depart, return, depart again. Years later, he had shrunk his book to but one volume, yet still the king could find no time for it. Ageing, ill-tempered, he was high above his people, so high that none could see him, nor could he hear them. His domains stretched from sunrise to sunset, his commands travelled the world, yet little was actually accomplished. At the very end . . . and see, I am fulfilling my promise, there really is an end . . . the tired old annalist was back in the palace, his hands empty. On the gigantic, resplendent throne crouched another old man, who greeted him wearily, stretching out a hand to receive the story of humanity. Then he peered closer. "But have you no book for me?"'

'"Nay," croaked his ancient friend, "for I can now tell you all my books in one breath. Respond to it how you will. The story of mankind is this: *They were born, they suffered, and they died.*"'

PART SEVEN

Darkness

A small boy, who was to live to a great age, once saw something he was never to forget. He survived the World Conqueror, forerunner of New Time, the son of Philip of Macedon, the Wonder of Centuries, who so briefly established the Empire of Greater Greece, Persia, Asia, Egypt. This, however, was not what the boy cherished until death. He would often speak of that distant morning on a wide street in Syracuse, itself lined with crowds calling greetings, familiar yet respectful, to an old fellow in a dusty robe, with a silver-crested staff, blind, led by a dog, escorted not by guards but by merry children, on his way to the Council.

A very curious stillness followed, as if at some apparition, benign but not quite mortal. It was as though he had witnessed some limping prince fulfilling an oracle that he would succour the land. His own life had been distinguished, but his pride of prides was that he had seen Timo of Syracuse, the Liberator.

A darkness existed behind darkness. Long ago Timo had learned at Eleusis that real life leads from the seen to the unseen, that dark Hades was an insufficiency of soul. By descending to the depths of self one climbed Olympus. Within his blindness a small sound swiftly enlarged to a bee, brilliant, almost overpowering. From a particular stir came a daughter, vivid amongst pomegranates; from another, a slave clearing the asphodel, his hands as distinct as his cough. He sensed shadow when a figure crossed through the glare; then coolness from a latticed window, another from an open

210

one. Melodies had shape, a tree could speak. The sea, usually distant, sometimes seemed very close. He could trace children's height by their voices, moods by their tread. Birds had become distinct: the oriole in the mulberry, the swallow under the thatch. Trees too had their separate voices: the creak, the rustle, the groan, the hushed stir. He could tell time by scents, coarse or pure, sweet or harsh, elicited by dawn, noon, dusk, moonrise. Silence had many depths and shades. Silence of an astrologer's waiting-room or executioner's pit; silence of a harp, of lovers, of a debt-collector's smile, the breath of a god; silence of a cave and the haunted field of Crimesus. Fingering a knife, he understood the intimacy of 'former people' with edges, surfaces, points, intimacy that became magical.

In his presence, voices lost impatience and reproach. Slaves were not servile, old opponents were amiable, Fates were kind.

He had heard, though from a poet, that the blind can trace colours on a pool, hear flowers unfold, understand the conversation of birds. He had not yet done so.

Driving in a mulecart through honeycomb air was enjoyable: to a temple, to a bay for the swoop of gulls and hum of the sea. Always, hands reached out to guide him, in their way praising him. That they might hold dagger or noose was insignificant. He trusted the intuition he still called Hermes.

Aigle, very simple, very competent, planned her activities by the moon; praying, singing, tending, according to its phases. Her style, demeanour, her being were now more substantial, as though released from mist. She knew when to enter his bed, when to refrain. Her nakedness was trim, soft, also subtle, yielding without beckoning. Another child might come, whom, never seeing, he might know the most profoundly. Yet how little he had ever known her, or anyone. Timophanes' instant of fear, in battle, a tiny shrug from Dionysius in defeat, a secret glimpse of Theodotos in soggy Kronian woods confiding to some secret animal, had revealed more than had long talks. However naked, Ismene had been almost as mysterious as Moira. He still wondered about her death, though covert inquiries had reached nowhere. His power ceased when reaching the important.

His own day was often crowded. He had long abdicated from the Council, yet no important law was resolved, no significant dispute settled, without his advice. Then the immemorial *The People of Syracuse have decreed. . . .* His ironic smile was borrowed from Ismene. Unchanged since Gelon, the formula disguised fraud, ambiguity, manipulation.

He refused to trouble the Council to journey to his home, would set out in all weathers. As usual, he would speak only when invited. Making a suggestion, he would request a vote. Sometimes this went against him, at which he would smile, in thanks for the others' forbearance. Last week they had hailed him as Master Craftsman of a building nearing completion and pleasing to gods and men, then, in tribute, ordained that, in any war, the command would be entrusted to a Corinthian.

An oracle had foretold that a Great One, a Son of Zeus, would shortly inherit the earth. 'Our Timo,' people chanted, and greybeards recalled that heedless chatter of 'the Arrival', 'a Great Year', perhaps less heedless now.

Strangers continually arrived, with gifts, odes, dedications, to the Father of Syracuse, Lighthouse of Sicily, Spirit of Hellas. Invitations begged him to honour Festivals, Games, Processions, though, pleading his age, he courteously refused.

Each day had its geography: contours, plains, promontories; mainstream and tributaries, eddies and foam; peaks and vales; small, blocked ravines. Petty disputes, elaborate reconciliations, quiet repasts and meandering debates: caressing of children, hearing their requests and complaints, their summer moods, listening to slaves' chatter about a snake in the porch. Did they know that this might signify the attention of Fate? Slaves' knowledge was as deep as minerals.

He would feel his way about the farm, still occasionally bruising himself against a seat or two, though impatient at offers of help. Life retreated, revived; was now blurred, now radiant, the universe inexorably fining down.

A wheelwright reported the passing of Dionysius, the Canary. In what Ismene had termed the witticism of time, Dionysius, cruel, cowardly, unscrupulous, had rebuilt himself into the affable teacher learning from his pupils much that he should not, but apparently greeting death with creditable unconcern.

In that brief talk outside Syracuse, Dionysius had accepted defeat with a shrug, not abjectly but with some dignity. Parting, he had joked about atoms circulating in the void. 'Syracuse will remember me.' His smile was without levity or sadness. 'But as a void. It will not please my father.'

Today was simple. He sat under a cool walnut tree, the aroma of jasmine, blackberry, bark, floating towards him. As always, visitors gathered at the gate. He seldom ordered slaves to disperse them, though, he reflected, he loved people more than he liked them, and had loved few. The present visitors were talkative, straining vigorously to interest him. Deafness was convenient though, as voices loudened, he contrived to halt some unpromising praise from a Theban mathematician tracing the Reconquest to some sky pattern. A Cretan, juggling with overdecorated words, told five jokes, none of them comic.

None had disposed of bores more deftly than Ismene, achieved with the grace with which she entered or left a room. A flowing impression of movement within stillness, giving others the sensation not only of receiving but granting a favour. She had read aloud Pindar: *Seek not my soul, the life of the immortals; but enjoy to the full the resources within thy reach.*

Etna was quiet, biding his time. Syracuse uneventful, the Constitution, the balance of factions, still held, though the Council remained grappling with all-aspiring Philip, the Captain-General. The Persian invasion was still delayed: another Great War would deliver Hellas either to Persia or Macedon, whose agents were everywhere. Probably only his Name prevented the rise of some despot dealing with new times in an old way. Like Philip, he would seem to give shade. He himself, blind and powerless, yet restrained Philip, bloated with conquests though watched by jealous gods. Macedonians had reached Byzantium, controlled the Straits, controlled Athenian food supplies. Temples, long empty, were now filling with prayers beseeching Hecate of the Crescent Moon, the Three in One, to protect the cities.

He and Philip exchanged secret letters. Continually he warned against extravagance, against war. Philip often seemed grateful, admiring, generous, but did not disband his swollen armies. He might see himself as a Dionysos, set to intoxicate Asia, his bullyboys swarming over Persia, over India in drunken greed for Empire, yelling that they were delivering the gifts of Hellas.

Queer tales abounded. Never quite forgotten was the ancient belief that Dionysos was fated to succeed Zeus, cleansing blood tainted by the Titans. A doubtful thesis. A new Empire won by a renewed Great War would be no more than despotic disorder. If, in his unknown correspondence with Philip, he was procrastinating, he deserved well of the city-states, despite lack of brazen lungs, glib catch-phrases and open money-bags. For Philip, puzzled, ever hopeful, in uncomprehending love for Hellas, ignorant of the Idea but loving words, dreaming of new times, he had a certain affection. He too, like the poor, deposed King of Syracuse, could have become a friend.

Aigle sang shyly of swallows and love, children came to hear a story. 'In the woods of Thrace lived a man who could also be a wolf. . . .' Then a neighbour, something of a philosopher, joined him. He always brought some wad of unnecessary information, like overripe apricots. Today one learned that a hollow horse symbolised death and rebirth, especially if made of yew. What wonders! Then in evening sunlight they listened to plucked strings and flutes, reminders of rare Orphic moments when savagery is stilled and Achilles weeps with Priam.

Later, in air still warm, he sat alone, Aigle within call, content with his thoughts.

Let there be one single man who personally controls a city, and he will create the ideal order about which the world is so sceptical.

The world was wise. Plato had learned little from fellow-men, nothing from rulers. One intelligence commanding an Ideal State would be atrophy, by renouncing which he had benefitted Syracuse more than she yet realised. He was known as Timo the Great but – here his old face winced – people revered not a live, troubled man but a statue. Virtue had left him, unbeknown, not in his callow joy at overthrowing Timophanes but in his butchery of Hicetas' women. This had not been punishment, not mere brute appetite, but apathy. To the screams, the dumb appeals, hideous blood, the applause of all Sicily, the hilarity and screeching, he had been indifferent.

The Macedonian too might be dogged by such feats, perhaps more easily forgetting them.

Darkness gave more time for essentials. He had recently received an Indian traveller and had learned of a long dead 'Sower of the Word', a prince who had renounced power and riches. His teachings were suggestive. You found that blindness sharpens memory, and words remained clear as if carved: *A man buries a treasure in a deep pit which, lying hidden, profits him nothing at all. Yet a treasure lies in the human heart, a trove of piety and love, moderation and restraint; a treasure so solid that it can never dissolve. When a mortal departs from the transient wealth of this life, the real treasure he bears with him thereafter.*

He had demanded to hear more. The Indian, much gratified, told him that the Sower, undergoing self-doubt, had been tempted by Mara, a god of evil. This god was unknown on Olympus, where bad behaviour was common, wickedness too often condoned, evil long past. Mankind must, however, improve on the gods.

Mara had dangled before the wandering Sower the possession of all the world, and had been refuted by the argument that, if alert and inquiring, we possess the world already.

Timo, hoarder of stories, cherished another, told by the Indian on departing.

The Sower had trudged to an outlandish unpronounceable region, and met a hermit.

'The people of this place are most hostile. If they revile you, what will you do?'

The Sower reflected. 'I shall return no insult.'

'And if they attack you?'

'I shall offer no blow.'

'But if they strive to kill you?'

'Death carries no evil, it conveys no hardship. Many actually crave it, to escape suffering or worldly conceits, or to satisfy curiosity. As for me, I shall neither delay nor hasten my end.'

He had, admiring the hermit but not wholly agreeing, advised the wise Indian to bear this tale to the mighty, all-conquering Captain-General, who hastened the ends of so many and was certainly resolved to delay his own.

How sad, though, that on reaching Syracuse the Indian had been arrested for indecency, and that in his baggage was found a golden vase presented by Sicilians to 'the Friend of Demeter, the Liberator'.

Liberator! Little was ever liberated, even by serene hermits and plausible sowers, though the effort should be maintained. His day was over, though Philip had the grace, the restraint, the acumen, to pretend that it was not. Nevertheless, for a blind old man the lights of Hellas had never been brighter. In one, during a long, slumbrous afternoon, he saw a wraithlike, almost transparent shape stooping by a dry fountain. Himself.

Hermes, guider of souls, be with me. In Zeus, one in many, many in one, all things end.

He enjoyed pondering not the nature of luck, which he could not even define, granted the existence of gods, and *aura*, but its fact. Some, like Apelles, deserve it, yet receive none. Some deserve naught and win, or are granted, plenty. He himself had had rather more than he deserved, though of his famous actions – the murder of Timophanes, the destruction of the Citadel – few had been planned, many of them accidental.

The sun suddenly cooled with unnatural speed. He heard the swallows of childhood, then with dusk around him the tingle of spirits who dwell in doors and walls.

No trumpet called from the sky when, quietly, alone, calling none, Timo died, at about the same hour as the murder of Philip, High King, Captain-General, father of Alexander.